COERCED VOWS

AMARIE COLLINS

Editing: Jessica at Deep Roots Editing

Editing: Dr. Mekhala Spencer at All The Proof Editing

Proofread: Holly at Naughty Nook PR

Paperback ISBN: 979-8-9929896-6-3

Ebook ISBN: 979-8-9929896-5-6

To the single mother's who would do anything for their child.

CONTENT WARNING

PLAYLIST

Dark Paradise — Lana Del Rey
I am not who I was — Chance Pena
Recess — Melanie Martinez
I feel like I'm drowning — Two Feet
Movement — Hozier
Butterflies — Isabel LaRosa
Slow Dancing — Ari Abdul
Do I Wanna Know — Arctic Monkeys
You Put a Spell on Me — Austin Giorgio
Cringe — Matt Maeson
Waiting for it all to go wrong — Artemas
In My Feelings — Lana Del Rey
Do It for Me — Rosenfield
Dark Red — Steve Lacy
West Coast — Lana Del Rey
Be More — Stephen Sanchez
Always Forever — Cults
Clouds — BORNS

1

WILLOW

H ave you ever felt someone's gaze burn into you?

Not just a mere eye, but a look so intense it feels as if your chest is tightening and you can't inhale, while the hair on the back of your neck stands on end?

A gaze so fierce, so deep, you feel as if you could drown in the profoundness of it?

One that can sense your fears and insecurities, and is so acute you feel as if you're being stripped bare? Your very worth laid out for inspection?

That's what I feel as I peek through my lashes and come eye to eye with Gabriel Reed.

He sits at the head of the long, polished mahogany conference table, cluttered with stacks of manila file folders, laptops, and leftover takeout boxes.

The air crackles with energy from the latest news of Reed Equity's newest acquisition. A flurry of papers and hushed conversations passes between the accounting and finance departments, the rhythmic tap-tap-tapping of keyboards adding to the atmosphere; every eye in the room is on them, except Mr. Reed's, which is solely focused on me.

"Will that work, Mr. Reed?" Mark from finance asks.

Mr. Reed's gaze leaves mine, and I blink, the sudden release of tension causing a sigh to escape my parched lips as the pressure in my chest dissipates.

"Send me the documents, and I'll make my decision by Monday," he says while gazing at his watch. "This is a good place to stop for the night. Have a great weekend, everyone."

Thank God.

I silently organize my spreadsheets and folders before standing with everyone else. I can't wait to escape this place and relish my two-day weekend, far from his odd, unsettling stare.

"Miss. Smith ... stay back for a minute."

My heart plummets as I hear those dreaded words.

Shit.

A few of my colleagues cast quizzical glances my way, their brows raised in silent question, before filing out one by one after our late-night work meeting. Many voices murmur satisfied goodbyes, the sounds of relief and happiness mingling with the clatter of closing briefcases and the rustle of coats as they head into the weekend. Their cheerful tones are a stark contrast to the icy grip of uncertainty and dread constricting my chest.

A calculating glint shines in Mr. Reed's eyes as he sizes me up once we're alone.

His fingers delicately graze his full bottom lip and chiseled jawline, peppered with just a touch of dark facial hair. A silent gesture of deep contemplation, I've seen multiple times right before he unleashes his ruthless business tactics, leaving his opponents in ruins. Only now I'm the opponent he's about to obliterate.

I messed up ... and he knows it.

I subtly glance at the sleek metal wall clock on my right. It's ticking a quiet counterpoint to the room's unnerving silence.

The time is 11:17 p.m., and although five minutes have passed since the others left, it seems considerably longer.

A knot forms in my stomach, tightening with each passing second of his appraisal; I know I can't postpone the inevitable. The threat of punishment has loomed over me like an ax at my nape ever since I made that terrible decision. It's time to face the consequences of my actions, and despite being terrified, I find a strange sense of peace in knowing it's almost over.

With a deep breath and squared shoulders, I stare at Gabriel Reed, the intimidating owner of the company who takes great pride in crushing everything in his path.

"S-sir." I tremble.

"Sir," he repeats. A barely perceptible smirk plays on his lips before his face falls into an expression of the practiced indifference he wears so well.

His appraising gaze holds mine as the silence stretches, thick and heavy, a suffocating blanket in the air. Every muscle in my body screams, tense and coiled, begging for something— anything—to break the tension.

I should have known something was up earlier today when they summoned me from my sparse, dimly lit cubicle, where I spend my days crunching numbers as a lowly junior accountant. They've never invited me to a meeting, much less one that bled into the night. And I'm practically new. I've only been an employee for a few months.

How could I have been so blind?

With a deep sigh, Mr. Reed rises from his seat, his eyes never leaving mine. Methodically, he unbuttons his navy suit jacket and drapes it over the chair. Then, with a soft pop, he loosens his tie; the knot coming undone, and lays it carefully beside his jacket.

He flips through several folders with long, deft fingers and a practiced flick of the wrist, the sound of paper rustling softly against each other before he pulls out a single sheet, the paper stiff and new.

A deafening roar fills my ears, a high-pitched scream battling to be heard over the rhythmic tap-tap-tap of his expensive dress shoes, echoing like a drumbeat against the polished black marble floor as he approaches me.

I hold my breath and let my eyes fall to my half-eaten cranberry and chicken salad from earlier this evening.

A sharp thud cuts through the silence as the paper and his hand hit the table in front of my face with such force that I flinch.

My vision swims with hot tears, the world a hazy blur as I close my eyes and let the overwhelming sense of defeat rush over me once more.

Desperation left me with no choice but to use the company's financial resources.

Darren, the father of my six-month-old Grayson, and the man I foolishly considered my partner, spent every penny of my disability checks on alcohol and gambling before disappearing without a trace. I was broke, unable to pay rent, and facing a shortage of essential baby supplies—diapers, wipes, and formula—after stress dried up my milk supply.

I went to the county office seeking aid, but they denied my application because I received family leave disability checks. I desperately tried to explain how my ex had taken the money, but to no avail. With a heavy heart, I had to return to work earlier than planned, sacrificing what was left of my precious maternity leave time with my baby, only to have my position phased out due to budget cuts three weeks later. They gave me a severance package, but it wasn't enough to catch up on bills and sustain Grayson and me while I looked for another job.

I was fortunate enough to get a job here at Reed Equity through my best friend Aella, whose father is a high-ranking executive in the company. Until a month ago, I was doing well, clearing bills, buying groceries, and getting all the essentials for Grayson, but that changed when I came home to find three menacing figures, their faces obscured by black masks, waiting in my apartment for Darren. He owed the Chicago Mafia one hundred and seventy-six thousand dollars, and they came to collect.

I told them I hadn't seen him in months, since just before Grayson was born, but they didn't care. They threatened to seize my son until Darren repaid his debt. By heaven's grace, they granted me twenty-four hours to pay, and that's exactly what I did. I came to work the next day and withdrew enough to settle his debt.

My eyes open to the white paper with a yellow-highlighted entry detailing my theft. A theft I wouldn't be able to pay back for the next decade at least. "Sir, I—"

"I don't want to hear your bullshit excuses." A low growl rumbles in his chest as he leans closer, his finger jabbing at the highlighted area as he emphasizes each word. "My company took a chance hiring you when you had little experience, and this is how you repay my act of generosity? By being a fucking thief!"

The sound of his furious rumble, like distant thunder, causes me to shrink farther into my leather seat. Fear constricts my throat, and my heart hammers a wild rhythm against my ribs as I dare to gaze up at him. "I'm so sorry. I was going to pay it back—"

A sudden, sharp tap on the glass slices through the tense moment, making me whip my head toward the sound. The floor-to-ceiling windows of the meeting room offer a clear view of two uniformed officers.

Blood roars in my ears, a deafening rush drowning out all other sounds, as my nails dig into the hard, worn leather of the armrests.

Oh my God, I'm getting arrested. They're going to arrest me. What am I going to do?

But worse, what will happen to my baby? He's the only one I have, and I'm the only one he has. The thought of never seeing him again, of him becoming an orphan, like me, fills me with a profound sense of heartbreak and dread. My biggest fear, the one that's haunted my dreams, is now my harsh reality.

"Please." My voice trembles as I stare up at his towering figure. "I'll do *anything* to make this right."

The corners of his mouth curl into a chilling, predatory grin, making me immediately regret my words. "*Anything*, huh?"

2

GABRIEL

Her wide, cognac-brown eyes, like those of a doe, hold a captivating mixture of bewilderment and innocence, the sight both enchanting and heartbreaking. But the raven-haired woman beside me is neither innocent nor enchanting. She's a thief who'll be held accountable for her crimes and punished accordingly.

She's rendered speechless as the predicament she got herself into worsens, and the police stare at her. The look of stark terror on her face is a sight I enjoy greatly.

A knock at the door interrupts the moment as Henry, my assistant, presents a man dressed in a black suit with a pristine white collar.

"Excellent." I smirk.

"What is ... what is this?" she whispers, eyeing them skeptically.

With a sigh, I lean against the cool, smooth surface of the table, crossing my arms tightly over my chest. "You see, Miss. Smith, you stole money from me, and there are only two ways to rectify the situation. Prison." I point to the boys in blue beyond the glass. "Or an arranged marriage."

Her eyes flicker between the two options, a silent debate waging within, before settling on me. "I don't understand."

"The innocent look doesn't suit you," I chide. It annoys the fuck out of me when women feign ignorance to avoid taking responsibility for their actions. She knew what she was doing when she stole the money from me.

With a frantic shake of her head and tears welling in her eyes, she chokes out a whisper, "I can't go to prison."

"Marriage then."

"Marriage ... I—"

With a sigh, I close my eyes. I don't want to waste my time on her fabricated confusion.

"Time is running out, Miss. Smith. I'm not a patient man."

"But who will I have to marry?"

"Me."

With a gasp, her eyes widen in horror, as if marrying me is the worst thing imaginable. "There has to be something else. I—"

"Prison it is." With a beckoning gesture, I motion to the officers.

"No! I can't." She clears her throat and gazes at me from under her wet eyelashes. "I'll do whatever you want."

Those words from another would have sent me soaring; from her, they're utterly repulsive. These types of women are all the same.

"Henry." I signal my assistant to retrieve the legal documents my lawyer prepared the previous day, outlining my carefully conceived plan.

A suffocating non-disclosure agreement so severe it will ensure her descendants will stay under the poverty line if she breaks it, a prenuptial agreement born from my mistrust of women, and a contract meticulously outlining her rules and compensation beyond mere freedom. In my opinion, it's more generous than she deserves.

8

"Sign this." I toss the pen onto the table with a sharp clack, making her flinch.

For someone who so brazenly stole over a hundred thousand dollars, she's damn good at acting like a delicate flower.

"What is it?" A single tear escapes her eye, tracing a path down her cheek as she chokes out the question. Although the tears are a welcome addition, they won't elicit an emotional response from me. I learned my lesson with that manipulative tactic a long time ago.

"A prenup. I think you've taken enough of my money."

"I don't want your money," she rasps with a hint of defiance before bringing the pen to the paper and signing the line with a little more force than necessary.

"Yeah, sure you don't," I mutter as I wave the police away. The scare factor was perfectly balanced, and I'll compensate them generously for their time and any inconvenience.

"Father," I motion to the pastor to step forward. "We're ready."

His gaze flickers between us, his eyes searching. "Would you like to stand and hold hands so we may begin?"

I gaze down at Willow with her bloodshot eyes and pink nose from her soft crying. Serves her right. The only positive is that her pillowy red lips are even juicier now.

Jesus, Gabriel. Stop thinking with your dick.

I should head to Obsidian after this before I do something idiotic. I haven't been to the exclusive sex club downtown in weeks. The lack of intimacy is probably why I find Willow's lips so delectable, and I can't help but imagine them quivering as they wrap around my cock. Would she still play innocent with tears rimming her eyes as her mouth opened or ...

No. No. No.

I clear my throat and bring my hands in front of the growing bulge in my pants. "No, Father. We'll stay just like this."

He eyes us skeptically before opening his little black book

of lies. "Very well." With a dramatic throat-clearing, he speaks in a voice loud enough to fill a stadium, despite only four of us being present. "Dearly beloved, we are gathered here today to witness the union of Gabriel Reed and Willow Smith in holy matrimony."

A sense of dread settles in, like a noose tightening around my neck. There's no going back now.

He continues his tiresome lecture about love, faith, and trust. All concepts are hollow and clash in this forced union. The ceremony concludes without the traditional exchange of rings, and I sure as fuck avoid the customary kiss.

"Can you stand?" Henry's voice, far gentler than I would have used, asks Willow.

She nods and rises. Her porcelain skin seems to have lost even more color after the lengthy ceremony, sending a chilling wave of satisfaction through my veins. I hope she realizes how fucked she is and her mistake in taking money from me.

"If you two can stand next to each other and smile," Henry says, holding a camera in the air.

God, I hate pictures. I blow out a breath of discomfort and remind myself that this was my idea and an important part of the plan.

As I approach Willow, I notice how tiny she is beside me—a delicate contrast to my six-foot-four frame. Her head barely reaches the middle of my chest.

"Closer," Henry instructs from behind the camera.

A frustrated grunt rips from my lips as I pull her rigid body against mine. "Believe me, I hate this just as much as you do," I whisper in her ear, causing her to suck in a sharp breath as my lips brush against them slightly.

"Just a little closer and a little less stiff," Henry urges. "Like a prom picture, but less cheesy and formal."

I roll my eyes at his analogy, but I have to admit, Henry

deserves a raise; he's a silent worker who always delivers, no matter how challenging or odd the task.

"Why do we have to do this?" Willow whispers through her forced smile.

"You don't deserve answers. You just do as I say," I sneer. "Now smile."

A flurry of flashes from the camera leaves me momentarily disoriented before Henry pulls back, a self-satisfied nod replacing his intense focus.

I gaze down at Willow, stock-still, her head bowed low, face still flushed and blotchy from crying. *Lovely.*

"Please edit the photos to show us in wedding attire, and adjust her eyes and face so they don't appear red or teary. Email them to me when you're done, and then we'll discuss the time-line of when we'll send them to my parents and the press."

"Right away. Have a good night, Sir," Henry says before giving Willow a sympathetic nod and walking out.

"Let's go home," I say, gazing at Willow.

A gasp escapes her lips. "What do you mean?"

I pinch the bridge of my nose and take a deep breath. Her constant questions are grating on my nerves. "Did you not just hear what I told you?" When she stays mute, I continue, "To make this believable, we must maintain a convincing facade." Now she's not only mute but also as still as a statue, as if she truly doesn't understand. "*Meaning*, every detail counts. If you had read the contract you so blindly signed, which was stupid, by the way, you'd know this."

With her arms folded across her chest, as if consoling herself, she gazes at me with wide eyes and whispers, "I can't live with you."

"Do you want to go to prison?" I ask, picking up my suit jacket, tie, and briefcase. When she remains silent, I stop at the door without a backward glance. "Be at Ash and Vine tomorrow night at seven so we can discuss the contract and what's expected of you."

"But—" I storm out, silencing her words with the slam of the meeting room door. I'm too busy to deal with her disingenuous apologies and unconvincing confusion.

"Three years," I whisper. The words are barely audible above the ding of the elevator.

Three short years of enduring this sham marriage, and then the company, its assets, and influence will finally be mine, and mine alone.

3

WILLOW

A symphony of creaks and groans erupts from the old wooden steps under my frantic sprint on shaky legs to my apartment door. I swing the door open and look for my best friend, Aella. "Elle, I'm so sorry for being late. I—"

"Oh, don't start," she says, rising from my couch, but stops short. Her hazel eyes appraise me with concern. "Hey, what's wrong?"

"I honestly don't know where to begin," I whisper, the words catching in my throat as a strangled, hysterical laugh bubbles up.

She comes to me and grabs my hands in hers before walking us back to the couch. "You're scaring me. Did Darren come back? Did he harass you? Hurt you? I told you I can find someone to take care of him."

Right now, my idiot ex is the least of my worries.

"No ... I think I got myself into something much worse." I groan. "Mr. Reed found out about the money."

"Shit, Wills. I told you I'd give you the money to pay it back before anyone noticed."

"I couldn't have you ask your dad for the money. You already sacrificed enough by having him get me the job."

"It's not that big of a deal. Just a few *family* dinners a month and church every Sunday."

She says *family* with a scowl etched on her face. Her dad left her mom years ago and got a shiny new family, which created a tense and difficult relationship, full of misunderstandings and hurt feelings she ignores, though I know it bothers her. She shouldn't have to sacrifice herself by asking him for help for me. I couldn't let that happen again.

"This was *my* mistake," I say, pointing to my chest. "I'm the one who got myself into this mess."

"No, this was your asshole exes doing. It's not your fault he took advantage of your trusting nature. I always knew something wasn't right with him."

"I guess it doesn't matter now. The damage is done."

"We'll find you a better job. One that gets you away from all those stick up the ass corporate dicks."

A small smile forms on my lips before a frown takes its place. "I don't think that's possible." I look into my best friend's worried gaze and attempt to find the words in my jumbled brain. "He ... I'm not even supposed to say anything," I mutter, licking my dry lips, while thinking about the non-disclosure agreement I signed.

"What did the bastard do?"

This is what I love so much about Aella Marks. She's so unapologetically herself. She's loyal and fierce and free and doesn't care who you are. We met six years ago on our mutual first day of college, and have been inseparable ever since. She and I share a bond unlike any other I've ever had; we're essentially sisters, not just friends.

"Talk to me. Please." She squeezes my hands tighter.

"He forced me to sign paperwork and marry him."

Her eyes widen. "Excuse the fuck out of me ... what did you just say?"

"It all happened so fast." I tell her every detail of our *coerced vows*, down to the weird photos, and the dinner I'm supposed to meet him for tomorrow night.

Her brows furrow in a brief moment of contemplation before smoothing out into something close to satisfaction.

"You know what this means, right?" She asks with a gleam in her eye as she throws her wavy golden-brown tailbone-length hair into a messy bun.

"That I'm totally fucked."

"No ... he is." A devious smile curves her lips as I furrow my brow.

"I don't follow."

"He needs you." I give her an incredulous look, and she continues. "For what? I have no clue, but him going through the trouble of planning this night with potentially bribed officials, and a pastor, screams premeditation and deep-seated, hidden agendas. I doubt the late-night work meeting was even necessary. He just needed an excuse to get you alone. We need to figure out his angle and use it to *your* advantage."

I groan. "Don't romanticize this into some suspenseful show of corrupt leaders, secret pining, and mystery. It doesn't make me feel any better." My voice cracks as I bury my face in my hands, the despair and uncertainty heavy and suffocating.

With a gentle tug, Aella pulls my hand away, and I angle my head to look at her self-assured stare. "It means you hold the power. Use that shit."

Aella and I spent another hour meticulously planning my dinner with Mr. Reed. She bids me goodnight, promising to collect Grayson and me tomorrow and bring us to her upscale inner-city apartment so I can borrow a dress and she can babysit.

I retreat to my room and find Grayson on my bed, nestled

comfortably between two pillows. I was supposed to get him a crib, but I haven't been able to afford one. With a sigh, I slip off my heels and black blazer, then remove the right pillow, and snuggle in beside him.

The urge to wake him is overwhelming. I long to see his face break into that sweet smile of recognition, a reward making even the toughest days worthwhile. Instead, I gently trace the soft, downy skin of his chubby cheek with the back of my index finger.

"Mommy made a huge mistake," I whisper as tears blur my vision, "and I don't know where it will lead us." The last part ends on a shuddering sob, and I try to calm myself with slow, deep breaths, the air catching in my throat.

Even though he's asleep, I always try to be as positive as I can, even when I feel like giving up. Babies are intuitive and can perceive emotions better than most adults. I don't want him to feel the emotional turmoil that's currently eating me alive. Clearing my throat, I continue, "I love you with all my heart, and I promise to do better for you from here on out." I wipe the tears from my eyes with the top blanket. "I'm sorry I wasn't strong enough to leave your father before he left us destitute, and I'm sorry for what I had to do to make things right."

A fresh wave of hot tears stings my eyes as I push myself up from the bed, put the pillow back in place, and stumble toward the kitchen, desperate for the warmth of a cup of chamomile tea to soothe my churning stomach.

Curled up on my teal second-hand sofa, with the steam from the tea warming my face, I gaze around my dimly lit apartment. Smoke-stained yellow walls, peeling brown linoleum, and the unsettling green shag carpet, likely full of asbestos. This is no place for a baby who will be crawling any day now.

I wish I could rewind my life like a movie and analyze the choices I've made to see where I went so wrong.

A relentless series of difficulties and setbacks filled my early years. The hardships I endured cast a long shadow over my young life, yet I was able to overcome them, so why is everything so messed up now?

My birth parents abandoned me at the Chicago Fire Department when I was only six months old. The foster care system was like a carousel of temporary homes, some more frightening than others, until my adoption at age five. Bob and Ginger Smith, a sweet elderly couple whose love filled my childhood with hope, were tragically taken from me in a plane crash when I was eight, which brought me back into the foster care system.

Unfortunately, I wasn't lucky enough to have another Bob and Ginger enter my life. I stayed in group homes until I aged out of the system, leaving with nothing but a trash bag containing two outfits and my brown teddy bear, which had lost its stuffing and an ear years earlier.

Despite everything, I steered clear of trouble, achieved academic success, and secured a scholarship with the aspiration of becoming an accountant, like Bob was. After my externship and graduation with a shiny bachelor's degree, I was fortunate enough to accept a permanent position at a well-known grocery chain, but I was let go and later got the job with Reed Equity.

Which now brings us to the present, where I was forced to marry my boss or go to prison. The uncertainty of my and Grayson's future gnaws at me, but the image of my baby being snatched away and him enduring the same childhood trauma I faced is unbearable.

My fingers fly across my phone as I bring up the search engine and type Gabriel Reed of Reed Equity. The first article praises him for his good looks and mentions his reclusive lifestyle. This article wrote a whole damn paragraph about his beauty alone. From his tall frame and broad shoulders to his symmetrical features, piercing dark brown eyes that bore into your soul, a chiseled jaw peppered with the perfect amount of scruff, full kissable lips, and dark, silky hair that appears seductively bedroom tousled.

One even quotes him as "The most eligible bachelor for the past decade, a man shrouded in mystery yet undeniably appealing to all."

Undeniably appealing to all? Gag me now.

He's shrouded in mystery, all right. Most men with his level of wealth would boast of expensive cars, designer clothes, and beautiful women at their side. Yet, he does none of these things from what I've seen at work and now online. Never married, no engagement photos.

Maybe he likes men?

No, I didn't get that vibe from him. I should have pressed Aella for more details; she's known him since her preteens.

Lost in the labyrinthine depths of the internet, I tirelessly continue my search, desperately hoping for enlightenment, but all I see are more glowing reviews of my asshole husband.

Husband. Ugh.

He's a philanthropist with hospital wings, children's libraries, and even a few park benches named in his honor.

But what no article speaks of is his cutthroat work ethic or how he makes grown men cry from ruthlessly dismantling their empires.

You also won't find a story about him catching an employee stealing and then issuing a bizarre ultimatum: forced marriage or imprisonment, instead of the standard dismissal and legal action.

What could be his reason for proposing marriage?

The only time I spoke with him since being hired was during two brief elevator rides, each ending with him asking me to press his office floor and nothing more. The only thing putting me in his orbit was my theft; otherwise, I was invisible to him.

Great going, Willow.

I drink the rest of my tea and type a question that scares me more than Gabriel Reed.

How long could you go to prison for taking one hundred and seventy-six thousand dollars from your employer?

The first word that catches my eye is embezzlement, which sounds a lot worse than taking.

Jail time for workplace theft (embezzlement) is not fixed. The amount stolen significantly impacts the sentence, as do your location (state and country laws vary) and whether it's treated as a misdemeanor or felony. This results in sentences ranging from minor penalties to lengthy prison terms.

The key factors affecting jail time include the amount stolen. Smaller amounts are likely to be considered misdemeanors with shorter jail sentences or fines, while larger sums can lead to felony charges with longer prison terms.

Minor theft, like pocketing a few dollars from the register, could lead to a small fine and perhaps a short period of probation—no jail time involved.

Moderate theft, such as repeatedly stealing a few hundred dollars, could lead to a misdemeanor charge and a few months in jail.

Large-scale embezzlement, involving the theft of significant company funds, can result in felony charges and lengthy prison sentences.

I drop my phone in my lap and put my head in my trembling hands. If I had chosen differently tonight, I would have become a felon with a lengthy prison sentence and never seen Grayson again.

Aella's words about my power over Mr. Reed echo in my ears, but the chilling uncertainty gnaws at me, a stark contrast to her confident pronouncements.

One thing is for sure: I need to tread carefully with Mr. Reed.

4

WILLOW

"You got this, Wills," Aella encourages from the driver's seat, a confident smile on her face as we smoothly pull in front of the moody, upscale Ash and Vine.

I shake my head, the strands of my curly hair dancing around my shoulders as I exhale, letting out a long breath. "I wish I shared your positivity."

"Remember, you're in control, and you set the rules. Don't let him bulldoze you with his aggressive asshole behavior, the way men like him often do."

How do I not let that happen?

"I'll try my best," I say with a sardonic smile.

"I haven't seen any photos of you two online yet, but once they're there, he's fucked and can't take it all back. Just bide your time until then."

Biding my time is easier said than done.

I chew on my bottom lip.

Aella grabs my hand and squeezes. "I know this is totally fucked, but I think this is the best way to get what you want." I raise a brow but let her continue, "You've always fought like hell to survive. Your strength and resilience have always left me in awe, but the time has come for you to take what you deserve. Use the resources being married to him will provide to give yourself a leg up in this life. For you and Gray."

Her words sink in, and I nod. Every home I've ever gone into used me as a money chip. They took everything they could, leaving me with only the tiniest, most insignificant scraps. Always hungry. Always cold. Darren was no different. He took and took until I had nothing left.

Leaning in, I kiss her cheek before opening the car door and stepping out. "I appreciate you."

"Appreciate me by going in there and showing the mighty Gabriel Reed who's boss." She grins.

"Mr. Reed *is* my boss, though."

"Don't you dare call him *Mr. Reed*. He's Gabriel to you. He doesn't deserve the formality or respect."

Snorting, I mutter, "You're absolutely insane."

"And you love it..."

I glance at Grayson, his small body nestled in his car seat, happily chewing on the new sensory toy Aella bought him. "Thank you for watching Gray for me."

"Auntie Elle loves her little man." She gazes back, her grin wide, a playful baby voice bubbling from her lips before her eyes narrow at me. "Now stop stalling and get in the damn restaurant."

"Okay, okay." With a click, I shut the door and turn to the four cobblestone steps guiding me to the entrance.

I can do this. No matter what tonight brings, I will endure anything for Grayson. His future rests on me being able to make this work. I can't let him down again.

An employee opens the door before my hand touches the antique brass doorknob and welcomes me to Ash and Vine.

Just as the photos online show, the inside is moody and gorgeous; the air is thick with the scent of delicious food and polished wood. A brick-inlaid ceiling, evocative of a wine cellar, displays crystal chandeliers dripping like vines, illuminating the black-and-white checkerboard marble floor and the elegant black and tan tables and chairs below.

I'm so glad Aella convinced me to wear her stunning black midi dress; the sweetheart neckline and thin straps are flattering, and the designer heels add a touch of elegance. If I'd worn my clothes, I wouldn't have experienced the same surge of confidence this outfit provides or felt like I belong; the dress makes me feel powerful and ready to take on anything, which is what I need.

Informing the host of my dinner with Mr. Reed, he leads me through a quiet corridor to a private room. The gentle murmur of conversation from the main area fades as we enter the dimly lit space.

A soft, warm light from wall sconces and a single candle in a floral centerpiece bathes the table, creating an almost romantic ambiance if not for the circumstances.

"Mr. Reed has yet to arrive, but he made preparations for you to dine in this room. A server will be with you shortly. Please enjoy your evening." The host bows, his movements precise and graceful in his black suit and tie, and I only stare, my eyes wide with surprise. Never have I been to a restaurant where they bow.

With the host gone, I release a shaky breath and sink into the plush chair. An uncomfortable silence, thick with anticipation and the scent of sweet wine, descends upon the room, scattering my frayed nerves as I wait for my unsettling dinner guest to appear.

My clammy palms run across the starched white tablecloth in my lap. It's crisp and immaculate, just like Gabriel Reed's persona to the world.

Ugh, this is going to be a mess. I can already feel it.

A clumsy thud echoes as my elbows knock against the table

while I prop them up, scattering the excessive silverware with a metallic clatter.

What in the Pretty Woman is this? And how did I not notice it sooner? Surely you don't need this many forks to eat.

I pull my phone from my borrowed black satin clutch and check the time. He's late. As I open my messages, the bright glow illuminates my face and makes me squint in the dimly lit room while I type a message to Aella.

> WILLOW
>
> It's twenty past seven, and he's not here.
> When would it be acceptable to leave without this all blowing up in my face?

> AELLA
>
> That dick! He's probably trying to show his dominance. 😒

> WILLOW
>
> So I should wait another ten minutes and then leave???

> AELLA
>
> Absolutely not. Order the most expensive entrée, dessert, and bottle of champagne first.

I snort.

"Is something funny?" The sudden rumble of his deep voice makes me gasp in surprise.

"Mr. Reed ..." Fingers fumbling, I place my phone on the tabletop and give him a tight smile, which does nothing to comfort the nervous flutter in my chest as I gaze at him.

With a sigh, he unfastens his pristine gunmetal gray suit, revealing a form-fitting black dress shirt underneath, and sinks heavily into the chair opposite me, the proximity almost suffocating.

"Miss. Smith."

The silence hangs heavy, thick with unspoken tension, until the server arrives. The clinking of glasses momentarily shatters the smothering stillness as the server sets down our drinks. A sparkling glass of chilled white wine sits before me, its condensation catching the light, next to a glass of amber liquor, rich and dark, in front of him.

Although I'm sure the wine would be delicious, I don't think it's a good idea to drink alcohol around him. I need to stay sharp and aware.

"Excuse me?" The server eyes me. "May I have a glass of water, please?"

"Of course, ma'am." She arrives seconds later with a glass of water and a crystal pitcher, which she sets on the table near me.

"Thank you."

My eyes return to Mr. Reed, his gaze sharp and unwavering as he swirls the amber liquid in his tumbler before bringing the glass to his lips and polishing off the contents in one go.

Darren used to do the same with his can of beer, and it looked sloppy, especially when he belched after. Mr. Reed does it, and it looks sophisticated. I guess all you need is the right looks, an asshole personality, and money seeping out of your pores. Who would have known?

He clears his throat as he reaches into his pocket. "I have the contract on my phone, and we'll go over the specifics of our agreement."

Right to business. Maybe this won't be so bad after all. I reach for my glass and take a long sip of the cool water.

"The arrangement will last three years."

In a startling, undignified burst, I choke. The water sprays from my mouth, and I'm almost certain some of it hits him across the table. I hastily dab my mouth with a napkin and attempt to catch my breath as I cough. "Three years?"

"I don't enjoy repeating myself, but yes, three years unless I determine it needs to be ... modified."

"Modified? What does that ..."

I fall silent as his lips press into a tight line, a reaction to my echoing of his words, like a mockingbird.

Jesus, what the hell did I get myself into? Three years? I'll be twenty-eight by then, Grayson, a preschooler. And modified? Does that mean it can be longer than three years? Or does he mean shorter? Let's hope it's the latter, but knowing my luck, it will be the former.

"May I continue?" He raises a brow.

I nod slowly, my mind reeling and crumbling in on itself from the unexpected revelation.

"There is no relationship outside of what we show everyone else."

There's the silver lining. He and I are in complete agreement about that.

"Do you understand?"

Duh.

"No catching feelings or acting as a couple unless it's for show. Believe me, I have no problem with that." I shrug while trying to maintain a neutral expression when I really want to roll my eyes because I don't plan on touching him, or any man, even if it would save humankind. The thought of being with a man, following all the misery I faced with Darren, fills me with a deep sense of revulsion.

His gaze roams my face, and I give him a tight smile.

"No men."

Is he for real?

"Given that we're married, I thought it was an obvious expectation."

He scrutinizes me, his elbow planted firmly on the table, long fingers stroking the scruff on his jaw, thoughtful contemplation etched on his face.

Great. What type of verbal torment does he intend to inflict next? And why can't he just say what's on his mind instead of dissecting me from the inside out? It's so damn uncomfortable.

Without realizing it, my fingers tighten around the cool crystal stem of my wineglass; I twist it slowly, the motion soothing against the tremor in my hands caused by his unnerving, silent gaze.

I'm about to fold like a deck of cards, and we haven't even eaten yet. Aella would be so disappointed. And did I call him Mr. Reed earlier? I think I did.

Her voice echoes in my head.

Keep it together, Willow.

You've endured hardship, emerging stronger and wiser, refusing to be controlled by another man. Don't back down now.

I inspect the wine's clarity to waste time and get my head right. When Aella taught me this, I felt like it was a bit pretentious. Why not just drink the damn fermented grape juice? But now I'm grateful. Angling the liquid to catch the dim light, the rich aroma fills my nose as I give it a small swirl, then I survey its color once more, and finally, I sip. All the while knowing his gaze still pierces through me.

Damn. Of course, the wine would be the right amount of sweet and crisp.

"And you?" I inquire, cocking my head to one side.

He raises his brow with what seems to be a hint of amusement in the curl of his upper lip. "What about me?"

"Will there be no women for you?"

His head cocks to the side, mimicking me. "Is that what you want?"

Why the hell would he ask that? I truly don't care what he does with his private time, but a little voice in my head, most likely Aella's, tells me I need to make this fair. Get back some of the power. "It's not about what I want. It's about fairness."

27

A slow smirk stretches across his face, crinkling the corners of his eyes. "Very well."

Did I win my first small victory against Gabriel Reed? Yes, I think I did.

We continue our discussion—mostly him lecturing me on expectations—until a plate of elegantly arranged finger foods, each bite-sized morsel a miniature work of art, appears.

To momentarily escape the chill of his tone, gaze, and the unexpectedly extensive terms of our agreement, I cautiously choose a morsel from the plate, hoping desperately it isn't snails or fish.

The smell of steak, garlic, caramelized onions, and cream cheese fills my nose. A tentative bite follows, and I moan. It's a delightful explosion of flavors and juices, like a tiny celebration on my taste buds.

Next, I lift a cracker with a dollop of creamy white sauce and peculiar black beads. The revolting stench of the sea hits my nose seconds later, and back on the plate it goes.

How can they sell things with such a repulsive odor, a smell so pungent it makes your eyes water, and people still pay top dollar for it?

"Did the Caviar and Crème Fraiche tartlets offend you?" Another smirk plays on Mr. Reed's lips as he asks.

Why has he suddenly become somewhat bearable?

"No, sir." Feeling a little embarrassed, I quickly grab the safe steak option and shove it into my mouth.

"Moving on," he mutters, his voice flat with boredom as his index finger mindlessly swipes across his phone screen. How his long finger looks so elegant as it moves, I'll never know. "Your allowance will be ten thousand a month with an extra ten-thousand-dollar bonus after every year completed."

A large chunk of steak lodges in my throat, a painful, suffocating sensation, until I frantically grab my wine and wash it down. Why does this keep happening?

"Dollars? Did you say ten thousand dollars?" With wide, questioning eyes, I ask. Surely, I heard him wrong.

"I'm assuming the amount will keep you satisfied, so no more of my money goes missing," he says, the ice clinking softly in his glass as he sips.

"If I'm allowed to keep my job, I won't need your ten thousand dollars a month."

"As my wife, you can't work for the company anymore."

That makes no sense, whatsoever. I know a few coworkers who are married and work together.

"Why not?"

"Because *my* word is law."

I don't like the sound of that one bit. His monthly *allowance* will feel like the cold, hard press of icy chains against my wrists; a heavy, restrictive weight crushing my already limited autonomy. I don't want him anywhere near those chains, and certainly not with the keys.

"Our time is up. I have somewhere to be." With a mix of bewilderment and dismay, I watch Mr. Reed rise from his seat, questions pounding through my brain as his chair legs scrape against the polished floor. He grabs his second tumbler of amber liquid and quickly finishes it before making his way to the exit, his voice echoing as he calls over his shoulder. "I expect you at my penthouse tomorrow, no later than ten in the morning."

Before I can utter a single syllable, he vanishes, leaving only unnerving silence in his wake while I sit stupefied.

The insistent beep of my phone slices through the quiet minutes later.

UNKNOWN
367 West Beach. PH #1 Chicago, IL 60649.

UNKNOWN

You need to show your ID at the reception
desk to get your key. Be there on time.

UNKNOWN

The right wing of the penthouse is yours. Stay
away from the left wing.

5

WILLOW

The penthouse entrance is a breathtaking sight with dark wood floors, metallic gold, and matte black accents creating a sophisticated and luxurious ambiance.

Overwhelmed with awe, I pause to take in the immense space. Plush, black cloud-like sectionals and a state-of-the-art entertainment center dominate the middle, with a professional-grade kitchen resembling a showroom floor off to the left and a terrace built for entertaining beyond the floor-to-ceiling windows to the right.

Like the biting wind of a Chicago winter, a sharp, cold whisper echoes in my mind. A painful reminder of my place as an outsider and a fraud, urging me to retreat and go back to where I belong.

"Why'd you stop?" Aella asks over our video call. She was adamant about seeing the devil's lair. Her words, not mine, although with each passing day, I'm agreeing with her assessment of him more and more.

Despite Aella's high hopes of me bringing him to his knees, I don't stand a chance. Last night's dinner felt like a losing business deal. He commanded every detail down to what I drank and ate while barking orders in his harsh, no-nonsense tone, which had me recoiling when I opposed anything.

Then there were his somewhat playful smirks and amusement, which left me dumbfounded. What the hell was I supposed to do with that side of him?

"Earth to Wills ..."

"I'm going. I'm going," I mutter. The straps of my overloaded backpack bite into my shoulders as I adjust them and head toward the right wing, as Mr. Reed ordered, while Grayson, in his carrier, gently bumps against my leg.

"Wait, I want to see the view!"

"I'm not going any further." Trepidation fills me as I eye the floor-to-ceiling windows. I'm absolutely terrified of heights. An unfortunate fear that started as a small child when one of my foster homes had an older son who pushed me off the second-story balcony, resulting in a broken arm and a lifetime of dread when I come into contact with anything higher than a stepladder.

Of course, my luck would have me now living in a penthouse on the seventy-first floor. I hope the elevator doesn't suddenly fail, sending me plummeting to my doom, or that a strange accident doesn't shatter the windows, sucking me out. I wonder what the building's rating is for wind resistance? Will it sway this high up? My chest tightens, envisioning all the potential yet absurd outcomes of my demise.

"Just a little closer, you scaredy-cat."

Grumbling under my breath and rolling my eyes, I carefully set the carrier down, then cautiously move three feet from the massive window, extending my phone as far as my arms allow to capture the view. "This is as good as it's going to get, so enjoy."

"That dick! He would have the best views of downtown."

With a knot from being so close to the window tightening my stomach, I hurry back to where I left Grayson, snatch the carrier, and head to my wing. How pretentious does that sound? *My wing.*

"What did you expect, Elle? A dark dungeon with chains and a sacrificial fire?"

"Yes, actually."

Snorting, I say, "Yeah, I guess I kind of did, too."

Stumbling into the first room, I lay Grayson down on a bed far larger than my old one. The pristine white and black bedding is luxurious; the heavy, expensive pillows surrounding him feel like a king's ransom. Once he falls back to sleep, I step into the connecting bathroom with a massive walk-in shower, easily the size of my apartment, and a luxurious Jacuzzi soaking tub offering a stunning city view.

Is this really going to be my life for the next three years?

At Aella's insistence on seeing the rest of the penthouse, I quickly learn it has panoramic views, encompassing both the sparkling waterfront and the sprawling cityscape, and is within easy walking distance to the aquarium, park, and the children's museum.

Despite her plea to see Gabriel's wing, I refused. I won't risk making him angry by invading his personal space.

6

GABRIEL

"I won't let you dismantle my life's work, you fucking snake!"
With a sigh, I lean back. The worn leather of my chair groans softly as I absentmindedly tap my pen against my desk. The rhythmic click is a dull counterpoint to the monotonous tone of Frank Renner's self-aggrandizing tale of corporate failure.

He's lucky I begrudgingly swooped in to make it my investment. It was dead in the water before I came in to revive it.

A quick, obnoxious set of knocks has my gaze rising to the door where Kennedy, my childhood best friend and business partner, strides in with an equally obnoxious smile and putter in hand.

I hold a finger up to Kennedy as Frank continues to berate my character. A triumphant grin stretches across my face as his dull and pointless words fall flat, their intended effect lost in the victorious thrill coursing through my veins.

He's at my mercy, as I prefer all company owners to be, and like all of them, he knows I hold all the cards. His little tantrum, complete with loud shouts and dramatic displays of frustration, and I'm sure a stomp of his foot on the floor, will soon be over,

34

followed by his customary retreat and the waving of a metaphorical white flag.

I'm what they used to call a corporate raider, but I like to think of myself as a strategic investor. I purchase enough stock to control the future of a failing company. A maximum return is my ultimate aim. If not, it turns into a breakdown. With top executives replaced and operations downsized, the news of the company's liquidation was the final straw, prompting Mr. Renner's furious outburst.

The high of dismantling empires, burning the useless pile, only to rebuild them to my liking, is like a drug. I pride myself on my relentless pursuit of identifying weak points in the corporate giant's armor and exploiting them for change.

Kennedy leans against my desk before activating the speaker on my office phone and filling my office with Mr. Renner's yelling. "What are your actual intentions with my company?"

I roll my eyes at his idiocy, making Kennedy smirk. "Money, Frank," I say, both bored and restless. "Now it's time to break it apart and sell off the pieces. In the last six months, my guidance has made you extremely wealthy, but I know when to cut my losses. Do you?"

"You piece of—"

"Our allotted time is up. I'll draft the paperwork and send it to you later this week. Bye Frank," I mutter, then hang up.

"I knew he was going to be a fucking pain," Kennedy groans.

"It doesn't help that you slept with his granddaughter at the Christmas party last year," I say, rubbing my temples.

The sooner I can get this deal over with, the better. I was doing my grandfather a favor by playing easy with his old friend, but that time has ended. Frank Renner's partnership has been nothing but disastrous since it began.

"God, don't remind me. I wasn't expecting her to get all

clingy and stalk me. I swear I thought I saw her in Japan two days ago. It made me spit my drink all over my date."

Ignoring all that, I ask the only thing that truly matters to me.

"How did the meetings go?"

"Excellent, per usual. The mismanagement of Charter One is astounding. The deal should garner us right under a billion. I'll have the papers for you tomorrow." Kennedy says, taking a ball out of his pocket and placing it on the floor before doing a few practice swings with a rhythmic whoosh.

"If the rest of the year is as successful as this first and second quarter, we could expand."

"Or go on vacation," Kennedy mutters as he swings again.

With a frustrated shake of my head, I wave one of the many thick black folders littering my desk, this one filled with the details of the oil mining company I want to acquire. "There's no time for play when there's always so much work to do."

Kennedy groans as he points his putter in my direction. "You know, you were more fun in college. If I had known you'd become such a bore over the last decade and a half, I would have made sure you had more fun."

"That's the last thing I needed after Eryn," I mutter, mentioning my ex, who fucked me over royally in my early twenties.

"I hope the bitch is rotting in a ditch by now," he mutters while lining up to take his shot. "Speaking of bitches, whatever happened to that employee who stole from us? Is she in prison yet?"

"I married her."

The ball, a projectile of fury, flies across the room. Its trajectory is a death sentence for my bar area. In the moments before impact, a low, ominous hum vibrates through the room. Then, the crash—a thunderous explosion of sound and splintering glass.

Among the casualties was my nearly million-dollar, fifty-five-year-old Yamazaki single malt Scotch whisky, which I planned to enjoy after making a multi-billion-dollar deal. I close my eyes and pinch the bridge of my nose.

I know there's a lesson to be learned in savoring life's simple joys instead of delaying gratification, but that's a problem for another day.

"Why in the hell are you using golf balls instead of foam balls inside?"

"The golf ball and booze are the least of your worries." Kennedy runs his hands through his short blond hair. "I think I'm losing my fucking mind because it sounds like you said you married the thief."

"I did," I mutter as I sit back and rub the scruff on my jaw.

A strangled, guttural sound escapes his lips, part choke, part gag. "Jesus fucking Christ. Tell me you're joking."

I knew he'd disapprove, so I never told him about my plans. I'm well aware that marrying her was a reckless decision, a desperate gamble to appease my father and get the company, but it felt like the only way forward.

"I wish I were."

"Why'd you marry her?"

"You know why. It's the only way my father will give me the company. He wants me to settle down. Besides, I'm more approachable to future companies as a mid-thirties family man."

"Are you high? You could have anyone in this city. Hell, in the country."

"I don't want anyone," I mutter.

"You should have called me before doing this." He shakes his head and takes a seat across from me. "What if she steals everything you got?"

"That won't happen. I have her right where I want her. She

signed the prenup and posed for our fake wedding photos, petrified and shaking. She won't be a problem."

But in the back of my mind, I recall her attitude at dinner last night. Initially timid, a newfound strength emerged within her as the night progressed that I continually had to snuff out. Maybe it was the liquid courage of the wine that had her trying to assert herself? Though ineffective against me, the execution was rather entertaining.

"At least you were smart about the prenup. Where is she now?"

"My penthouse. I got an alert about an hour ago."

"Fuck. Is she going to be living with you? Tell me she's at least young and hot?"

"Young, yes, in her mid-twenties."

"Fuck, robbing the cradle."

Ignoring his words about our eleven-year age gap, I continue, "As for her appearance, I didn't look closely."

He snorts. "You fucking liar. She's hot ... I can tell."

I roll my eyes.

"What about kids? Your parents will expect grandchildren. My mom keeps hounding me for them."

I recoil at the mere thought of kids. They aren't part of my plan.

"I'll tell them we want to wait and enjoy our time together. Once the company is mine, she and I will file for irreconcilable differences and be done."

"Just like that?" he asks.

"Just like that," I repeat.

"You make it sound so clinical and detached. What if you catch feelings for her or some shit?"

Leave it to my best friend, who has never settled down in his whole adult life, to ask these questions.

"Feelings are the last thing I'll ever feel for her ... unless irritation counts."

A wicked smirk creeps across his face, his eyes gleaming, and I know the question he's about to ask will get an immediate refusal.

"Can I take her if you don't want her? Or we can share?"

Fake wife or not, no one touches what has my name on it.

"I doubt your fan club would approve." His secretary, Aella Marks, whom we've known since she was in her preteens, has been relentless in her pursuit of him. She's one of the executive's spoiled, high-maintenance daughters. I'm glad I avoided that potential disaster.

"Stop reminding me of my misfortunes." He grumbles with a look I can't decipher and then smirks. "Are you at least planning to fuck her?"

This asshole never gives up. If he redirected half the energy he puts into chasing women toward brainstorming new business concepts, we'd have already started our expansion. Maybe even started our own company, so we don't have to answer to my father anymore.

"Your secretary? Absolutely not. And you shouldn't either," I say, grinning to deflect any thoughts of Willow with her pillowy lips from my mind.

——————

WITH A WEARY EXHALE, I lean my tired back against the cool, smooth metal of the elevator. The soft hiss of the closing doors is a welcome sound as it begins its gentle ascent to my penthouse.

The moment I finished my work at the office, I should have headed home. I haven't slept in over forty-eight hours, and the three potent glasses of scotch Kennedy bought me at the club are blurring my vision and muddying my thoughts.

The elevator pings, announcing my arrival, but the sigh of relief I prepared catches in my throat as a baby's cry pierces the silence. I stop mid-stride. The world fades as I close my eyes and slowly count to ten, willing my heart to slow its erratic beats and my muscles to release the tension from the unwelcome noise.

If my mind plays this game as it has many nights before, sleepless anxiety and sorrow will fill tonight.

A heavy silence follows as I open my eyes and cautiously move into my penthouse.

From the right wing, Willow's form appears and heads for the kitchen, her small hand clutching a baby's bottle.

So, am I *not* hallucinating?

The only sounds besides my heart beating in my ears are the soft taps of her hurried footsteps.

I come up behind her as she stands at the sink.

"What the fuck is going on here?" I growl.

Willow turns with wide eyes and a hand on her chest. "Shit, you scared the crap out of me."

The piercing cry begins again, and Willow rushes through her cleaning of the bottle and heads back to her wing.

"Hey, I asked you a question," I bark while following her quick pace into the bedroom.

My eyes fall to the small child, maybe six months old, with jet black hair, nestled in the middle of a wall of pillows on the bed, its tiny chest rising and falling with each cry. Why isn't he in a crib? But more so, why is he here? My gaze drifts, searching for answers, until it settles back on Willow, who gently picks the child up and rocks him back and forth, while patting his back rhythmically and humming a gentle lullaby, which calms the child down instantly but puts me even more on edge than before.

Shell-shocked, I stand frozen and wonder if my mind is still playing games and Willow isn't really standing here with a baby in her arms.

"Whose is that, and why do you have it here?" I ask in a

deceptively calm tone, even though I'm seconds from losing my shit.

Willow shoots me an incredulous look. "He's my baby."

Fuck. Fuck. Fuck.

"Why the hell didn't you tell me?" I yell, causing the baby to wail again.

I rake my hand through my hair; the strands catch slightly before I tug hard, but the usually satisfying sensation is absent, as I feel my plan crumbling the more her son cries.

Willow shakes her head, her dark hair swaying, then coos at him before returning her gaze to me and whisper-yelling. "I tried to tell you on Friday and then last night. Both times, you rudely cut our meeting short."

I let her words echo in my mind, each syllable a sharp beat against the dull throb behind my eyes.

Jesus Fucking Christ. How could I have fucked this up so royally? My usual PI was out of town and swore his nephew, Peter, would compile all the intel he could on her ... fucking fired and blacklisted. A fucking child ... what am I going to do?

In hindsight, I recall a subtle scent of wildflowers and baby powder emanating from her as I held her for the pictures on Friday. The scent was sweet and nostalgic, and now I know why.

A sharp ding from my phone jolts me, and I reach into my suit pocket with trembling hands to retrieve it.

HENRY

> All news outlets have received the wedding photos. I'm sure they'll run pieces by tomorrow morning at the latest.

"Fuck!" I mutter.

How could I have forgotten?

I gaze over at Willow, who watches me with concern and skepticism, and then at her son. There's no turning back now.

Everyone will know about our marriage within the next twelve hours. How am I going to explain a child to my parents and the world? The timeline's accuracy is already crucial, and throwing a child into the mix makes it much more difficult.

No. Not difficult. Fucked. So fucking fucked.

He has dark hair like mine and hers, so it should be believable to the outside world ... but still.

What if the child's father tries to come back into the picture?

The child has seriously complicated the fuck out of this, and I'm not sure I can handle it.

No, I know I can't handle it.

It fucking hurts.

Why does it still hurt so much?

"Is everything okay?" Willow whispers, nestling the now quiet child against her chest.

"Stay on your side of the penthouse," I bark before turning and striding out to the sound of her son crying yet again.

This is fucked.

7

GABRIEL

COLLEGE AGE 20

My feet scream in protest as I stumble into the dorm, drenched to the bone after a furious thunderstorm turned our practice into a muddy battle. However, Coach didn't seem to mind the wet, chilling wind as he huddled under the thin cover of the dugout. It was a punishment for the party that the team got caught at last night. Being the team captain, I know better than to party before a game.

We lost badly, and the scouts in the stands witnessed my worst performance ever. The air following the game was thick with the scent of stale sweat and defeat, and I felt the weight of the team's disappointment settle heavily on my shoulders as their leader.

My parents said little, but I knew my poor performance disappointed them. I know better than to let a drunken night shatter my dreams.

Playing professional ball is my goal, and my father told me to follow that dream, but our family's company would be my safety net if I changed my mind. The pull to join the company is strong, and I'm working hard with my business and economics studies, but the thrill of baseball is too deeply rooted—it's an essential part of who I am and who I plan to be.

"There you are. I've been waiting for hours," my girlfriend, Eryn, says as I open the door.

My heart fills with warmth and speeds up as I see her lying in my bed, wearing only a raglan shirt with my name across the back. She's so perfect, and for some reason, she chose me.

"Sorry, babe. We had practice after the game. Coach was pissed about last night."

"I don't get why a little partying is such a big deal."

"It's about discipline and keeping our word. We play the best when we're rested and without alcohol coursing through our veins."

"Whatever," she says with a shrug of her shoulders.

"Are you okay?"

"I'm fine," she clips.

Stroking her cheek, I lean in and give her a chaste kiss.

"Gross. You're all wet!"

"Shit. Sorry, babe." I rub the few drops of rain from her face. "Is everything okay?"

"Everything's fine."

I pause. She's said fine twice now. I've learned from my mother that when a woman says everything is fine, it's usually not.

I take her soft, rosy cheeks in my hands. "Tell me what's wrong so I can fix it."

Eryn pulls back and hands me a gift bag with crumpled paper on top, puzzling me since it's neither my birthday nor Christmas. "What's this?"

"Open it."

Smiling, I say okay, then lean over to kiss her again. I seriously can't get enough of her.

I take out a tiny doll outfit and chuckle. "Babe, I'm afraid this won't fit."

"Read it," she whispers.

I quirk a brow. "Daddy's MVP?" My eyes return to her. "I don't understand."

"I'm pregnant, baby," she says, wrapping her arms around my neck.

The shock leaves me breathless, rooted to the spot, as if the very ground is about to vanish beneath me. Pregnant? We've been extremely careful. She's on the pill. I've worn a condom every time religiously. Although I know both options weren't completely reliable, I'm stunned by the outcome.

She pulls away and frowns. "You aren't happy?"

God, I hate when she looks upset. I only want to make her happy. I shake my head. "No, babe, I'm happy. I'm just surprised."

"I was, too. But now we're going to be together forever. You, me, and our baby."

8

WILLOW

"Are you sure you remember everything?" Gabriel asks from the driver's seat of his black Mercedes AMG.

My gaze drifts from the sun-drenched rolling hills outside with the last hints of summer to his unnerving stare.

Does he ever allow himself a moment of ease, or is his life a constant, high-strung performance, the kind that makes you wonder when he'll finally snap?

"I'm waiting."

I take in his crisp white Henley, which stresses his well-defined arms and hugs his torso. The contrast against the low-slung dark denim is striking. Then I gaze back up at his tense arms, the muscles bunching, knuckles stark white as he grips the wheel, his face etched with irritation.

Despite his relaxed attire, he's just as dictatorial and unpleasant as usual.

"For the millionth time, yes. You all but made me flashcards and drew me pictures," I snap.

His behavior has been unpleasant ever since he learned of Grayson's existence almost a week ago, leading to a cycle of negativity and equally rude responses from me.

46

I pull down the visor and look to the back seat, where Grayson is fast asleep. Thank goodness. Why Gabriel is so bothered by him, I'll never understand. It's not like I've asked him to change a dirty diaper or watch him.

"Where did we meet?"

Annoyance prickles me. I slam the visor shut, the sharp click echoing in the quiet car, and gaze forward at the ever-growing mansions, each one more breathtaking than the last, their immaculate lawns stretching out like green carpets. "A company party."

"Who approached whom?"

My jaw grinds. I find his "version" of our first meeting that he made up to be utterly unbelievable.

"I approached you ... though I never would," I mutter the last part.

"Excuse me?"

"I approached you," I repeat.

"Yeah, I got that. What was the last part?" His amused tone has me gazing back into his eyes, which now sparkle with the same mirth as they did over dinner the other night when I was giving him shit.

Is this the trick for him not to act so beastly? I need to be sarcastic and bitchy?

His gruff attitude is something I've learned to navigate by giving it back to him, but these rare moments when he acts playful—a smirk here, a light jab there—throw me off.

With a nervous lick of my parched lips, I stare into his eyes, attempting to project an air of indifference. "I would never approach you."

His lips pull into a slow grin. "What's wrong with me?"

Looks-wise, absolutely nothing, unfortunately. Personality-wise, too much to count on one hand.

"Not a thing, Sir." I smirk.

An iron gate creaks open, and as we proceed up the long,

twisting driveway, the rhythmic crunch of gravel under our tires blends with the rustling leaves of the trees lining the way.

"Don't call me sir in front of my parents."

The swift change in his demeanor leaves me with a mild case of whiplash.

Hello, mood swings.

"What would you like me to call you then?"

His face twists into a mask of nausea and revulsion. "My mother will probably expect a pet name."

"Do you have one in mind?"

He lets out a heavy sigh as he shifts the car into park. "I detest them all, so no. Just pick one."

Jerk? Dick? Asshole? Tyrant?

With a sharp click, he unbuckles his seatbelt and pushes the car door open. A wave of cool afternoon air washes over me, which is a welcome relief from the car's intense interior temperature from a certain someone. With a forceful slam, the door shuts, and the vibrations make me grumble under my breath.

"What a romantic ..." I mutter as I watch him circle the car with a swagger I envy, each step radiating self-assurance. It's rather irritating.

He opens my door and extends his hand like a true gentleman, and it takes everything in me not to roll my eyes.

I reach for his hand, stepping out onto the uneven cobblestones, and go to take another step, but my heel catches. I twist, my feet tangling, and face-plant into his hard chest with a surprised, breathless huff. The scent of his citrus and woodsy cologne, warm and comforting like a weighted blanket, fills my senses as I inhale deeply.

"Falling for me already, *wife*?" A hint of amusement colors his whispered words.

Wife? Kill me now.

"Ugh. Not in this life or the next. Let me go," I grumble,

steadying myself and smoothing the imaginary wrinkles from my flowy yellow and blue floral dress as Gabriel steps back to give me space.

Not wanting to face him after the embarrassment, I turn and reach for the back passenger car door, but Gabriel's hand swiftly covers mine, causing me to raise a skeptical brow.

"I'll get it."

Ah, I forgot; he's in performance mode.

"He's a *him*, not an *it*." I squeeze between Gabriel and the car to lift a stretching Grayson from his car seat. "You can get the carrier and diaper bag since you want to be so helpful, *baby*."

"Do not call me that," he snaps, a sour look on his face, before wrestling the overflowing blue diaper bag and bulky carrier from the trunk.

Geez.

"Then maybe you should've picked the stupid pet name, you dictatorial asshat," I mutter to myself.

He leans in toward me and whispers. "I'm beginning to think you like to talk shit under your breath."

I hold my tongue before I say something I might regret, like, *Yeah, dick, what of it?*

"And were you expecting an overnight trip with how heavy this bag is?"

"I got nervous. I wasn't sure what to expect." Looking at the new diaper bag about to explode, a small smile touches my lips. "Thank you again for all of Grayson's new stuff."

The night Gabriel came in, found Grayson, and left so upset, I didn't know what to expect by morning, but it sure wasn't a new diaper bag, carrier, crib, and a mountain of toys and clothes ranging from six months to a year. It was unexpected and thoughtful, and completely contradicted the way he's acted for the rest of the week.

Again, mood swings.

His only response to my thanks is a curt nod.

Okay.

Together we climb the steps to his parents' enormous, ornately carved wooden door, which is easily ten feet tall, flanked by hornbeam topiary spirals and a cute welcome doormat with a big cursive R in the middle.

My stomach lurches, a sickening twist of anxiety that brings on a wave of dizziness and the metallic tang of vomit to the back of my throat. Meeting his family is nerve-racking, but deceiving them is far more unsettling.

The question I keep asking myself is: Why go to these extreme lengths? What prize, what ultimate goal could possibly be worth the high price he's willing to pay? And what happens if it all falls apart?

He pushes open the heavy oak door; the hinges groan in protest, and I hesitantly follow.

If I thought his breathtaking penthouse, with its panoramic city views and sleek, modern design, was impressive, his parents' house was simply magnificent.

It evokes a sense of timeless elegance with soaring high ceilings, intricate crown molding, crisp white walls, and gleaming polished mahogany floors. All that's missing are little cherubs painted on the ceiling while lying on fluffy white clouds.

"Let me see my grandbaby." A woman with chin-length brown hair in an elegant, crisp white pantsuit rushes toward us, smiling, as we walk into the entryway. Her energy washes over me in a warm wave, a comforting yet intense sensation that brings a nervous but happy smile to my lips.

"Mother—"

"Don't you dare mother me," she says, giving him a kiss on both cheeks before pushing him to the side and giving Grayson and me her full attention. I move from one foot to the other as I hold Grayson to my chest, wrecked with anxiety.

What if she hates me? What if I mess up and she finds out this is all a lie?

She smiles. "Oh dear, you're gorgeous, the spitting image of Snow White. Your wedding photographs didn't do you justice."

"Th-thank you, ma'am."

"Vivian, but call me Mom. Not Mother like this one over here. He's always so formal." She rolls her eyes, making me smile. "And my grandbaby, oh, my grandbaby," she coos as she holds her arms out.

I'm usually nervous about handing him off, but the pure love and wonder coming from Gabriel's mother's blue eyes both put me at ease and make me want to cry at the same time. The absence of grandparents left a hole in my heart and a fear for Grayson, but now I see a different future for him, one full of love.

The delusional thought makes me shake my head. There is an expiration date on our contract. One I should remember.

"He's so precious and has your nose and dark features, Gabriel. I need to get your baby pictures out so we can compare." I steal a glance at him. Silent discomfort emanates from his rigid spine and furrowed brows. "I can't believe we leave for a trip abroad and this is what we come home to. A daughter-in-law and grandbaby. I would've loved to have been at both important events."

"I didn't want to ruin your long-awaited trip. You've been planning it for years."

"The trip isn't as important as family, son. I want to be a part of every milestone you have. You know this."

I feel awful as I witness Vivian's eyes glass over with unshed tears. If she only knew what was really going on. I'm sure she would be even more upset than the prospect of missing her son's wedding and her grandbaby being born.

"I'm sorry, Mother."

"We will find a way to fix this, won't we, Grayson?" she

whispers, her touch gentle as she kisses my son's head and rubs his back in small, comforting circles. "Let me at least see the ring."

My hands, clammy and restless, twist in front of me until Gabriel's cold, assessing gaze forces me to clasp them awkwardly behind my back.

"We're waiting to get it back. It had to be resized." The lie rolls off his tongue so effortlessly, it's scary. He really has thought of everything.

"Well, I can't wait to see it. Let's go to the sitting room. Your father should be done with his business call soon," Vivian says before turning around with Grayson and walking away.

Gabriel looms over me like a gloomy cloud. "You need to keep it together."

"I'm trying," I say as we both follow his mother down a long hall.

Gerard, Gabriel's dad, strolls in from another hallway just as we step into the sitting room, and it's as if the room has suddenly gained a window to the future. Gerard and Gabriel both share the same tall, imposing physique. His symmetrical, sharp jawline is framed by jet black hair, speckled with gray, and the same familiar eyes as Gabriel's bore into me.

"Son," Gerard says, his voice thick with emotion as he pulls Gabriel in for a hug before stepping in front of me, which fills me with dread once more, but the feeling fades as he smiles. "Willow, it's a pleasure to meet you. Welcome to the family."

"Thank you, Sir," I say, feeling the firmness of his grip as he takes my hand.

"Call me Gerard." I nod and decide he might not be as warm as Vivian, but he's still not frigid like Gabriel.

He turns and affectionately rubs the top of Grayson's head.

"Isn't he just the cutest?" Vivian asks Gerard with hearts in her eyes. "He reminds me of Gabriel when he was a baby."

"Grayson's cuter," Gerard says, a remark that draws a laugh

from me, while Gabriel's expression is unreadable, hard as stone.

Geez.

I spent the next hour admiring Vivian's home as she showed me around, all while making small talk as she asked me about Grayson, while Gabriel and Gerard animatedly talked about baseball. Meeting a family is new and intimidating, especially since Darren was an orphan too, but I felt like things were going well—or so I thought.

As the day progressed, Gabriel's mood seemed to darken. The air crackled with tension during dinner as Gabriel and his father clashed over a business Reed Equity bought shares in.

The client, an old family friend, is facing Gabriel's notoriously tough negotiating tactics. It doesn't surprise me. But what does is how Gerard, despite his retirement, remains so heavily involved in the business. It seems he isn't happy with any decision his son makes, and he has no problem letting him know. Repeatedly.

Although Gabriel can be a real asshole, I don't think he deserved to be chastised like that during a Friday night family dinner.

The absence of family is painful, but I can imagine it's almost worse to endure a parent's constant disapproval and disappointment.

Vivian then requested a photo of the three of us, and to Gabriel's obvious displeasure, he had to hold Grayson. I handed him over while noting Gabriel's stiff posture and uncertainty. Then his father made a comment about how it looked as if Gabriel had never held him. It was unbelievably uncomfortable and only seemed to piss Gabriel off that much more.

The entire ride to his parents' house, Gabriel was worried about me messing something up, but he's the one who acted strangely. And if his parents catch on, it will be because of him.

After dinner with his parents, Gabriel dropped Grayson

and me off in the dimly lit parking garage under the penthouse. Without so much as a goodbye, he peeled out, using the lame excuse of 'plans.'

It sounds suspiciously like cheating, from the way he was acting, but I didn't call him on it. If he chooses not to stick to his word, that's on him, and if I were a different person, a petty person, I'd probably pay him back out of spite.

9

GABRIEL

The sound of Frank Renner's laugh, like nails on a fucking chalkboard, sets my teeth on edge. I glare at his condescending smile aimed at me, while my father, who sits at the head of the conference table in my chair, barks out a laugh in return.

At this point, I don't know whose kneecaps I'd like to bust with a baseball bat first. Frank, who's radiating smug self-assurance about his new business deal, versus my father, who offered Frank a lousy business deal behind my back.

They blindsided me an hour ago when they both showed up for a meeting I knew nothing about, a meeting I had every right to be a part of and have a voice in.

With every ounce of self-control I possess, born through years of discipline and respect for my father, that's diminishing by the second, I remain composed, but on the inside, I'm burning with rage.

I've poured over thirteen years of my life into this company —and what have I got to show for it? Nothing but a father who treats me as if I'm still that sixteen-year-old boy who sat at his desk, fumbling to make sense of all the paperwork.

I've generated hundreds of millions through tireless work and innovative strategies. I deserve to feel appreciated for my efforts and contributions, instead of being treated like a disposable placeholder. Yet here we are, with Frank about to sign a contract I didn't agree to. One I wouldn't agree to in a million fucking years. Setting fire to the money and watching the ashes fall would be a more appropriate use; that's how I envision the next year unfolding as Frank squanders it, just as he did in the past, before we intervened.

One thing I've learned over the years, as I've wrestled control from countless companies, is that people are creatures of habit; their ingrained behaviors are resistant to change, especially someone as set in their ways as he is. He's stubborn, clinging to methods from four decades past, believing they still hold relevance. They don't. Something my father also believes, which is why profits have soared since he left the company to take my mother on their extended vacation. A vacation I wish he was still on.

Their pens scratch across the paper, a sound that echoes the weight of the disastrous decision and binds Reed Equity to a two-year partnership with the failing company.

"I believe congratulations are in order?" Frank says while giving me a shit-eating grin.

I give him one of my own, my mind racing with schemes to get us out of this contract once the storm has passed. *Car accident? House fire? Unfortunate cardiac arrest by scaring him to death? Mugging gone wrong?* The possibilities are endless.

"Congratulations." With a silent toast to Frank Renner's impending demise, I lift my glass of scotch in the air before I drink it in one long, satisfying gulp and stand. "If you'll both excuse me—"

"Stay back, son." I gaze over at my father, who gives Frank a curt nod, his eyes lingering on Frank's retreating back before returning to mine. "You seem to have quite a problem with the deal."

"Because it's a giant mistake. I told you this over dinner last night. His company—"

"Needs our help," my father says, placing the signed documents in a manila folder and closing the metal clamps.

"Which I've given him."

"We need to give him more. It's not always about making money, son."

My eyes widen, and I throw my hands up in exasperation, staring at him as if he's sprouted a second head. As my father has aged, he's become more sensitive, which has affected his business decisions, making them less practical. If I allow his argument to continue, I foresee myself being the sole person frantically scooping water as the ship gradually sinks.

"You had no right to make that decision without consulting me. I—"

He says something, but I can't hear shit over the grinding of my jaw and the fresh wave of furious anger boiling inside me as I'm cut off for the third time in the matter of one minute. I clamp down hard on the inside of my cheek, the sharp pain and copper taste a welcome distraction from the words threatening to escape my lips.

It's crazy to think I used to crave his approval, validation that I was good enough to be his son, a need that now feels distant and absurd. All my hard work means nothing.

Once I see his lips stop moving, the ringing in my ears fades, and I do what I always do when I'm not in the mood to argue.

I grit my teeth, forcing a smile and mumble, "You know best, Sir." The words taste like ash in my mouth.

Turning, I grab my belongings and leave the meeting room before he can utter another word. With a sigh, I stride to my office and go straight to the mini-bar, but stop short when I remember the reason for being here today. The Reed Equity Annual Employee Appreciation Party.

My hand fists the neck of an aged Macallan. I yearn for the oblivion the bottle of liquor promises; I'd even welcome the burn of the alcohol as a temporary solace. My eyes close, and I squeeze the glass before letting it go and face my office.

None of this is mine. Not the desk, nor the chair, nor the file folders sitting on top. Not even the fountain pens.

It's still my father's.

What was the fucking point of dedicating so many years to this company?

What was the fucking point of marrying Willow if it didn't convince my father to relinquish control of the family business as he promised once I settled down?

What was the fucking point?

The office door slams louder than intended as I storm to the elevator, descending to the second floor, where the muffled sounds of laughter, music, and clinking glasses from the banquet hint at the lively party.

One hour. That's as much as I can handle today, and then I'm gone.

I appreciate my employees' hard work, but the exhaustion and resentment are affecting my judgment, and I lack the energy for small talk. A sharp pang of guilt pierces me—I owe them my time, considering their commitment of five, sometimes six, days a week. My father might not appreciate my work ethic, but I appreciate theirs.

"Finally, you showed up," Kennedy says, handing me a glass.

The champagne bubbles tickle my nose as I take a drink and savor every second as my gaze sweeps over the hall. A wave of joyous laughter and upbeat music fills the air, mingling with the aroma of the buffet.

Some employees move on the dance floor, others are currently cramming into the photo booth, while some are happily piling their plates high. My hardworking party staff quietly move through the sidelines, carefully setting up the raffles and games and replenishing the dessert bar.

"Frank Renner showed up for a meeting with my father."

"Shit. How'd it go?" Kennedy asks.

My eyes scan the room until they fall on a group of employees huddled together in a circle off to the right side of the dance floor. My eyes linger on a killer ass in a tight navy dress. Her backside is perfection, and I'm tempted, so fucking tempted.

I shake my head and gaze at Kennedy.

"That fucking bad, huh?"

"I'll find a way out of it, and if I don't, I'm gone," I say, my gaze falling back to the woman in the dress that has the power of making me fall to my knees.

"What about your legacy?"

I snort. "Over the years, I've deluded myself into believing it would be mine, working as hard as I fucking can to prove myself when really, it'll always belong to my father. His saying he'd hand it over once I settled down with a family is a crock of shit."

"Fuck, man," Kennedy murmurs as he clears his throat. "You know, I miss my dad more than anything, but I'd hate for him to be up my ass about work. Constantly criticizing my choices and sabotaging my deals. It would drive me crazy. I don't know how you keep sane."

Through his trust fund, my father founded and financially backed Reed Equity, with Kennedy's father being my father's right-hand man and closest companion until he suffered a heart attack many years ago. They made a deal early on, which dictated that if one of them were to pass, the other would keep the position vacant for their child to inherit. My father remained true to what he had said and gave the position to Kennedy after he finished college.

"I haven't. I've reached my limit, and I believe it's time to seriously consider moving on. Starting my own company—"

"I'm down."

"You'd come?" I quirk a brow. "I haven't even given you my proposal."

"*Proposal* ... I hate that fucking word. And fuck yeah, one of my younger brothers can take over my dad's position. Kayden would be the best bet since he actually works for the company; Kade is too busy with cyber bullshit, and Knox is still in college. I want a fifty-fifty partnership, three months off a year ... no, make it four, and I get dibs on picking my office first."

"Anything else?" I say while observing the woman in the navy dress lean closer to Greg Thompson as if the words spewing from his lips are gospel. He works in accounting, but his ridiculous antics make it clear he's far better suited to clown school. Luckily for him, he's still good at his job.

"I want my name first."

"What?" I ask, gazing over at Kennedy.

"Heartwright and Reed. Not Reed and Heartwright."

With a snort, I tear my gaze away and refocus on the group. "I'll think about it."

"She's got a nice ass, huh?" Kennedy asks as I sidestep, angling for a better view of the woman.

Shit. What am I doing?

My thoughts are a jumbled mess, and I really should go, but I can't look away.

At the last moment, she subtly shifts her weight toward Mr. Thompson, and a sudden chill runs down my spine.

"Surprise!" Kennedy exclaims with a laugh.

Fucking Willow.

My fists clench, and a burning rage boils inside me like lava as I watch her stand too close to him, him gazing at her with a smile that deserves to be messed up. He might get into clown school after all. His arm wraps around her shoulder, and my feet move on their own.

Who the fuck does he think he is, touching what's mine?

10

WILLOW

I *lied.*
I am petty and spiteful.

Leaning closer to my old co-worker Greg, the thick, almost sickeningly sweet scent of his cologne assaults my nostrils, causing my nose to wrinkle. However, I hold my position as the weight of Gabriel's intense gaze burns into my back; I can practically feel the heat radiating from his eyes.

Despite no longer being a Reed Equity employee, I wasn't going to miss the annual party, and when Vivian asked to watch Grayson, I agreed because he deserves the love and attention of a grandma, no matter how fleeting that may be.

Since arriving in Reed Equity's opulent banquet hall, amidst the sparkling chandeliers, lively chatter, and clinking champagne glasses, I've avoided Gabriel like the plague—a task made easier by his recent arrival just five minutes ago. But the second he walked in, I felt a tangible shift in the atmosphere; the air crackled with a hushed energy.

After his 'plans' which kept him out until well past two this morning, I made up my mind.

I'll play the game, but I won't be his fool, which is why I'm being a bit petty by standing a little too close to another man.

I'd never cross the line, but a bitter resentment fuels a reckless decision to flirt with the edge, toeing the precipice, tempting my fate, which is in Gabriel's hands, with a spiteful grin.

It's a cheap thrill, yes, but it ignites a feeling of empowerment with a small flame of defiance burning bright.

We made a deal, but he didn't keep his end of the bargain. So here we are.

Aella's eyes dart between Greg and me, her mouth forming the silent question, "What the fuck are you doing?" from across the noisy, crowded circle of six. A mischievous grin stretches across my face as I shrug, enjoying the sight of her smile widening as she downs the champagne in one go and then mouths, "That's my girl," and does a little dance.

My snort rings out, perfectly timed to follow Greg's weak joke, but he remains oblivious, basking in the attention of us five girls.

Although the air vibrates with the bass-heavy classic music, punctuated by shrill peals of laughter and the constant, murmuring chatter of the crowd, all I feel is the intense weight of Gabriel's stare boring into me.

It's a strange mix of fear and excitement, a delightful yet unnerving feeling.

"So, when were you going to tell us, Willow?"

I blink out of my haze and gaze over at Hally. The resident gossip queen of Reed Equity. She's in her mid-thirties and thrives on everyone else's juicy business. "Tell you what?"

"Umm, hello? That you were with the boss. All those times we all discussed his—"

"I'd watch your words, Hally," Aella warns. "She's your boss now, too."

Hally bites her bottom lip before directing her light blue

eyes toward me again. "It just doesn't make sense; you're practically new, and he's never shown you any attention. I've never even seen you two talk."

"Yeah, I thought you were going to give me a chance, Willow," Greg says as he places his arm around me, and it makes my stomach roll.

A surge of anxious adrenaline shoots through me as I feel like they've caught on to our deception, but Aella's face, as she sneers at Hally and then Greg, tells me I have nothing to worry about. She has my back.

"It doesn't fucking have to make sense," Aella snaps while pointing her champagne flute at first, Hally, then at Greg. "Many of us prefer privacy and dislike nosy individuals like yourselves prying for information they'll spread to others. And you, I'd stop touching your boss's wife before he rips your arm off."

"I hope I'm not interrupting," Gabriel says, pulling me closer to him and possessively placing his arm around my waist, causing my stomach to drop.

Four things happen instantaneously. The palpable shift in the air is immediate as Hally, Ginger, and Beth from the other side of the circle slowly melt with heart eyes for Gabriel. *Gag.* Greg's retreat is abrupt as he takes a large step away from me. *Smart man.* Aella's hostile gaze locks onto Gabriel. *My best friend is the best.* Finally, the nearness of my pretend husband, holding me close, leaves me paralyzed. His arm, shockingly, is more comforting than Greg's and, weirdly, feels right?

No.

"You aren't interrupting at all, Mr. Reed." Hally smiles seductively, and I kind of want to throat punch her.

"Excellent. I'd actually like to have a moment with my *wife* if you'll excuse us," he says while pulling me away.

The way he says *wife* ...

Gabriel places his hand on the small of my back and guides

me out of the banquet hall before rushing me into a storage room off to the right, filled with racks of cleaning supplies.

"What the fuck are you doing here?" he whispers with his face inches from mine.

"Enjoying the party at the company I spent months working for."

"You mean stealing from."

My teeth clench as I glare into his dark brown eyes, which look sinister in the dim light of the room.

Is this going to be something he brings up constantly? I've repeatedly apologized and readily accepted all his conditions. I'm so over it. It's not like I stole from him to buy frivolous items. I did it for the survival of Grayson and me.

Since the night he coerced me into marrying him, I haven't felt the need to offer an explanation because I know he wouldn't believe me or wouldn't care. Which is why, even though I'm curious, I haven't asked what his motive is for marrying me. It's not like he'd tell me anyway. But this—this I can't stand anymore.

"After my ex spent all my money and left me, three men in masks came to my house and threatened to take Grayson if I didn't pay them the money he owed. They held guns to his head while they threatened me. I was terrified and just wanted to save my son. That's why I stole the money. I've apologized to you countless times. I've agreed to everything you've asked. What more do you want from me? I have nothing left." My hands tremble, a furious energy coursing through me as I barely breathe the last sentence.

I bite my bottom lip as tears well in my eyes before studying the black-and-white speckled linoleum floor so he doesn't see the defeated look on my face.

As silence descends in the small, bleach-smelling storage room, a wave of icy dread washes over me. I expect a harsh rebuttal, a declaration that I'm lying or that I've brought this on myself, but nothing comes, and the silence that follows is deafening.

Gabriel clears his throat, and his voice is more of a murmur and less of a sharp snap. "I didn't want us to have our first outing as a married couple yet."

I nod. "I understand."

"Look ..." He sighs. "I—"

The doorknob jingles melodically, then swings open with a flourish as Aella pokes her head in, her bright eyes sparkling with mischief. "Oh, I'm sorry. I didn't know anyone was in here." Gazing from one of us to the other, she registers our proximity, and so do I. The scent of his cologne blanketing my senses and the touch of his hand on my elbow is a sudden, heavy feeling.

Has he been holding my arm this whole time?

"You okay, Wills?"

"Yeah, Elle, I'll be out soon."

With a withering look toward Gabriel, her eyes blazing with contempt and simmering anger, Aella slams the door behind her, the sharp click echoing in the silence.

Gabriel's slitted eyes pierce me. "I'm assuming you broke the non-disclosure agreement and told Aella Marks."

Shit.

"I—"

"Just ..." Exasperated, he shakes his head and lets out a shaky breath. "Forget it. I need to get the fuck out of here."

As he grabs the handle and opens the door, I find my voice. "She won't say anything."

"You don't know that."

"She's my best friend."

He snorts and walks out. "Of course she is."

My hand slams against the closing door, and I walk out to see Gabriel waiting by the bank of elevators.

"Hey, what's going on?" Aella asks from my side.

"I don't know."

"Where's he going?"

"I don't know that either," I say, watching him get into a waiting elevator.

"Let's find out," Aella says as she grabs my arm and pulls me toward the stairwell. "We'll lose him if we have to wait for another."

"I don't know if this is a good idea."

"This is the best idea. You think he's cheating. Let's go find out."

Three flights of stairs later, with my heart racing and legs burning, we burst into the cool, damp air of the dimly lit underground parking garage.

Gabriel's black AMG peels out just as the stairwell door closes behind us.

"Shit. Let's hurry before we lose him," Aella says.

I race after her, my breath catching in my throat, as she sprints to her car. I jump in with a squeal just as she reverses and shifts into drive.

"Geez. Let me get my seatbelt on." I'm jostled around like a rag doll as she hits the speed bumps without applying the brakes.

"Where do you think he went?" She asks as she stops at the opening of the parking garage and looks first right, then left.

I gaze to the right and see the back end of his car turning two stoplights ahead. "There."

Aella makes a hard right and skids to the side. "Jesus, Elle! I'm not ready to die."

"The only person who will die is Gabriel if he's off to be with a mistress."

She makes another right at the second stoplight and eases off the gas as we're now two cars behind him.

Now that my mind has caught up to the fact that we're actually following him, doubt creeps in, and a knot of unease forms in my stomach. "What are we even going to do if he is?" I whisper.

Aella gazes at me with sympathy before locking her eyes on his car again. "What do you want to do?"

"I don't know."

Aella leaves me with my thoughts after that, and I'm grateful. Even if this relationship is a sham, the betrayal will still sting. The feeling of inadequacy will fester and take root deep within me, poisoning the next three years.

We continue following him for another thirty minutes into an industrial area of Chicago. One I wouldn't be caught dead in at night. With the sun gone, the concrete buildings stand stark and silent against the somber sky, their empty windows like vacant eyes, creating an eerie, desolate atmosphere.

I gaze at Aella, her lips pressed into a thin line, knuckles white as bone as she grips the wheel.

"Elle, what's the matter?"

She shakes her head solemnly. "I'm sorry, Wills."

"For what?" I say, gazing around as Aella stops and takes out a key card before placing it against a screen that opens a gate to the underground parking garage. "What is this place?"

She blows out a long breath as she parks in a spot. "A sex club."

My eyes widen as I point a finger upward. "Here?"

She nods.

"How do you know about this place?"

She sends me a sardonic smile.

"Oh my God, Elle. Why haven't you told me?"

"What was I supposed to say? Willow, I just went to a sex club and had my uterus scrambled in the best way possible?"

A heavy silence hangs in the air before we both erupt in laughter, the sound echoing around us, and it's exactly what I need to temper my rising anxiety. "Okay, maybe not."

"Yeah, I thought so."

A thought sobers me. "Have you ever seen Gabriel here?"

"Absolutely not. I would've told you right away."

I nod. "I know. I'm sorry for asking. I'm just shocked but also not shocked ... you know? Well, I'm shocked about you coming here, but not Gabriel."

"There's no reason to be sorry. Do you want to go in or leave?"

Ringing my hands in my lap, I survey the parking garage with gleaming chrome and polished paint of at least thirty luxury cars. Gabriel's being one of them.

Of course, he'd be somewhere like this. The secluded high-end property is hidden away, perfect for indulging in debauchery while maintaining a flawless public image.

"They have a bar with a club-style setting in the front. No nudity or penetration whatsoever. That's behind closed doors. We could have a drink and dance the night away." When I say nothing, she continues. "When you were with Darren, you were never able to go out. Never able to be free. Now, you have the opportunity. How often are you out by yourself? To be *just* Willow? Not the kick-ass single mom or the smart as hell accountant, or—"

"Okay, fine," I say, laughing at her attempt at sweet-talking me. If Gabriel's here to be with a woman, I doubt he'd be on the dance floor. Hopefully, I won't see him at all.

After signing another non-disclosure agreement, agreeing to the club's rules, getting a high-tech bracelet placed around my wrist, and feeling like I'm completely out of my depth, we're on the dancefloor.

The music's powerful beat courses through my veins; sweat slicks my skin as crimson beams dance across the smoky club. A smile touches my lips. This feels amazing.

I feel exhausted yet so alive.

Chained but free.

Darren never let me go out, and if he did, he would hover

and make the night absolutely miserable. Everything would always start out fine, but as the night progressed, he'd get upset about something that never happened. It's like the fight came out of thin air. I'd cross some invisible line, and then I'd have to leave. After years of his control, this feels like a fresh start, a tiny step toward freedom.

And although I love Grayson and miss him, it's nice to be *just* Willow for once.

Aella mimics drinking with her hand, and I shake my head. I've had one shot already, and I still have to go home and replace *just* Willow for the kick-ass single mom, as Aella so eloquently put it. She mouths she'll be right back, and I nod, then close my eyes and let the music wash over me.

A moment later, a searing heat radiates from behind, accompanied by the pressure of a body against mine. I hesitate for a single second while the word cheater rolls around in my mind before shrugging and continuing to dance.

Since arriving, Gabriel's absence is deafening; it can only mean one thing—he's cheating somewhere in this club. One innocent dance with a stranger pales in comparison to the gravity of Gabriel's far worse deeds behind the club's closed doors.

The music swells, and as we dance, I feel the heat radiating from my dancing partner's broad chest while his muscular forearm, corded with muscle, holds me securely around my waist. My fingers graze the back of his neck, nails lightly scratching, sending a wave of goose bumps across his skin. The intoxicating aroma of him—wood-smoke, amber, citrus, and a hint of fine scotch—fills my senses with an odd sense of recognition as his nose skims my neck until his lips linger near my ear, eliciting a soft moan from my mouth.

"What the fuck are you doing here, Willow?"

My eyes snap open, and a gasp escapes my lips as Gabriel's voice, sharp and clear, pierces my thoughts.

No. No. No.

I try to pull away, but his arm cinches around me tighter. "Ah, ah, ah. Where do you think you're going?"

"Away from you," I spit back as I gaze up at him. I feel played and so incredibly stupid right now. This was supposed to be an innocent dance with a stranger. Not with my fake asshole husband, who just made me moan seconds ago.

"Why? Are you trying to meet someone tonight?" He gestures toward the bar, with its dazzling wall of liquor and disco balls that bounce light around the room. "Maybe that asshole who bought you a shot twenty minutes ago? Or maybe Mr. Thompson, who you blatantly flirted with earlier at my company party."

"You've been watching me?" I ask incredulously, then shake my head before gazing back up at him. "You know what? Forget it. What's it to you, anyway? I'm the one who followed you to a sex club. Seems like you're the one trying to meet someone tonight."

Gabriel's eyes hold mine as he rasps, "Seems like I did." His mouth almost brushes mine before he grinds himself against my backside.

My eyes widen in shock, not only from the very hard and impressive bulge but from his brazenness. This isn't like him. I gaze into his eyes, red and glassy and slightly blown. He's drunk, but I don't call him on it. Instead, I pucker my lips and say, "Seems like you aren't following your rules."

"Seems like I'm dancing with my wife."

Wife. There's that word again. Only this time, it sounds strange on his tongue, lacking the sharp edge it held earlier.

"Why don't you run along? You didn't keep your promise and, to be honest, maybe I won't either."

"Promise?" He quirks a brow.

I snort. "Of course you wouldn't remember that you promised not to touch other women."

A serious look etches itself onto his features. "I haven't touched anyone since we got married."

His sincere tone, though slightly strained and slurred, makes me hesitate. But years of horrible luck have taught me to distrust a man's smooth words that may seem genuine. Besides, the evidence is all around us.

"Yet here you are ... at a sex club. I knew you were an asshole, but I didn't expect you to be a cheater and a liar, too."

He steels his eyes as his jaw clicks. "I am many things, *Willow Reed*, but a cheater and a—"

"What's going on here?" Aella yells over the music.

Without taking his eyes off me, Gabriel yells, "Miss. Marks, fuck off."

"Excuse me?" Aella asks with a hand on her hip.

"Fuck ... off, Aella," Gabriel repeats.

"It's okay," I say, begging her with my eyes to drop it.

"I'll be over there. Not fucking off, but watching your ass," she spits at Gabriel as she turns and stalks back to the bar.

"She's gonna be a problem," Gabriel says with another slur of his words.

"Not if you start treating me with some decency."

His gaze is unnervingly long, heavy, and intense, pinning me in place until a slight sway in his posture gives me a sliver of relief.

To save my stiff neck, I shift in his embrace, exchanging the view behind me for a look at him. Surprisingly, he releases me. "Let's get you home."

"I don't want to," he murmurs softly, his voice barely audible as he pulls me to him, his body molding against mine yet again. "But you shouldn't be here. You can't be here."

What the hell does that mean?

Trying to separate my body from its current position, I push against him, but he pulls me closer, impossibly so, with a firm grip and an even harder body. "What does that mean, Gabriel?"

"Not right now," he murmurs, his fingers silencing my lips. "Just feel me against you. The way my cock throbs to take you. I can practically hear the sweet sound of your moans in my ear as I pound into your tight cunt."

My eyes widen; my breath catches in my chest as his words hang in the air like a sexually sinister mist. My fingers claw into his biceps, a desperate grip anchoring me against the torrent of words and his close proximity. Resisting the intoxicating feel of his body pressed against mine takes every ounce of my strength, a delicious torment after being starved of intimacy for so long.

He licks his lips as he eyes me with a gleam, and the grin that follows is predatory in a way that makes my stomach flutter and a wetness slick between my thighs.

This can't happen. I can't dance with the devil and like it.

"It's time to go, Gabriel. You're going to regret this tomorrow, if you remember ... that is," I say, taking hold of his arm. "I know I will."

"Which part?" he asks.

I gaze up at him. "What?"

His eyes search my face. "Regret this or remember it?"

"Probably both," I say.

His gaze drifts away, which is a rare occurrence for him, and I take that as my cue to pull him along.

As we pass the bustling bar, I mouth that we're going home. Aella rolls her eyes, but adds, "Drive safe," and requests a text upon arrival.

After collecting his keys and my handbag from the reception area, we head to the parking garage. Down here, the only sounds are the uneven, almost comical thump of Gabriel's feet and of me repeatedly hitting the alarm to locate his car, which is a stark contrast to the otherwise overwhelming stillness.

With a gentle push, I open the passenger door and help Gabriel settle into the seat. His head immediately lolls in the opposite direction, a soft sigh escaping his lips as if he's exhausted, and as I survey him, I think it's true.

The normally sleek perfection of his hair is gone, replaced by a tousled, windswept look, as if he'd run his fingers through it a million times in frustration. The shadows under his eyes are so dark they seem to absorb the surrounding light, and the white dress shirt beneath his slightly askew suit jacket is unbuttoned, revealing a glimpse of his hard, tanned chest.

I shift from foot to foot, the silent battle between convenience for me and safety for him raging. With a heavy sigh and the decision made, I snatch the seatbelt, place my right foot in the car between his open legs, and lean against his warm body to buckle him in, the plastic click clasping loudly in the quiet car.

His head snaps my way with surprising speed, momentarily stunning me before he snatches a strand of my hair, brings it to his nose, and inhales deeply with his eyes squeezed shut.

I stand frozen, my face inches from his, my heart pounding in my chest as time passes, unsure of what to do or say until his eyes open.

A warmth spreads through me as his gaze meets mine, its usual intensity softening with time, or perhaps it is merely a trick of my mind.

"I'm sorry," he whispers.

I raise a brow. "For what exactly?"

Maybe rubbing up against me so indecently it bordered on dry humping? Or for perhaps the seductive words that I never imagined he would say to me.

He shakes his head as if regretting the apology before licking his lips. "I had a business meeting with the owner. He's my friend. I didn't cheat. I'd never cheat." His hand holding the strand of my hair captive falls to his lap, and his eyes close once more.

11

GABRIEL

I drag myself into the entryway, a carry-on in tow, weighed down by exhaustion and a migraine from hell, but the tantalizing scent of a greasy burger and cheese fries with onions covered in thousand island dressing from my thermal container, fights off my desire to go straight to bed. Though I could have eaten it fresh on the West Coast, I chose the solitude of my place over the crowded airport.

Above the mantle, the television flickers, casting a muted light on the room as the credits of a children's movie roll.

Squinting, I spot the black remote on the cool marble table and stride toward it.

My hand halts inches from the remote as Willow's form comes into view on the chaise lounge, Grayson nestled on her chest, his head tucked under her chin, her arms a tight embrace as if even in sleep, he might escape.

I haven't seen her like this—in a restful slumber or anything remotely peaceful. Dealing with me always brings a frown and an irritated notch between her brows.

Her dark hair cascades over the pillow, forming a halo,

while her long lashes rest against her always slightly rosy cheeks.

It's not yet winter, but I still gaze around the living area with the need to find a blanket to cover them in. A small tan blanket adorned with brown teddy bears lies over Grayson, but I doubt it provides enough comfort and warmth. Only decorative pillows made for aesthetics line the couch, but not one blanket is in sight. I've never really used the space and had just requested my mother make it resemble a model in case I wanted to sell it quickly. But now I think having one in the living area could be beneficial for instances like this.

After dropping my bags in the kitchen, I creep to the linen closet right outside my bedroom. I reach for a black plush blanket, still crinkling in its wrapping, which my mother gifted me last Christmas. It feels buttery soft, with a comforting weight to it.

Returning to the couch, I observe Willow, whose red lips are pursed in a small pout, as though she can sense my looming presence.

Leaning over, I carefully drape the blanket just under where her hands hold Grayson, avoiding any physical contact, before finishing by covering her feet while making slight adjustments to keep her lower half warm.

As I stand upright, my gaze follows the line of Willow's small feet up to her face, where her eyes are open and observing me in question as I stand over her like a creep. I clear my throat, the sound echoing softly, and then avert my eyes to the floor.

My hand runs against the back of my neck. "I ... ah ... didn't know you were in here. I was going to turn off the television ... but then I saw you and thought you might be cold, but maybe ..."

I stop because now I sound like a babbling idiot who seems

like he got caught doing something bad, even though my thoughts and actions were pure.

"Sorry," she says as she gracefully rises to a sitting position with a still sleeping Grayson on her, making the blanket I just laid over them fall to her waist. "I must've dozed off for a minute."

I take a step back to give her more space. "It's not a problem."

Her fingers absentmindedly trace the soft, textured blanket before she rises to her feet. Reluctance washes through me at the thought of her leaving when this is the first time I've seen or spoken to her since the embarrassing drunk moments I had at the club with her four nights ago. I want to know we're okay after my behavior.

"You don't have to leave. I just got home from the airport, and ..." I look to the kitchen as if it will bring me some sort of enlightenment and spot my thermal carrier. "Have you ever tried In-N-Out?"

The indent between her brows I know so well forms as she stands before me. I wonder if she's remembering the other night or if she's just confused by my out-of-left-field question. I wait, my anticipation thick in the air.

As she analyzes me, her intense scrutiny feels like a slow burn, a form of torture.

Oh, to be on the other side of someone's unwavering scrutiny.

"Animal style?" she asks.

My lips twitch before they pull into a smirk.

"Is there any other way?"

Her lips curve into a small smile, causing the tightness in my chest to dissolve.

"Let me put him down, and I'll be right back."

I watch her carefully glide down the hall, and I know in her mind she's hoping it's a smooth transition from her arms to his crib without him waking up.

By the time she returns, I've nuked our food and taken out two sodas.

"That smells delicious," she says, walking into the kitchen.

My head tilts as my gaze quickly sweeps over her, taking in her tan pajama set with little bears that look to be the same pattern as Grayson's blanket.

She stops dead in her tracks. "What?"

"Your pajamas match Grayson's blanket."

She pulls on the long-sleeve shirt as if shy, surveying the pattern, before muttering, "Uh, yeah. Aella bought us a mommy and me set."

I nod as if I understand what that even is before she bounds toward me and groans as she dips her head to sniff the delicious food.

"This is a bucket list food item. It better be as delicious as everyone from the West Coast boasts about."

I quirk a brow. "You have food on your bucket list?"

"Of course," she says in a way that makes me feel like I'm an idiot for even asking.

"It's not as good now as it is fresh, but I can tell you right now, it's worth it." Her tongue pokes out to lick her full bottom lip in a way I want to ignore, but can't. "But I'll tell you a secret. You can't tell anyone, though; I could get stoned in the streets," I say dramatically.

As she peers up at me and waits, a playful grin spreads across her face.

"Their fries are awful unless they're covered in cheese and toppings, and even then, they're still just okay."

She fake gasps. "I'm telling everyone!"

A grin pulls at my lips. "You promised you wouldn't say anything."

"I did no such thing."

I snort as I take the knife and cut the double cheeseburger in half before pushing the plate toward her. "For your silence."

Without hesitation, she grabs it and takes a large bite. The moan that follows should be criminal, or maybe the thoughts that come to my mind are.

"Well?"

She smirks. "I'll keep your secret."

A cry breaks through the moment, and Willow darts out of the kitchen. I inhale the remaining half of my cheeseburger and a few fries without tasting them before setting up the baby glider near the island and grabbing the bottle and formula just as she returns with a fussy Grayson.

"How much and for how long?" I ask, holding up the bottle.

Her brows scrunch together as if she's hesitant to accept my help. "You don't have to—"

"Another round of the burger in the microwave will probably change your mind about it being worth it."

"Are you sure?"

I smile, attempting to make her feel at ease. "Yes."

Another beat of silence echoes around us as she eyes me skeptically. I get it. I have been of little help, and I definitely haven't been kind.

"That's ... sweet of you. Thanks."

I stay silent, simply nodding, while she details the perfect formula-to-water ratio and how long to warm it.

As we wait, I decide it's time to clear the air. "About the other night ... I—"

She raises a hand to stop me. "Don't worry about it. We'd both been drinking, and some of the night is hazy."

"You sure?" I ask skeptically, feeling like I'm getting off far too easily. I mean, fuck, I ground my hard cock into her and laid everything out in explicit detail, and we're not exactly a happily married couple. In college, I had to put more than one teammate in their place after they'd crossed the line with a woman. I may be many things, but I don't want to be that type of man.

Once Grayson is settled, Willow eats the remainder of her

food and even agrees with me about the fries. Go figure our first agreement would be about food.

She offers me a thank you before heading to her room with a now-sated Grayson in her arms, and I feel like this may be a sort of fresh start.

12

WILLOW

"Willow?" I hear his distant, grave tone and shudder.

Please tell me this is my sick, delusional imagination and not Gabriel standing near the bathroom entrance watching me vomit.

"Willow?"

A sudden wave of nausea washes over me. My mouth salivates, and my skin prickles with icy sweat as I lurch toward the toilet.

Ugh, this is the absolute worst.

Overwhelmed and exhausted, I hang my head over the bowl while violent shakes rack my body and warm tears run down my cheeks.

I don't hear Gabriel, so he must've fled once he saw me throwing up, which is probably for the best. Though he apologized for the strange encounter at the sex club days ago, I still feel off-center when I think about it and him.

For me, that night got filed away as one of those you never mention; a blur of sexual tension, mortifying moments, and strange muffled apologies.

I wasn't myself. For a brief moment, I enjoyed the warmth and strength of a man pressed against me. A scenario I vowed I'd never entertain again.

And he wasn't himself. He was a paradox.

Rather than dwelling on the reasons behind it, I opted for grace and filed it away immediately.

But then, he placed the soft blanket over Grayson and me. He shared the meal that he had saved from across the country with me. He helped me feed Grayson. For some, it's insignificant, yet to me, it's monumental in its attentiveness and generosity. Gabriel Reed and those two words were never something I'd connect.

As I lift my head, a cold, damp cloth is thrust near my face. I fall back onto the cool, smooth floor with a thud, gazing up at Gabriel's towering frame.

"Mr. Reed." I grab the cloth and wipe my mouth and under my eyes. "Please don't come any ..." My palm smacks against my lips, and I rush for the bowl yet again and throw up until I'm wracked with the worst case of dry heaves.

I take my earlier statement back. Throwing up isn't the absolute worst. Gabriel Reed watching me do it is.

He doesn't need to witness this repulsive, sickening spectacle; the stench alone should be enough to make him sick.

"Do you have something for your hair?" I hear him ask as he rifles through the bathroom drawers.

I nod but opt to say nothing as I continue my interaction with the toilet bowl.

A soft touch on the side of my ears causes me to pause as it continues to move through my hair.

He's ... he's pulling my hair back?

Once my hair is secure, Grayson bellows out another cry. Having fed, bathed, and changed him, my worry that he might also be sick has me crawling toward him.

"Stay put," Gabriel's gruff voice instructs as he touches my shoulder. He stalks toward Grayson, lifts him into his arms, and then pats his back with the confidence of a seasoned professional.

What happened to his stiff, uncomfortable posture?

I rub the cool, damp cloth across my burning forehead, wondering if this is a fever dream. The world I know doesn't contain this version of Gabriel; his unexpected tenderness and compassion feel foreign and unsettling.

When Grayson lets out a blood-curdling scream, Gabriel flips him over. His head rests against Gabriel's inner elbow, with Gabriel's palm against Grayson's stomach, while he pats his back firmly.

Springing forward, I shriek, "What are you doing?"

His brows scrunch. "I'm doing the football hold. Your son has colic. That's why he's crying. Now stay there like I said."

I collapse onto the floor. The impact is jarring, and I tell myself it's dizziness, but a cynical little voice in the back of my head scoffs at my excuse.

Instead of getting caught up in those thoughts, I ask, "How do you know he has colic?"

"He cries after you feed him. He brings his legs to his stomach as if in pain, and if you place your palm against his stomach, you can feel the bubbles."

"What would you know about babies?" I ask, crossing my arms over my chest.

His help is appreciated, but it only amplifies my guilt. I can't shake the feeling I've failed my son by not noticing this earlier. Has he been in pain this entire time? He's always fussy after his meals, but I just thought it was a baby thing until he got comfortable. The thought of my neglect wrecks me more than any sickness can.

Gabriel's quiet before he sighs and says, "I know they aren't supposed to cry after eating. Why don't you get in the shower, and I'll take care of him?"

When I continue to stare, he walks out of the room while patting Grayson, who is almost back asleep.

Definitely a fever dream.

13

GABRIEL

My home—a peaceful haven and productive workspace —feels invaded and unusable since Willow moved in.

Despite the two thousand square feet separating our wings, her son's cries carry into my silent space.

Since returning home from the office around midnight, his wails have tormented me. A constant high-pitched sound lasting until around two in the morning. Right as I typed out my last email, the child's blood-curdling scream pierced the air, replacing my irritation with a surge of alarm, like an intuition.

Did something happen to him? To her? I practically sprinted across the penthouse to her side.

The sight of her small frame shaking and groaning in pain as she hovered over the toilet broke something inside me.

Then I saw Grayson lying in the portable bassinet next to her. Toys, snacks, and bottles lined the floor. She was sick and still trying to take care of him.

It reminded me of a time when I was sick and all by myself with Jack. His name still pierces a piece of my soul when I think about him. Eryn was out with friends that night, and when she got home, instead of helping me with our son, she went to bed.

I watched over him all night while running to the bathroom every couple of minutes after a severe case of food poisoning. That night should have been my first sign that she was selfish and irresponsible.

So now, here I lie in Willow's bed, her son's weight surprisingly comfortable on my chest, while she showers and hopefully finds relief.

I gaze at the child softly snoring on me, his face peaceful after tiring himself out. So much time has passed, I've forgotten —or more accurately, blocked out—their small features, how a simple, funny sound can bring a smile to their face, and how quickly they grow.

I've been a cold, distant man, neglecting to give the warmth and connection others deserve. The perfect world I had carefully created came crashing down, not because of Willow or Grayson, but because of a materialistic woman's insatiable greed. And I need to remember that.

The values instilled in me during my childhood don't align with who I am now. If my mother knew the circumstances of Willow and my relationship, how I orchestrated everything, she'd be horrified and disappointed. Shit, I'm horrified and disappointed in my actions.

We're in this predicament now, and I need to do better for myself, Willow, and Grayson. She and I need to figure out our normal, and Grayson needs a father figure. To teach and guide him in ways only a dad can.

I wholeheartedly believe Willow is capable, but growing up with both parents highlighted the distinct advantages of having a mother and a father's guidance in certain areas. *But it's only for three years*, my mind whispers.

Willow's throat clears, and I eye her standing near the entrance to her bathroom. A red silk robe clings to her silhouette. "Thank you."

"Anytime," I say while giving her a once-over. Despite some

improvement, the lingering effects of her illness are clear in her bloodshot eyes, dark circles, and pale skin.

She takes her bottom lip between her teeth before blowing out a breath and stalking toward the bed. Hesitantly, she reaches halfway toward Grayson, her arms outstretched, before she pulls them back empty, a sudden wave of uncertainty washing over her face.

I raise a brow and glance down, only to realize I don't have a shirt on, only a pair of black silk pajama pants I put on after I got home and showered.

A heavy silence hangs in the air, thick with tension, as she stares at her child, her eyes wide, hands fidgeting while I survey her.

Because I'm not only cold and distant but also a dick, I wait for her to gather the courage to pick him up on her own. We've had physical contact, but only with me taking the lead, and it was all for appearances.

What about the dance at Obsidian?

Alcohol and irritation led to our encounter at the sex club. Nothing more. I lie to myself.

Still, I can't deny that I crave the sensation of her fingers tracing the contours of my stomach as she did with my neck the other night while we were dancing. It shot electrical currents through my body, and I want more. Something I haven't contemplated since my early twenties.

But why now? Why her? What's happening to me? Where did this thought come from?

One moment of self-reflection, a dance, and I'm prepared to let Willow closer than anyone has been in a decade?

Willow gently lifts Grayson, her touch feather-light as my warring thoughts threaten to overwhelm me. She was so stealthy I didn't even feel her touch, and it's probably for the best.

Rising from the bed, I silently gesture toward the cool glass of water, medicine, crackers, and plastic bowl on her nightstand just in case she's unable to make it to the bathroom quickly enough, and then walk out of the room without a backward glance.

My thoughts about improvement, particularly for Grayson's sake, are sincere, but I'm emotionally unprepared to delve deeper into the matter with Willow, and I doubt she is either after what I've put her through.

―――

AGE 20

"Gabriel, it hurts so bad!" I rush from the private hospital bathroom to Eryn's side as she has another contraction.

"Breathe through it, babe, just like the teacher instructed. I'll do it with you," I say, moving the blond strands from her face and tucking them behind her ear. Then grab hold of her hand so she can ground herself and know even though she has the pain, we're in this together; I love her so much.

One hour later, a piercing cry shatters the silence, the sound of my baby boy's first wails changing my world forever. As a father, I'll strive each day to be the most devoted dad I can be, showering my child with only affection and support.

"Ready to cut the umbilical cord, Sir?"

I nod, carefully walking around the bed to my son Jack; his skin still glistens with amniotic fluid, yet his face is the most precious sight I've ever seen. I made sure we delayed cutting the cord to allow more blood to flow from the placenta to the baby; I read in one of the countless baby books I've studied that this improves the baby's blood volume, iron stores, and red blood cell count, giving my baby boy a healthy start.

After the cut, and we've had skin to skin, they gently swaddle him in a warm, soft blanket and hand him to me. He's so light and fragile in my arms, and I'm terrified of hurting him, even though the nurse reassured me that babies are resilient and I'd do fine.

"Eryn, do you want to hold him?"

With a shake of her head, she turns away from the bassinet and grabs her phone.

"It's okay, little man. Your mom is a little tired from bringing you into this world, but she loves you so much. She and I both do," I whisper, slowly moving from one foot to the other to rock him.

My phone buzzes insistently, and I answer the video call with a huge smile. First Kennedy, then the rest of my old team's cramped faces light up the screen. They're on a bus headed to the championships right now and wanted to see my boy.

After finding out we were having a baby, Eryn and I talked it over, and we decided I should quit baseball. The baby needs his father at home, and I can't let my child down. Baseball was my everything, but now this little family we created is.

14

WILLOW

"S-U-N. Sun." I hold a deck of flashcards, their edges slightly softened from use, and enunciate the word to Grayson. His eyes are wide with fascination at the colorful, whimsical illustration. I flip to the next card. "B-A-L-L. Ball." I smile as his hands excitedly reach for the card while I flip to the next one. My throat feels as if it may close as I see an illustration of a man. I almost skipped it, but decided not to at the last second. "D-A-D. Dad." Grayson makes a few babbling noises and something that sounds far too close to Dada. "Oh, no, you don't, mister!" A sad, wistful smile plays on my lips, but I quickly switch to a brighter, more genuine smile as I flip to the next card. "B-A-T—"

The elevator dings, and I quirk a brow as I check my phone, but it's barely ten in the morning, and Gabriel won't be back for hours.

"Knock, knock."

Crap.

The sound of heels distantly tapping against the floor causes me to leap from the couch. Frantically, I smooth my hair, sweep it into a messy bun, and wince as I glance down at my stained band tee and sweatpants, still dotted with rice cereal and pear puree from my first attempt at feeding Grayson solid food earlier. It was semi-successful until he decided it would be better all over his face and on the floor than in his mouth.

After being advised by his pediatrician, I'm hoping that switching him to a mix of solid food and less formula will help him with the colic situation.

"Mrs. Reed." I plaster on a smile, my hands clasp neatly behind my back, attempting to project an image of composure.

"Please, darling, call me Mom. I would love it more than you know." Vivian walks into the living area with shopping bags in her arms and a warm smile. "You know, I always wanted a daughter, but I was high risk and nearly passed while having Gabriel, so we decided not to ask for another blessing and be thankful for having a healthy, sweet baby boy. Now I get to have my wishes made with a daughter and a grandson."

Speechless from Vivian's sweet words, I sit on the couch and place a decorative pillow on my lap to hide the stains while listening to her speak softly about how precious my son is.

She drops her shopping bags to the floor by my feet and crouches down to kiss Grayson's cheeks.

"Hello, my sweet boy. Grandma missed you so much."

At the sound of her voice, he bounces up and down in his jumper, slapping his teether on the side of it in a frenzy.

My heart clenches, overwhelmed by the almost unbearable sweetness of the moment.

With a quiet grace, she sits across from me, her hands clasped in her lap, her light blue eyes holding mine, a subtle smile playing on her lips. "We haven't spent much time getting to know each other, and I'd like to change that. I'd love to know everything about you."

My heart beats faster at her request. I'm unsure of what Gabriel has mentioned to her and what I should or shouldn't say. "Umm ... there's not much to tell."

"Nonsense. I can tell you, and Gabriel are ... new to being together."

My heartbeat was irregular from her unexpected arrival, but now it feels as if it's ceased completely.

"I ... We—"

Shit. What do I say?

My mind runs through a kaleidoscope of recent memories. We're on the dance floor, with the music pumping, sharing a moment meant for lovers. The oddly enjoyable meal he and I shared. The bittersweet feeling of him caring for me while I was sick, when no one had in a very long time. And finally, the achingly swoon-worthy sight of him holding and comforting Grayson when I couldn't.

Though our time together has been brief, it also feels as if it's been a lifetime.

"Oh, dear, it's okay. I didn't mean it like that," she says, grabbing my fidgeting hands in hers and giving them a reassuring pat.

"Let me tell you a little story. My father betrothed me to a man of his choosing. He was stiff, boring, and not very good-looking. Then I met Gabriel's father by chance." She smiles, shaking her head. "Like a damsel in distress, my heel got caught in a metal grate while walking on a sidewalk in New York City. My love of shoes kept me from leaving the poor thing there. After pulling it in the most unladylike fashion, I fell back and right into the arms of Gerard, heel in hand. His charm was irresistible, and a passionate and all-consuming love affair began. We got married soon after I fell pregnant, and it's been the happiest thirty-six years of my life." With a wistful smile, she gazes into the distance, a thousand sweet memories probably flickering behind her eyes.

My heart aches, yearning for the radiant love she possesses —a love so intense it's blinding.

A wedding filled with the warmth of family and friends, and the joy of welcoming a child together.

I didn't get that. I was given an ultimatum between prison and a forced marriage. A wedding consisting of signing a prenup under duress and a photo that needed to be photoshopped to give the illusion of an intimate, beautiful moment. But worst of all was delivering Grayson into the world without the love of a partner by my side. Thankfully, Aella was there, but it's not the same.

"Anyway, what I'm trying to say is I don't care if your actions weren't traditional. I'm not traditional. I'm just happy to have two more people to love."

My heart shatters, and I feel like the absolute worst human alive as I look into Vivian's hopeful and loving eyes.

Clearing my throat, I whisper, "That's very sweet of you—"

"Oh, I almost forgot. I bought you and Grayson some stuff today. Once I started, I couldn't stop. Quality time, acts of service, and gift giving are my love languages, so get used to it," she says, handing me a few matte black designer gift bags.

Inside the first luxurious bag, nestled amongst tissue paper, lies a pair of unbelievably plush cream pajamas, smelling faintly of vanilla. The set's butter-soft texture is irresistible; I can't help but repeatedly rub the fabric between my fingers.

"Soft right? New moms need nothing but comfort."

Grayson becomes fussy, and I hastily set down the clothes to rush to him. "It's time for a bottle, and it looks like a diaper change as well," I say, gently lifting him into my arms.

"I'll take care of the bottle," she says.

"Are you sure? I can—"

Vivian waves me off as she heads toward the kitchen. "Nonsense. I want to help and get all the cuddles I can. I'll be right back."

I change his diaper and continue to rock him as Vivian rushes back into the room.

"May I?" She holds out her arms.

"Of course," I say, handing him over as she kicks off her high heels, the click echoing in the quiet room. She settles cross-legged on the couch with Grayson in her embrace while he fights to hold on to the bottle in his cute, independent way.

"Keep on opening bags, darling. I can't wait for you to see the dress I picked out for the charity event."

My brows scrunch. "Charity Event?"

Vivian sighs. "I swear he's just like his father sometimes. You two have a charity event tonight, and Gabriel asked if I'd watch Grayson. Hair and makeup should arrive soon."

Since my subsequent illness a week ago, Gabriel has kept his communication limited to short, distant texts regarding my health and nothing more.

"This is so surreal. I never thought this time would come. I was actually quite worried."

"Really?" I ask, intrigued since I know next to nothing about Gabriel.

"Gabriel, much like his father, has worn himself down with an unrelenting work ethic. The relentless pace started when his father began bringing him to the office when he was around sixteen. He had his detour in college." She frowns, but stays gazing down at Grayson as she continues, "He then returned to the company and hasn't stopped working since. I've watched his teens, twenties, and part of his thirties slip between his fingers like grains of sand, each year a fleeting moment for him. I'm so relieved he found you. I hope this helps him relax, find peace, and appreciate life's simple pleasures. Life is for living, not existing for work."

Pressure sits on my chest as the guilt eats me alive. "I hope so too."

And then a thought hits: why would she say he needs to find peace?

Vivian is so supportive and sweet and deserves better than

the lies we've given her. At first, I thought this would be possible, but the more time I spend talking to her, the more it guts me.

"Now, enough about Gabriel. Tell me about you and your family. How excited was your mom when she saw her grandbaby?"

A suffocating pressure builds in my throat, and I desperately try to swallow, but the lump remains stubbornly lodged. "I don't ... I'm an orphan."

"Oh dear, I had no idea."

"It's okay," I say automatically, but it's not okay. Now more than ever, I wish I had a mother like Vivian.

"Well, you're no longer alone."

The feeling of belonging and love flows through me, and for a second, I believe the lie. That I belong here, on this couch with my mother-in-law while she feeds my baby I had with her son.

WITH VIVIAN'S ASSISTANCE, I slip into my ruby red dress later that evening. Its hand-sewn Swarovski crystals catch the light with every movement. The structured bodice cinches my waist, and the incorporated push-up bra provides a lovely lift to my breasts within the sweetheart neckline. The left-side thigh-high slit evokes an unexpected sense of sexiness I haven't experienced in, well ... ever.

I stare at my reflection, my breath catching in my throat. I appear elegant and sophisticated, channeling old Hollywood glamour with bouncy vintage curls and a deep side part sweeping my hair behind my ear. My makeup is simple yet stunning, with black-winged liner and a stained red lip that matches the dress.

Even as I stand here, awestruck by my reflection, a harsh

voice screams in my head, *You don't belong here! You aren't worthy.* The words echo in my ears and make my heart pound.

"You are an absolute vision. I knew this dress would be perfect on your figure." Vivian smiles behind me. "And there's one more detail to add." With a gentle hand, she positions a cool, pear-shaped diamond solitaire above the swell of my breasts, its facets sparkling. "This was the necklace I got on my first anniversary, and I'd love for you to have it."

My hand goes to the diamond as my eyes burn with tears. A cocoon of acceptance and love encases me, and it breaks my heart a little more to know I'm lying, giving her the illusion of a daughter-in-law. "It's lovely, but I can't accept this."

Her hands rest on my shoulders and give me a reassuring squeeze. "Nonsense. A beautiful necklace for my beautiful girl."

My fingers trace the cool, smooth surface of my priceless gift. A heartfelt, choked "thank you" escapes my lips as I turn and envelop her in a warm hug, then grab her hands as we part, telling her thank you again.

Strong measured steps carry into the room, right before I hear Gabriel's deep voice. "We're going to be ..." In the floor-to-ceiling mirror, our eyes lock, and a flicker of something I can't quite grasp flashes across his face, accompanied by a subtle yet tense tightening of his jaw. "Late."

I whirl around, and time seems to freeze—before me stands my breathtakingly handsome fake husband, his hair styled short on the sides and longer on the top with a distinct side part and slicked back to mirror my old Hollywood hair style, and his all-black fitted suit molding to his body in all the right places.

"Now that's the look I was hoping for!" Vivian exclaims as she comes between us.

My eyes flicker shut, a blush creeping up my neck. I was definitely staring at him indecently.

What's wrong with me?

As he stands next to me, he clears his throat, and my eyes open. "Are you ready?"

"Yes, Sir ... Sweetheart," I say, then wince.

Luckily, Vivian had headed into the other room, so she missed my mistake.

His gaze darts to my neck, lingering on his mother's necklace. Confusion etches itself onto his features before being erased by chilling indifference. "We should leave—"

"Not until I get my picture." Vivian rushes in with her phone in hand.

"Mother—"

"Don't you dare. Now hold your beautiful wife and smile."

We hesitantly move close, but it's awkward at best.

15

WILLOW

Trapped in the back of a town car, leather and anxiety permeate the air. We follow the line of vehicles on their way to the St. Regis Chicago luxury hotel at a sluggish pace. The time gives me the opportunity to stress myself into a near panic attack.

What if I can't be convincing? What if I say something wrong and incriminate us both?

The back seat of the car becomes stifling; a wave of heat hits me as I reach for the air-conditioning vent, grasping it like a lifeline. Panic seizes me; my shallow, rapid breaths burn in my chest like flames.

"Hey." Gabriel's voice, sharp and clear, cuts through my rising panic. "Look at me."

I gasp for air. A ragged breath catches in my throat as I turn to face him.

His brows furrow, and a look of deep concern etches itself onto his face as he regards me. Whether the concern is for me or for himself, I can't tell. Probably the latter. I'm sure he doesn't want his image ruined by his fake new wife.

His hand reaches out to my thigh, but he thinks better of it at the last moment and balls his fist and places it in his lap.

"Everything will be alright. I'll do most of the talking. If I introduce you to someone, act like you've known them for years. And if all else fails, just smile."

I lick my parched lips and nod.

"Here." From the mini-fridge, he gives me a chilled water bottle, and I quickly gulp the water down. I focus on the sensation of the cold water making its way through my body and take a deep breath.

"Better?" he asks.

I nod. "Thank you."

He reaches into his jacket pocket and retrieves a small red velvet box before handing it to me. "For you."

With trembling fingers, I open the box to find a beautiful solitaire oval diamond with a skinny band; its facets flash like tiny stars, catching the light and sending sparkles dancing across the lid. "Oh my, this is breathtaking and far too much," I say as I move it around in the streaks of light.

"Most women would say it's not enough," he mutters as he keeps his gaze out the window.

"I couldn't imagine anyone saying that about this ring," I say, more to myself than him, as I marvel at its beauty.

I lift the ring from the box, its weight surprisingly light, and carefully slide it onto my fourth finger. A small gasp escapes my lips as it fits perfectly. I'm so relieved Vivian arranged for my nails to be done. My nails before would have looked so out of place, just like me.

No Willow. We aren't doing this right now.

A knock sounds on the window, and Gabriel exits the car. He offers me his hand, and I cling to it like a lifeline while hearing the screams of his name. He gives me a warm, reassuring squeeze before we head to a white tent and are instructed on how the red carpet will run.

There are four spots marked with a small black X on the carpet; these are where we will stand to pose for our photos. They're urging us to keep our time on the carpet to under three minutes to prevent congestion and long waits.

Three minutes ... I can do anything for three minutes. I murmur to myself, psyching myself up for the challenge ahead. Having experienced a twenty-three-hour delivery with Grayson, this should be a breeze in comparison.

"This way, please." An attendant with a clipboard and headset urges us forward.

With a stony, emotionless expression, Gabriel pulls me forward, his eyes fixed ahead, giving no hint of his thoughts.

Stepping onto the plush red carpet, I'm met with a deafening roar of voices, a blinding flash of lights, and the overwhelming sensation of a thousand eyes on me.

With a gentle pull, Gabriel's powerful embrace surrounds me as we stand on the first prompt.

"Hey," he murmurs while squeezing my side. Staring up at him, I'm hit with a mesmerizing, wide grin that lights up his face.

He lowers his head, and I freeze as I think he's going to kiss me. Instead, he rests his lips against my neck for a second before rising to my ear in what I can only imagine is a deceptive show of intimacy for the onlookers.

"Smile and count to one hundred. I promise it will be over soon." I give a small nod. "Now pull away and laugh as if I've told you something funny."

Pulling away, he resumes his practiced, fake smile, towering over me as he stands to his full height. I obey, my laughter echoing unnaturally in response to his command.

A cacophony of excited shouts and the clicks of countless cameras makes it nearly impossible to pinpoint their source in the dense crowd.

"Gabriel! Reed! Reed over here! This way, over here! Right here! Gabriel! Mr. Reed! To the left! Just like that!"

People chant this mantra over and over. This experience is terrifying—a relentless assault on my senses, and it leaves me drained.

Does he always experience this when he goes out? No wonder he's so reclusive.

I continue counting, a smile stretching across my face so wide I feel as if my lips and cheeks might crack as we stand on the next two Xs.

As we reach the final posing prompt, a wave of relief washes over me until I hear a word I wasn't expecting.

Kiss! Kiss! Kiss!

A sudden chill replaces the warmth of my smile as Gabriel's dark eyes meet mine. The air is thick with unspoken tension. His tongue sweeps across his lips before his gaze drops to mine, then back up to meet my eyes. A silent question hangs between us.

The ghost of a smile touches my lips as I give him my silent consent right before a nervous flutter hits my stomach. The heat of his hand on my skin, soft as a feather, melts into a caress before his fingers thread through my hair, drawing me in until our lips are nearly touching. His minty breath mingles with scotch and the scent of his woodsy aftershave, enveloping me in a seductive, intoxicating haze. With his other hand resting possessively on my back, he pulls me even closer.

His lips crash into mine in a passionate, overwhelming kiss, and it borders on indecent as his tongue seeks mine. We pull apart a moment later, still chest to chest with the rapid beat of my heart against his.

He clears his throat. "All done."

My eyes snap open. The cacophony of the city—car horns, distant sirens, and shouting voices—crashes over me in a jarring ripple of sound. With a final wave to the screaming crowd, Gabriel pulls me away from the flashing cameras and red carpet.

"You did well," he whispers. His voice is barely audible above the murmur of conversation and music as we pause behind another couple entering the opulent hotel ballroom.

With a slow nod, I deeply inhale the fresh air. That was intense, and it had nothing to do with the screams and flashes.

I glance at him from beneath my lashes, where a mask of indifference he wears so well sits on his face as if nothing happened.

Yet here I am, still breathless, reliving the gentle yet dominating way he claimed my mouth. I fight the urge to touch my lips, to trace the contours and confirm their sensitivity, to validate my memory of the way his lips and tongue ravaged my mouth.

"Look," he says, his voice hushed as he shows me his phone, where the picture of us on the red carpet gleams. It was when he was whispering in my ear. The press is already feasting on the fake moment.

"Is this good?" I ask, completely thrown off at the idea that my photo is on a famous sight already.

"It's excellent," he says with a wicked grin.

He played the reporters and paparazzi as he does with other company owners, with cold calculation to get exactly what he wants.

Which is something I should remember when we kiss again, and I foolishly want to touch my lips after.

———

COCKTAIL HOUR, despite its glamorous sound, mostly consisted of repetitive murmurs of congratulations and clinking glasses; a somewhat monotonous experience.

It was unusual to thank someone for their congratulations

on my forced marriage, but I did it anyway. I gave a big, blushing smile while touching Gabriel's chest or gushing about how romantic it was while staring into his eyes more times than I could count.

We sit down at our reserved table, and a double-take is necessary as I see my first name, paired with the surname Reed, printed elegantly on a place card in front of my seat. *Willow Reed.*

A man and woman I've seen many times in tabloid sites sits across from us, followed by an elderly couple, who Gabriel mentioned are friends of his parents, and finally, Kennedy Heartwright, Gabriel's business partner, sits to my right with a blond date who looks vaguely familiar next to him.

"Mrs. Reed," Kennedy says as he turns toward me, his eyes twinkling with mischief as he playfully grabs my hand and plants a light kiss on my skin.

With a pointed look, Gabriel murmurs, "Keep your hands to yourself."

A grimace stretches across my face as I struggle against his strong yet tender hold.

As the couple across the table gets Gabriel's attention, Kennedy leans closer to me. "Be good to my friend."

I look into his light blue eyes. The usual playful glint is absent, replaced by a sober intensity. One that seems uncharacteristic of what I've heard he's usually like.

At Reed Equity, my co-workers know him as the hot, approachable, funny boss, a stark contrast to the intimidating Gabriel, whose no-nonsense demeanor keeps employees at a distance.

"I will, Mr. Heartwright," I murmur sincerely, my gaze unwavering even as a knot forms in my stomach. Shouldn't he be worried about his friend being good to me?

"Call me Kennedy." He gives me a grin and frees my hand

before launching into a funny story with the famous couple across the way.

That was unsettling.

"Wills!"

I turn in my seat to see Aella standing behind me, the soft glow of the emerald-green satin dress catching the light. "Elle, you look beautiful!" I stand and give her a tight hug before whispering, "Thank God you're here."

"Aella. What are you doing here?" Kennedy asks from my left.

"Oh, Mr. Heartwright. I didn't see you there," she says with a bright smile that dims when she sees his date.

"Wasn't expecting to see you, Kate," Aella grumbled.

Kate? Shit, no wonder she looked familiar.

I glance at Aella's stepsister, who's a real piece of work, while she dramatically grabs onto Kennedy's arm like she's being swept away at sea. How dramatic. "Ken begged me to come. Who was I to deny such a request?"

"Yeah," Aella mutters. "*Ken* can be pretty persuasive when he wants to be."

There's an awkward silence as Aella downs the rest of her drink while Kennedy shoots daggers at her. Aella then winks at me and excuses herself from the table.

I attempt to follow, but Gabriel grabs hold of my arm. I gaze down at his hand as he whispers in my ear. "Let her go. People are watching."

With a sigh, I nod, then slump into my designated chair. I feel like the worst friend ever. I knew Kennedy's date looked familiar, but I couldn't place her. I shoot Aella a text, and she replies almost immediately with a thumbs up and a picture of a drink in her hand.

16

GABRIEL

"Are you enjoying yourself?" I whisper in Willow's ear. Her body's close, moving against mine in a slow, deliberate dance across the sparkling marble dance floor, which is far different from the way she danced against me at the club. This is formal, stiff, and stuffy in the worst kind of way.

She nods. "Yeah ... tonight's been nice. Thank you."

A deep, throaty chuckle shakes my broad chest. "You don't have to lie, Willow. I hate these functions."

Gazing around at the cackling attendants, their expensive clothes shimmering under the chandeliers, and the extravagant furnishings makes me wish we could leave this charity event. It all feels so fake, and I can't stand feeling like I'm on display, like a lab rat being observed.

"I'm not," Willow says while shaking her head with a serious look on her face. "I wasn't able to go to prom, so this is like a do-over. No ... not a do-over—"

The serious set of her mouth dissolves into a horrified grimace as mortification floods her features. I could take advantage of the moment, but I give her a pass. So instead I ask, "Why didn't you go to prom?"

"I was in a group home, and the lack of funds meant we barely had enough to eat, let alone money for things like prom."

"I'm sorry."

She gazes up at me with a wry smile. "Did *The* Gabriel Reed apologize to me for something he had no control over?"

I smirk. "Maybe ... don't get used to it."

"Oh, I wouldn't dream of it, Sir," she whispers the last part, making me grin.

I'm starting to suspect that she calls me "sir" just to get a rise out of me, and frankly, I find it quite enjoyable.

"Why do you hate these events?" she asks.

With a shrug, I scan the room. "It's a vulgar display of wealth. A pissing contest disguised as charity, where the goal is to outspend each other. This isn't out of the goodness of everyone's black hearts; it's a tax write-off and, for some, a way to wash dirty money. Most of these people are deplorable human beings who think that by dressing up in their fancy tailored tuxedos and flashy ball gowns, it will absolve them of their sins."

"That's ... I don't really know what to say."

"There are many awful people in this world, Willow. Most are among the richest."

Her brow creases. "Then why come?"

"I'd rather donate privately than be around all these pretentious people, but we needed to make an appearance."

She nods. "Right."

"And I'm one of them ... don't you think?" Her head tilts to the side as if confused. "I coerced you into marrying me as punishment when you truly had no other choice. If you ask me, that makes me the most deplorable of them all. I could have let you go, but here you are, in my arms at a charity event."

Her lips part as she gazes at me with a pensive expression. "I—"

"Gabe, baby, I thought that was you."

My eyes slam shut as a wave of nausea and bile rises in my throat at the sound of my ex—Eryn's sickeningly sweet voice.

Willow's hand tightens around mine, and I survey her unease as she eyes Eryn, and then I, too, gaze over to see Eryn in a plunging fuchsia mermaid gown, showing more than what's covered. I guess not much has changed. She always liked to be looked at, always the center of attention.

"Eryn," I clip, the word sharp and quick as I incline my head.

"Don't be like that after all this time, baby," she whines, her voice dripping with a manufactured sadness perfectly complementing the downturn of her overly inflated bottom lip.

My eyes track her hand as the sharp points of her long, pink nails rake along my bicep, sending a jolt of revulsion and anger through me.

I try to summon every ounce of calm I have, but I'm about to snap.

A public confrontation won't be great, especially at a charity event, but I won't entertain her unpredictable requests, which, given our past, are sure to come, nor will I provide her with the attention she seems to relish.

Her eyes sparkle when I don't make a move, like she believes me to be the same fool I was years ago. Tongue-tied and willing to do anything to appease her.

————

AGE 21

Today is an amazing day. It's Jack's first birthday, and he just took his first wobbly steps toward me. His blond hair is a chaotic mess of curls I'm trying to tame as he wrestles me to get back up and explore the balloons, streamers, and bounce house set up for his party starting in half an hour.

My mother is currently in the kitchen overseeing the catering. She offered to make the food herself, but Eryn didn't want to help and stated she wanted something everyone would remember.

Unfortunately, Eryn isn't present these days. With too many functions or girls' weekends to attend and as a millionaire's wife, she believes planners and caterers should handle it. Her words, not mine.

I've never been one to flaunt my wealth. My mother instilled in me the importance of humility and gratitude from a young age. Although my father's wealth could have afforded us help, my mother insisted on making every birthday cake, decorating for parties, and preparing each holiday meal. Her love shone through with every holiday we celebrated.

A sharp ring of the doorbell slices through the quiet, and I hurry to the door, excited to welcome our guests.

Instead, a courier hands me a manila envelope, which will alter the course of my life.

My old college teammate, Carter, believes my son is his.

He's requesting a paternity test.

ONE WEEK LATER

Results: You are not the father.

My world is shattered beyond repair, and I will never be the same.

———

PRESENT

"How about a dance, for old time's sake?" Eryn asks. "I know you want—"

"Ahh, Eryn. I thought I unfortunately saw you earlier," Kennedy says from behind her.

Thank God.

"Do you always have to be such a jerk, Kennedy?"

"With you, yes. Now, if you'll excuse me, Gabriel is having a dance with his beautiful wife, and I think I saw your husband, Carter, in the hall with his tongue down a server's throat. Blond hair, predatory gleam in her blue eyes, like she's about to come into a giant payday. You'd better hurry. She sounds a lot like you, and she might just replace your insignificant ass."

"Fuck you, Kennedy!" Eryn yells before stomping away.

"Not even with my enemy's dick," Kennedy mutters.

My gaze stays fixed on Eryn's back as she barges toward the exit, knocking over a few chairs and yelling obscenities in her wake.

"What a fucking bitch. I'm still disappointed you didn't allow me to make her life a living hell. It would've been so epic, and we could've reminisced for years to come. What a missed opportunity." Kennedy mutters, shaking his head and downing the rest of his drink before walking away.

A light caress against my tense shoulder causes me to gaze down into Willow's anxious eyes.

She's worried and uncomfortable, yet she's still comforting me?

Me. Her boss turned into a forced asshole husband. I don't deserve her care, her worry, or her comfort, but I savor it anyway.

My eyes crinkle at the corners as I give her the most genuine smile I think I've ever given anyone. She looks momentarily stunned, and it takes everything in me not to turn it into a smirk. Instead, I pull her close, and we sway as I apologize for the way Eryn acted and for my inaction.

"That's the second time you've said sorry tonight. Is Mr.

Reed turning a new leaf?" She raises her delicate brow with a grin, and I'm grateful for her attempt at lightening the mood.

The music changes, and I guide Willow to our table as everyone takes their seats for the auction portion of the charity. Only one more hour of this, and then I can be in the comfort of my penthouse. Away from these people and, more importantly, Eryn and the memories she brings.

As the bewilderment subsides, anger sets in brighter than before. She has a lot of fucking nerve coming up to me while I had Willow in my arms. I think I was more shocked by her brazenness than anything else. Her touch, raking across my bicep, felt like rusty nails and left a mixture of revulsion and hatred in its wake. This tux is getting torched once I get it off; a simple dry cleaning won't do.

The strangest part is that I haven't seen her in years, and she still came up to me as if time heals all. When in fact, it doesn't. She tried reconciling with me right after I found out Jack wasn't mine, and I almost fell for it, willing to raise him as my own, until I realized her girls' weekends were used to cheat on me. If I didn't want her then, what makes her think I'd want her lying, cheating ass now?

Leaving the life I created with her and the son I thought was mine was excruciating, and it still haunts me.

I gaze at Willow as she says something to the younger couple across from us and then glances at me. Her smile is a comforting beacon in the dim light, but I sense a storm of unspoken questions behind her eyes.

She deserves answers for no other reason than to be better prepared if this ever happens again. The uncertainty in her eyes, flitting from Eryn to me, was unmistakable, and I don't want her to think there's something going on between us. I made Willow a promise, and I plan to keep my word.

The auctioneer begins by unveiling two paintings, both hideous. An abstract take on what looks like faces run over by a bus, their ornate frames the only saving grace, gleaming under the bright lights. The bidding starts at a hundred thousand dollars, and if it weren't in the name of charity, it wouldn't be worth it.

A man at a table to my right and a woman near the center of the room engage in a silent but intense bidding duel as their hands rise with practiced grace. Their eyes dart around the room every so often as if someone else is going to come in and outbid them for the ugly paintings. The auctioneer's voice, crisp and clear despite its speed, is the only sound cutting through the tense quiet of the room.

The auction drags on, a whirlwind of escalating bids and hushed whispers, before the man concedes, leaving the woman triumphant with her two paintings, which cost more than half a million dollars, which is complete madness.

With a subtle arch of her eyebrows, Willow silently conveys her agreement to my thoughts as she looks over at me.

I mouth, "I told you. Pissing contest."

She rolls her eyes, and I snort.

A whisper from Kennedy behind Willow's chair causes me to shift closer, my right arm resting on the backrest, the scent of her perfume filling my senses as I lean in pretend to listen intently.

"Are you going to the club after this?"

Willow's body tenses at Kennedy's question.

I shake my head. "I'm going home after this," I say, then lean back in my chair but stay close to Willow and keep my arm on the back of her chair.

Willow visibly relaxes at my words until I stroke my thumb against her naked shoulder blade. The feather-light touch is supposed to be for show, or at least that's what I tell myself.

When her chest seems still, and her breaths imperceptible, I lean in close and whisper, "As a newly married couple who haven't been seen together, our closeness needs to be believable and frequent."

Is what I said true? Yes. But am I also driven by a selfish desire, savoring the way her skin feels against my fingertips? Also yes.

She audibly swallows before leaning into my chest. From an outsider's perspective, it looks as if she's craving her husband's warm embrace, which sends shivers down my spine and a jolt of electricity through my body.

Next, the auctioneer reveals a luxury waterfront home with walls of polished wood and expansive glass windows, promising views of a tranquil forest and glimmering lake.

I remain unmoved by what is essentially a cabin on the water until Willow gasps beside me, her eyes sparkling with wonder as she murmurs about its beauty.

Without hesitation, my hand rises, eager to place my bid.

Willow gazes up at me, but I keep my face a mask of cold stone as I get into a heated bidding war with an unseen opponent at a table behind us. The auctioneer's voice is a breathless rush, a dizzying climb to half a million dollars before a quiet hand gesture from me bumps the bid to six hundred thousand with a subtle flick of the wrist. Six hundred thousand for a one-week stay at a secluded cabin in the woods?

Have I lost my mind? Probably.

Do I regret it? Hell no.

17

GABRIEL

As the town car pulls up to the building where the penthouse awaits, the weight of the day finally lifts from my chest. It's always exhausting going to events, which is one of the many reasons I rarely attend them. We also stayed later than expected, lingering to write the check and gather information about the cabin I won.

I offer my arm for Willow to hold as we make our way up the stairs and into the lobby, but stop short as I see her tremble from the chill in the late evening air. I slide off my suit jacket, and as I place it on her shoulders, I see her eyes widen in surprise.

Damn, she must think low of me if she's surprised I'd give her my jacket while she's cold.

On the way to the elevator, I guide her to the front desk and pick up the pizza I ordered on the way here.

Willow's eyes light up when she sees the cardboard box being passed to me.

"Oh, thank God," she breathes.

I hold my smirk in as I grab the box. "I noticed you didn't eat much at the event and thought you might be hungry."

"Please tell me the pizza has sausage and onions."

"You'll have to wait until we get upstairs to see."

"Then we'd better hurry because I'm starving."

I smile. "Lead the way, Mrs. Reed."

Her cheeks heat the color of her dress as she marches to our personal elevator bank without a backward glance.

Once in the penthouse, we stalk into the kitchen, and I open the box. "Is this to your liking?"

She licks her red lips as she nods. "Most definitely. How did you know to get sausage and onion?"

"Lucky guess." I shrug. Peter, the useless PI, was a total fuck-up and completely clueless about her having a baby, yet somehow discovered her pizza preferences. Go figure.

"Maybe you should play the lotto," Willow says, her cheeks flushing crimson as a nervous giggle escapes her lips. "I didn't mean to say that. You obviously don't need it. Let's just leave it at a lucky guess. Okay, shutting up now."

A genuine smile stretches across my face as a wave of contentment washes over me. She doesn't see me as anything besides her pizza-eating companion, and it's refreshing.

Almost every woman I've come into contact with has given me the impression or shown me she's had ulterior motives. My money is their primary objective. Not Willow. And I know it might be because of our circumstances, but a part of me feels like she wouldn't be like them, even if our paths had crossed casually on a busy street.

She's a vision as she gracefully hoists herself onto the counter, legs crossed, her dress molding to her body in all the right places, while my jacket hangs off her. She brings a slice of pizza to her mouth, the aroma of garlic and oregano filling the air as a moan escapes her lips, followed by comments of the cheese pull, causing me to groan inwardly.

Christ. I need a drink.

With a soft clink, I retrieve two lowball glasses from the cupboard and make my way to the liquor cabinet for a bottle of whiskey. "Want some?" I ask, holding the bottle up.

Indecision etches itself on her face as she slowly chews.

"My mother won't bring Grayson back until eleven tomorrow. Something about a discovery activity center being delivered," I mention trying to sweeten the deal because the thought of drinking alone isn't as appealing as it usually is.

With her by my side, the night has been nice, enjoyable, and I want to keep it going as I uncover more of her personality. She has an easygoing way about her, where her sweetness is balanced by spicy wit and intelligent humor.

"Why not?" She shrugs.

"Excellent." I stalk back to the island next to her and prepare my drink. "Do you want it neat?"

"Neat?" She quirks a brow.

"Without an ice ball or with?"

"Dirty."

I snort. *That was cute.*

"What?"

"Nothing," I say, grinning like a complete idiot as I retrieve an ice ball from the machine and place it into her now *dirty* drink and fill it with whiskey.

I lift my glass and clink it against hers. "Cheers to surviving the night."

"That was insane, by the way," she mutters before taking a sip and shuddering with a hand against her chest. "Oh my, that is *strong*."

I snort before taking a bite of pizza and gazing back at her. "What was insane?"

"The amount you paid for that waterfront property."

I shrug. "It will go to a good cause."

My phone rings, and we both lean on the counter to look at

it. A picture of Kennedy and me from when we were in college sits on the screen, both of us in our baseball uniforms, holding up a one with our index fingers. It was the best and last game I played before everything went to shit and Eryn fucked it all to hell.

"Oh my God! Is that you as a teen? And Kennedy?"

"Yeah," I say as I silence his call and place it in my tux pocket. "It was college, actually. So, I was twenty."

"Your minor detour," she says with a mouth full of pizza.

I frown. "My what?"

"Your mom said you had a minor detour in college."

"Did she now ... what else did she say?"

She shrugs. "That you work too much."

I snort. "Yeah, I bet she did."

"So if you played baseball in college, you must've been pretty good."

My stomach drops. Baseball will always feel like the one that got away. "I was okay."

"I hate to break it to you," she says with a smile while poking my chest. "But you, Gabriel Reed, seem like the kind of guy that doesn't do anything *just* okay."

I try to keep my grin hidden, but the corners of my mouth twitch uncontrollably. "I might have been a little more than *okay*."

"See! I knew it!" she says as she sips her liquor and gives another shudder. "Why'd you stop?"

"Life."

She nods, but doesn't ask me to elaborate, and I'm grateful. This is another thing I find so interesting and refreshing about Willow. She doesn't push; she doesn't hound; she takes what you give her, and it's enough.

"Did you ever want to do something besides accounting? I'm sure crunching numbers wasn't your dream as a kid."

A mournful smile touches her lips. "Bob was in accounting."

"Bob?" I ask, although I already know who she's referring to, but I want to hear it from her.

"He was my dad for a little while, and he was an accountant." She gazes out the window overlooking the city before looking back at me. "I guess I was paying homage to him by going into accounting, but ... I also like it."

I'm not convinced. "What would you have done if it weren't accounting?"

She looks thoughtful as she studies the slice of pizza in her hand before she shrugs. "I ... I don't know. I've never tried anything. Isn't that sad and kind of ridiculous?"

I shake my head. "Now's the perfect time to find something you enjoy."

She chews thoughtfully on her lower lip; her brow furrowed in contemplation. Does she doubt her right to pursue something purely for herself?

Her continued silence makes me wonder whether she has ever pursued her own desires and dreams, or whether she has always been this kind and selfless.

"It doesn't have to be a major career shift, just something that brings you fulfillment."

A small smile creeps across her face as she looks at me. "Maybe I will."

Our eyes lock, and a hush falls over us; neither daring to break the silence with a word, and for once, I'm not dissecting her for any other reason but to admire her beauty.

Her eyes sparkle, reminiscent of the warm amber glow of a well-aged scotch. The dusting of light freckles on her small nose, soft and delicate, and unbelievably adorable. And the deviously delicious curve of her plump, red-stained lips as she smiles. She's a heady combination—intoxicating, and with a single glance, she erases all of my clarity.

My hand, moving with a will of its own, stretches toward hers across the counter, but before I can feel the electric tingle of nearly touching her, Willow shakes her head and places her hand in her lap, causing the charged moment to evaporate.

As the sting of rejection washes over me, my fingers automatically curl into a fist on the counter.

"Thank you for this." She holds up her piece of pizza and hops off the counter. "And thank you for the not-so-bad night, Mr. Reed."

"Of ..." I clear my throat. "Of course."

She grabs another slice of pizza before breezing past me, and I get this strange feeling of reluctance to see her go. The words linger on my tongue, asking her to stay a while longer, but I steel my lips into a rigid line.

She stops mid-stride and curses before gazing over her shoulder. "Will you ah ... will you help me? With my dress?"

Fuck. As if tonight couldn't get any more challenging.

"Yeah, of course," I say, pulling away from the island and stalking toward her as she slinks out of my jacket and places it carefully on the back of the couch.

I approach her from behind, and she remains still, her eyes locked on something in the distance.

As I gather her wavy hair to place over her shoulder, my fingertips brush against the warmth of her bare back. The temptation to lean in and suck the exposed skin of her neck, just under her ear, is fierce, but I hold back, fearful of being rejected again.

Rather, I gently run the back of my knuckles against her skin as I painstakingly find the back closure placed at the top of her dress in the center of her spine. The metallic snap of the clasp echoes like a bomb blast in the hushed silence.

With a deep inhale, I glance at our reflection in the giant mirror of a window that stretches from floor to ceiling. My attention is immediately drawn to Willow, whose midnight hair falls like a curtain, her eyes softly closed, and her lips relaxed yet slightly pouty, giving her a serene look in the soft glow.

I, on the other hand, feel the furthest thing from serene. I'm burning inside.

All night, the memory of the kiss we shared on the red carpet has replayed in the back of my mind.

The pace began slow and sensual, yet it quickly dragged me into its grip.

She dragged me into her grip.

Maybe I truly misjudged tonight, misread what I thought were heated moments?

No, she had to have felt something.

My fingers grab the small zipper, and as it descends, I let my knuckles trail down the soft skin of her spine, all while keeping my gaze fixed on her face. Hoping for a sign that she feels something, anything, the way I do.

Her eyes snap open as the zipper comes to a halt, and another heavy silence fills the space between us.

"Thanks," she whispers.

"Of course," I rasp.

How many fucking times am I going to say that?

A glimpse of red lingerie beneath the half-fallen dress is all I see as she stumbles away, one hand desperately trying to hold the dress up while the other protects her pizza slices.

When she's no longer in sight, I close my eyes, pressing my palms to my eye sockets, trying to rub away the tension caused by Willow, but the sensation of her soft skin lingers on my fingertips and the phantom of her perfume, a ghost of all things sweet, tempting, and off-limits to someone like me, still clings to the air and torments my senses.

I grab the jacket off the back of the couch and inhale her scent without giving a damn.

Maybe I should discuss the intimacy clause we agreed to. To

preserve what little sanity I have left, I desperately need some-thing, anything.

But what if I mention it and she refuses or decides she wants someone else?

The thought of her with another man is unimaginable, and I'm starting to think, me with anyone else, is too.

18

WILLOW

A heavy sigh escapes my lips as I stare at the canvas. The sunrise is a murky mess of clashing colors, the buildings' edges jitter and falter, their forms wavering, and the water looks less like waves and more like thick, swirling clouds of paint.

"This is just awful," I grumble to myself as I look for the black paint to cover this monstrosity.

"I would have to disagree—"

My heart leaps into my throat, a strangled gasp escaping my lips as I look up at Gabriel, my eyes wide with surprise. "You scared the crap out of me!"

"Sorry," he says, a smirk playing on his lips as he cocks his head, his critical eyes scanning my painting, the intensity making me fidget.

"So maybe landscapes aren't my thing," I mutter before he states the obvious.

"Again, I'd have to disagree. I think it looks good," he says while trying to conceal his smile and giving a nod.

I snort. "You're such a liar."

"Art is open to interpretation. Anything can be considered a masterpiece to someone with the right eye." He slips on his jacket and grabs his briefcase.

"And you have the right eye?"

"Definitely." He winks.

He's been doing that a lot ... winking.

The charity event marked a turning point for us, and since then, our relationship has been friendly and even a little bit flirtatious.

"When it's done, I'd like to put it in my office."

"To scare potential clients away?" I give a sardonic smile.

"Exactly."

"Well, maybe I'll make you a blanket to go with the painting," I say while gesturing toward the fuchsia ball of yarn I'm more than likely going to butcher after I clean these painting supplies up.

A few nights after our conversation over pizza following the charity event, a delivery arrived containing numerous boxes. Each brimming with materials for diverse hobbies: tubes of vibrant paint and canvases, balls of colorful yarn for crocheting, a sleek camera for photography, patterned scrapbook paper, gardening tools with pots and seeds, and even a violin.

The top of the first box held a small, neatly folded note; its message mirrored Gabriel's words from two nights prior. *"Now's the perfect time to find something you enjoy."*

I've never had anyone do anything so incredibly thoughtful.

"I'd like that," he says while checking his watch. "Shit, I have to go."

"Have a good day at work," I say as I continue trying to salvage the painting with lines of black. Maybe it just needs more shadows? Or white for more light?

When he says nothing, I turn to see him by the door, gazing at me. "Everything okay?"

A thoughtful silence envelopes us as he runs a hand

through his hair, then finally asks, "Would you like to go out with me tonight?"

Without thinking, I quirk a brow. "For a meeting or event?"

"No. Ah—" He runs a hand through his hair twice as he looks anywhere but at me.

He's ... nervous? But why? He's never nervous.

"I'd love to."

He nods, relieved. "Okay. Perfect."

"What should I wear?" If he wants us to have another public outing, especially after seeing the way everyone is when he's in public, I want to make sure I look decent.

"Something comfortable."

His phone rings, and he waves goodbye while walking to the elevator, barking orders to someone.

Comfortable? What does that even mean to someone like him?

———

SOLID STEPS LAND in the kitchen, and I gaze over at Gabriel— white sneakers, denim jeans slightly faded, a worn white and navy-blue raglan long-sleeve shirt, and a navy ball cap perched low on his head. "Are you ready?"

I breathe out a sigh of relief that my intuition was right, as I'm also in a comfortable pair of light denim, a cream sweater, and some white sneakers.

"Yeah," I say, hopping off the barstool.

"Where's my mother and Grayson?"

"She's sitting in the rocking chair next to his crib."

He nods. "Good. Let's go."

We descend in silence to the underground parking garage and, to my surprise, he opens my car door, a small, unexpected gesture I wouldn't expect since there isn't anyone watching us.

The car ride begins with him turning on some rock music,

the catchy tune a surprising change from our past drives in tense silence together, making me smile. He seems light, happy even.

We pull to the side of a dark road where a tiny food truck sits with a single window to order and pick up.

As he places the car in park, he eyes me. "It may seem a little sketchy, but these are always the best places."

Amusement tugs at my lips as he attempts his sales pitch, though it's utterly unnecessary. "I can smell the grilled onions from inside the car. I can't wait."

"They're the best Francheezie in town."

We grab our takeout food, the aroma of cheese and fried bacon clinging to the paper bags, and head back to the car since the small pop-up restaurant has no tables.

Once inside the car, we dig in. The first bite is heaven. The bun is soft yet sturdy; the fried bacon-wrapped hot dog has just the right amount of cheese and onions, and the dash of ketchup I added completes it.

"Oh my God," I groan around a big bite.

"Right ... the best."

"How did you even find this place? It's like a little hidden gem."

"I found it after leaving over there," he says, pointing to the back of a family fun park three buildings down.

I raise a brow.

"Would you want to go?" he asks while gazing out the windshield.

His behavior is so drastically different from what I'm used to, it's completely throwing me. He offers me the choice, but I can sense his anxiety in the way he avoids eye contact, as if I may turn him down, which makes my heart clench for some odd reason.

"Let's do it!"

As we pull around to the front, the emptiness of the parking lot is striking—just a few cars scattered across the expanse of asphalt.

For a Friday, the park is pretty dead. We haven't passed a single customer since walking through the maze of arcade games, bumper cars, and laser tag. "Are you sure this place is open? It's like a ghost town."

"I may have rented it out for the night."

My eyes widen. "You what? Is that even a thing? I thought that was only for children's birthday parties."

He shrugs. "The teens always hog the cages."

"You know, you're kind of intense. And what if I had said no earlier?"

"My hope was that you wouldn't."

We reach the outdoor batting cages, past the other noisy activities, where he grabs a few bats and a helmet from behind a dusty counter that smells of worn leather.

Once inside the batting cages, he turns on a machine, which he tells me feeds baseballs for him to hit.

He adjusts his cap backward, settling into a batter's stance at the makeshift home plate. Gripping the bat, he takes a few smooth, powerful practice swings. The sharp whiz of aluminum cutting through the air echoes around us.

The first thought that comes to mind is how at home he looks. Comfortable yet powerful and more in his element than in his pristine, polished suits.

The worn, backward cap, a hint of a smile playing on his lips, the thick veins bulging on the back of his clenched hands, the fabric of his shirt clinging to his broad physique, and the denim molding to his powerful muscles all reveal his raw physicality.

The next thing I hear is a sharp, high-pitched beep, and then the ball shoots out with terrifying speed—but he's ready, and the resounding crack as he hits it makes me wince.

That was sexy ... in a way I can't explain.

I try to imagine Gabriel as he once was. Was he like the jocks I knew in high school? Was he an asshole and felt superior? Or was he confident and loved the game?

I'm starting to realize he may be the latter; the crack of the bat vibrates through me as he sends another ball soaring with a grin.

Damn, he looks good.

"Do you want to try?" he asks, holding out the bat.

I shake my head. "I've never tried any sports."

"This is the perfect time. Come on. I'll turn the pitching machine down."

He bounces on the balls of his feet, practically vibrating with excitement; it's impossible not to share in his exhilaration.

"Okay."

After turning the machine down, he picks up a helmet and places it on my head. "Is the fit okay?"

"I think ... I'm not really sure how it should feel."

His eyes pierce through mine as he holds the sides of the helmet by my ears. "Secure but comfortable."

"Uh ... it feels a little weird, but not bad."

He grins, and his dark brown eyes sparkle. "Perfect. Here's your bat."

With the bat in hand, I walk to the home plate, focusing on duplicating his stance, but it all feels awkward. "Like this?"

"Can I help you?"

"Sure."

His body presses against mine instantly, his breath on my neck sending chills across my exposed skin. "You need to be balanced yet relaxed." His muscular hands move to my shoulders, then expertly reposition my arms and hands. The warmth of his touch is both comforting and precise, but it feels more like a massage than an adjustment of my posture. "Just like that," he murmurs.

His warmth seeps under my clothes as I nod, while his whispered words send a strange thrill through me.

The feeling is identical to what I felt when he unzipped my dress the other night. Nerves mixed with a dangerously delightful need for more.

"Your feet should be slightly wider than shoulder-width apart. Knee's bent and more weight distributed on your back leg than your front," he says in a tone that sounds right out of an erotic novel. Grave and deep and so sexy.

I swallow the lump in my throat as I try to mimic his words, but they're coming out sexually in my head.

What is happening to me?

It's as if a chaotically dizzy dance of butterflies is fluttering in my stomach.

"Like this?" I ask breathlessly.

The feel of him is gone until his hand circles my left knee, eliciting a sharp gasp from me as his touch sends a jolt of awareness through my body and a warm rush to my core. He continues his exploration, his hand moving slowly down, adjusting my feet until they're positioned as he likes.

"How does that feel?" he asks, standing to his full height and coming up behind me again.

Like every one of my nerve endings is firing at once.

Like I'm dying and being reborn at the same time.

I clear my throat and rasp, "Good."

"That's what I like to hear," he whispers.

My eyes widen, and I'm thankful for him being behind me because I can imagine how flushed I probably look.

Is he fucking with me? Because what in the hell is going on, and why am I enjoying it so damn much?

"Are you ready?"

I nod, as words are impossible.

His heat fades, the air growing cooler around me as I stand coiled, my senses heightened and ready. The electronic beep sounds, and the ball approaches, slower than Gabriel's had been, but still with considerable speed. I close my eyes, swinging at the last moment.

The sound of the ball meeting the bat was a thunderous crack that made my hands vibrate and left me grinning.

With another one of his heart-stopping smiles, Gabriel rushes toward me, engulfing me in a hug. "That was amazing."

All I can think is, *Yeah, you kind of are.*

19

GABRIEL

My vision swims from exhaustion. The screen's brightness is a harsh contrast to my dim home office, and though it's well past midnight, sleep is impossible.

I take a slow sip of the amber liquid in my tumbler; the smoothness warms me from the inside out while I survey the blueprints of my newest investment, a chain of sprawling luxury resorts on five different islands along the Mediterranean Sea. The revenue streams could catapult me to my billion-dollar goal if I keep the company intact, but possibly more if I dismantle it.

This is the investment I've chased relentlessly for years—a shimmering, elusive prize that's finally within my grasp, but I'm conflicted. An emotion I've never experienced until these past few weeks.

The powerful urge to strip it down and sell everything is battling with a sense of attachment.

Part of me imagines taking Willow and Grayson on vacations to the islands for swimming and sandcastles by day and candlelit dinners by night, which is worrisome. This marriage was for show. *Was.* I'm already thinking of the reason for this fake marriage in the past tense, which is again worrisome.

This marriage was supposed to be simple. Transactional. A ruse to get control of the company—nothing more.

After Willow stole from me, she made everything so easy; I had every step planned, but now, it's far more complicated.

She's more than just the employee I forced to marry me. Willow's a woman burdened by a difficult past, struggling to raise her child alone after her ex screwed her over. She isn't Eryn. I've observed her closely since she moved in—a short time, but long enough to know she's honest and straightforward, not manipulative and deceitful at all.

Her interactions with my mother are sincere and attentive. Each gesture and word of Willow's shows genuine interest in what my mother has to say.

Willow's a present, selfless, and loving mother even while sick.

Her humor is infectious, and with her, I feel comfortable enough to be myself. Going to the batting cages with her was unforgettable. Her radiant energy, eyes sparkling with excitement as she watched me hit the ball, and then the joy when I got to teach her. It was the best night I've had in a very long time.

Lastly, she's exceptionally beautiful.

With a click, my document closes, replaced by the familiar image of us on the red carpet outside the charity event three weeks ago.

The sight of her, radiant in her shimmering red gown, left me speechless. It was the first time I had let myself fully admire Willow's beauty.

In the beginning, I pushed those thoughts aside, but the need returned that night with a vengeance and has lingered ever since, a persistent ache to have her.

I keep telling myself that if I hadn't kissed her, I wouldn't be plagued by these thoughts of her soft, pillowy lips. If I hadn't held her so close, I wouldn't have had thoughts of her body writhing against mine. But I would, because she is so much more than that.

And I'm the asshole who can let her go at any moment, but I don't want to. Not now, not ever.

With a sigh, I stretch, willing the tension in my neck and shoulders to subside.

I'm a creature of habit, a stickler for schedules. This unplanned turn of events is unsettling to my preferred discipline and organized approach, and I have no clue what to do. Or if I even want to do anything to change it.

A gentle tap, tap, tap on the door, barely audible above the quiet hum of the computer, interrupts my contemplation as I continue to stare at our beaming faces on the screen. "Come in."

Willow pokes her head in with a warm smile on her face. "I know I'm not supposed to be on your side of the penthouse, but—"

I clear my throat, sit up straighter, and then exit our photo on the screen before waving her in. "It's okay. Forget what I said; you can come over here whenever you want."

With careful steps, she enters, balancing a white plate piled high with food and a glass of something sparkling in her hand.

"I haven't seen you since breakfast, and figured you would be hungry, so I made you some food."

"Really?" I raise a brow. Besides my mother, no one has ever made me food.

And more, she was watching out for me?

Not like that asshole. Exhaustion is getting things mixed up in my mind.

Willow stops short, and her face falls. "I'm sorry, I should've asked."

"No ... I'm just surprised, is all." I rise and move my laptop, the file folders, and loose papers from my desk to the side to make room.

With a gentle clink, she places a plate of steaming chicken and rice on my desk and, next to it, a tall glass of sparkling water. The rich, savory scent of the food is intoxicating, prompting an immediate growl from my hungry stomach.

With a fork, I spear a juicy piece of chicken, then gather a spoonful of rice, spinach, and what appear to be caramelized onions and place them in my mouth with a satisfying sigh.

"If you don't like it, you don't have to eat it," she urges with wide, nervous eyes.

Willow has nothing to worry about. The food is delicious, but even if it wasn't, my mother taught me manners. I would have eaten the entire plate, maybe even asked for seconds, with a smile on my face because it's the thought that matters.

"It's good," I say, taking another mouthful.

Willow visibly relaxes. "Good."

She takes a step as if she's about to leave, and the same strange reluctance I always get rushes through me. I don't want her to go, and this time I won't let her.

"Stay a minute." I point to the seating area off to the right with a brown leather sofa and a glass table.

As she sits, her red silk robe rides up, revealing a tantalizing view of her toned thighs.

With a sigh, I look away. Maybe this isn't a good idea. I reach over and take another sip of my whisky before gazing at her again. "Did you eat?"

She shakes her head while surveying my office. "No, I ... I wanted to do this as a thank you."

Curiosity tilts my head. "A thank you for what?"

"For looking after Grayson and me, both when I was sick and when we were well ... for everything you've done."

With the plate and drinks in hand, I make my way over to her on the sofa.

Her eyes lock with mine as I sit next to her, and the warmth I feel contrasts with the cold formality of our first meeting in the brightly lit meeting room. Her doe-like eyes hold no trace of tears or fear, only a dash of uncertainty and ... lust?

No, it can't be. But what if it is?

I angle my body toward hers as I spear another piece of chicken and carefully place it before her luscious red lips. Her eyes flicker down to the fork before she looks back at me and, just as I brace myself for her refusal, she parts her lips in acceptance.

Good girl.

No, not good girl.

Jesus.

Suppressing a groan, I watch as her lips curl around the fork, while struggling not to react as her tongue sweeps over her lips in the next moment.

"Thank you."

I clear my throat; the sound echoes slightly in the charged silence, and I stab at another piece of food to distract myself.

Does she sense the same exhilarating electric tension between us as I do? It feels like being in the batter's box, bases loaded, in the ninth inning—the weight of the world on your shoulders as you grip the bat, ready to swing at the ball.

Placing another forkful of food in my mouth, I savor it *that* much more, knowing her moist lips touched the same utensil moments before.

Okay, I need to collect my thoughts; otherwise, I'll make a complete fool of myself.

"What were you doing up so late?"

"I was editing some really great shots of Grayson I got while in the park earlier today, and time just seemed to fly."

The realization that she genuinely loves photography brings me rare happiness, and I'm thrilled to be the one to have made it happen. Without my purchase, her secret passion may never have come to light.

"What about you?" Willow asks. "It's late for someone who has to work in a few hours."

I shrug. "I couldn't sleep, so I decided to do a little work."

"You never stop working, do you?"

"Never. I think I'm addicted."

She nods. "There are far worse addictions out there, I suppose. What are you working on tonight ... if you don't mind me asking, of course?"

"I don't mind." I grin. Discussing work is a safe topic and something I love. "There's a chain of luxury resorts on a few islands." I rise and grab my laptop before settling down beside her and propping it on my lap. I click through a few pages, making sure I don't accidentally click on our photo, then find the videos of the resorts.

She leans in to get a better view, and I take the opportunity to inhale her floral and powder scent that drives me crazy yet also puts me at ease. It's like running through a flower field, with the warmth of the sun on your face, the sweet scent of blossoms filling your lungs, and petals softly brushing your skin.

"Oh, this one is breathtaking. Look at the view of the sunset above the water from the balcony of the dining area. It's like a dream." She bites her lip before gazing at me. "What are you planning on doing with it?"

Leaning my head back, a chuckle rumbles in my chest. I'm sure even without asking, she knows my plans for the properties from my track record.

"I haven't decided yet."

She continues to look at the video as it runs through the many amenities with hearts in her eyes.

I lied.

I have decided.

Right here, right now.

I'm keeping them.

For her.

"What would you do with the resorts?" I ask.

"Why would you ask me?"

"You're a young, intelligent woman who graduated at the top of her class."

Her brows furrow. "Why would you add the *young* to that sentence?"

I pause, setting the laptop on the table, and stare at her, confused. "You are *young* and intelligent. Why are you worried about the young part?"

She looks down at her hands in her lap. "Nothing ... It's stupid."

I raise her chin with my thumb and forefinger. "Nothing you say is stupid. Why?" I ask the last part sternly.

"One of the news outlets said I was a lot younger than you, and that's the reason you married me. Obviously, it's not the reason, but they believe it to be and said some pretty mean stuff."

Interesting.

"Does it bother you knowing we have a decent-sized age gap?"

"I didn't even think of it, to be honest. You look pretty young for an old guy."

I snort as she smiles.

If only she knew the countless ways I could demonstrate my youth to her.

"No more looking at those stupid gossip sites. Over the years, I've learned that for every five people with positive feedback, there will be twenty with negative. I can save children from a burning building and get praise, yet also be chastised for not knowing and fixing it with my money beforehand."

"I've never seen one bad thing written about ..." Mortification rushes across her face.

"What was that?"

"Oh God, nothing. Forget I said anything," she murmurs with a bright red blush and eyes darting everywhere but at me.

I put a hand on my chest. "Did *Mrs. Reed* Google me?"

"Please say you'll forget I mentioned it."

No fucking way. It's engraved in my mind forever.

"If you tell me what you've read, then maybe."

She contemplates it for a moment.

"They mostly spoke of your good looks, reclusive lifestyle, and something like 'universally appealing to all.'"

I grin. "And that assessment bothered you?"

"At the time, yes." She laughs.

"And now?"

She nods as her cheeks flush. "I think they got it right."

So, she agrees with their assessment of me? Am I appealing to her?

No, I can't ask her that. My ego can't take another hit. So, I change the subject.

"What would you do with the resorts?"

She smirks. "Logically or illogically?"

"Both."

"Logically, a venture is only worthwhile if it aligns with sound reasoning and yields a profit."

"I don't need a definition, Willow."

She rolls her eyes. "Illogically, it looks like paradise, and I'd keep them."

I nod, gently guiding another forkful of food toward her lips.

"What do you think?" she asks before opening her mouth so I can guide the food in.

"I like your illogical thought," I murmur, my thumb

brushing her full bottom lip, dislodging a single grain of rice, which I then suck into my mouth.

As her eyes meet my lips, a soft, pink blush spreads across her chest.

Fuck it.

I run my fingers across her cheek, down her neck, and across her chest. The feel of her soft skin makes me bite my lip until I taste blood, with a thrill that shoots straight to my cock.

I want to touch every goddamn inch of her. Consume her. Make her desire me like I desire her.

Continuing my exploration down her left arm, I finally reach her exposed thigh.

She gasps, eyes hooded, "Mr. Reed—"

Her addressing me so formally nearly makes me laugh. I've realized it's something she does when she gets nervous, but right now I yearn for our previous intimacy, where her inhibitions are lowered so she can feel what she wants without nerves taking center stage.

"Gabriel. Just Gabriel," I breathe, as I lean in to taste her sweet lips.

This time, there's no need for a pretentious display of affection with a crowd of spectators. There's just Willow and me. Side by side, with an unwavering connection I know she can feel, causing a sense of timelessness and euphoria as we finally give in.

With one hand tangled in her silky hair, fingers tracing the delicate strands, and the other hand around her waist, pulling her impossibly closer, I deepen the kiss, our tongues a frantic dance.

Slowly, I guide her beneath me on the sofa, our bodies intertwining as I continue to explore her neck with my tongue and teeth, eliciting soft moans from her plump lips.

Leaning back and kneeling between her legs, I untie her

robe and marvel at the way the thin silk dress delicately hugs her flawless frame.

I gaze into her eyes, searching for a sign—a flicker of hesitation, a subtle shift in her expression, anything that would tell me to stop.

Her eyes only smolder with desire as she hesitantly runs her fingers over my chest before deftly unbuttoning my dress shirt. Once off, her eyes take me in, and I smirk. "Not too bad for an old guy?"

Willow visibly swallows and shakes her head, making me chuckle. I may be older than she is, but I've taken care of myself.

"I would've never expected this under the suits," she murmurs as she traces one of my many tattoos. "When I was sick, and you were lying on my bed, I thought I was hallucinating."

My eyes momentarily flutter shut, a groan escaping my lips as her fingers, feather-light yet intensely intimate, lands on skin untouched for over a decade. I grab her hand as it reaches my sternum and kiss each of her fingers.

Although she came here to do something thoughtful for me, tonight is for her.

I lean back as my fingers travel down her magnificent body. From her slender neck, to the juncture between her breasts where her nipples strain against the fabric, to her exposed belly button where her dress rode up, and finally to the small, wet black triangle of fabric covering her.

"Do you want this?" I ask while trying only to look into her eyes, but finding it increasingly difficult with the way she looks and feels under me. "Not because I made you marry me. Not because you feel you owe me. But because you feel a burning desire that consumes you, and you want this just as much as I do."

She nods.

"I need words, Willow. I won't touch you any further without words."

"Yes," she moans. "I want this ... I want you."

Thank fuck.

Biting my bottom lip, I let my eyes roam the perfection that is Willow a little longer before asking in a raspy tone, "Do you know how crazy you made me the day of the annual party and then at the club?"

She shakes her head.

I grab her left leg and hike it over my right shoulder as my fingers trace the smooth, warm skin from her ankle to her calf. My gaze remains locked on her eyes, glittering with desire, her chest rapidly rising with anticipation. "I was going out of my mind with jealousy and want."

Continuing their exploration, my fingers glide past her knee and up her thigh, eliciting goose bumps on her flesh and a gasp from her parted lips.

"The thought of someone else touching you, kissing you, fucking you ..." I pause and inhale deeply, then exhale as I shake my head, working to soothe the pressure in my chest before carrying on, "The second my body fused to yours on the dance floor, I felt as if heaven replaced hell and your touch was my salvation."

My fingers find the hem of her nightdress, and I pull it higher, exposing her porcelain skin inch by agonizingly slow inch as if edging not only her but myself.

"I wanted you more than I've wanted anything in a very long time," I say as I finally spot her pebbled nipple coming into view. "And more, I want you to want me just as much."

As I rub my thumb along her hardened peak, she arches toward me, letting out a soft moan, while her hair falls behind her and her hand tries to pull me close.

I shake my head and smirk. Surrendering to the moment,

letting my body become one with hers, would bring this to a close much faster than I'd like.

"Open your mouth," I say, sticking my thumb against her lips.

She opens without hesitation, the warm wetness of her lips now around my thumb, while her tongue slowly caresses my finger. Her eyes bore into mine as my cock pulses with the growing intensity of her suction. The moment is erotic and hypnotizing, and I can't bear the intensity much longer.

Pulling her thong to the side, I tease her wet entrance with gentle caresses. She's soaked. My fingers dance over her clit, coaxing a moan from her lips that quivers against my thumb. I keep the tempo slow and delicate, moving from her clit to her opening until she's writhing, desperate for more pressure, desperate to be stuffed with my cock.

I gaze at her intently as I find her core once more with my fingers, finally penetrating her tight heat. A gasp leaves her as I pump in and out with my two fingers curved to hit her sweet spot. As I keep up the pace, her moans grow more intense as they bounce around the room. The wet suction on my thumb is driving me wild. Her hand finds my wrist, and she grasps it tight as she bucks against my fingers. Her back arches, causing my thumb to leave her mouth as her body convulses in the throes of her orgasm. As she comes down, her glossy eyes meet mine once more, a shy smile touching her lips while a blush covers her cheeks.

The sight of her, so innocent yet satisfied, ignites a deeper desire within me, conjuring images of how I could bring that look back over and over again.

"You're breathtakingly beautiful, Willow Reed," I breathe before I lean in, and my mouth meets hers. "And all mine."

Our fingers entwine, and I gently lift her arms above her head to rest on the armrest of the couch while my hard cock presses against the juncture of her thighs.

I breathe in her wildflower and powder scent as I bite the soft skin between the base of her neck and ear while rocking my body against hers. "I want to feel you."

"I want to feel you too," she breathes.

Her thighs clench around my waist, and that's all the motivation I need. I move my hands from the comfort of hers to my pants. Releasing my throbbing cock and spreading the pre-cum across the head before positioning it at her entrance.

For a fraction of a second, our eyes connect, and then my hand closes around her throat as I surge in with one hard thrust.

Her eyes widen with a gasp, back bowing, nails digging into my back as she chants, "Oh God."

My eyes close as I savor the feel of her sheathed around me.

So fucking tight.

So fucking warm.

So fucking right.

As my eyes open, I recoil, then lunge forward with another powerful thrust.

"Fuck, you feel so fucking good," I groan as my pace picks up.

With one last squeeze, my fingers move from her neck to her breast, where I then give her nipple a firm, yet pleasurable, squeeze. A gasp quickly morphing into a moan escapes her lips as shock battles delight.

Fueled by the sound, I hoist her legs onto my shoulders, adjusting the angle as I sink deeper. She lets out a throaty moan as the new angle sends a jolt of pleasure through her.

I watch, unable to look away, as her eyes seek mine. She moans deeply, her black hair cascading around her face, and her fists clenched tightly as pleasure takes hold. My hand sinks between her legs, seeking her clit again as I feel her walls clamp around my cock. She's close, and so am I. The pleasurable burn spreads through my body as I vigorously stroke her clit.

"That's it, beautiful," I groan through thrusts. "Come on my cock."

Her eyes widen as her orgasm hits her, and it spurs my own. I continue to fuck her through mine, ensuring every last drop is released deep inside of her. Our eyes never waver, our bodies remain intertwined, and the connection feels deeper, more intimate than anything I've ever felt before.

As I watch her descend from the euphoric state I brought her to, the rosy blush on her cheeks, eyes swimming in a blissful haze, and a smile of immense pleasure spoke to me again.

Her hand reaches up to move a lock of hair that fell into my eyes, and I relish the soft touch.

The connection resonates on a deep, unspoken level.

She doesn't know it, but she has collapsed the first of many walls I know she'll demolish as our time together continues, and for once, I'm not terrified.

20

WILLOW

My steps falter as I walk from the hallway leading to my bedroom into the main penthouse area where Gabriel stands before the range as the smell of sizzling bacon and just-brewed coffee invades my senses.

I watch the pale blue of his dress shirt stretch and strain as his broad shoulders move.

Last night's events replay in my mind as if in slow motion—the charged air as he asked me to stay, the intimate graze of his thumb against my bottom lip, the deep, visceral pull in my abdomen as he ate the grain of rice from his thumb. Each tattoo on his body—a tiny window into his past, held a story I yearned to uncover. The way his body moved against mine. The way he meticulously gathered my shattered fragments, mending each piece with such care, made me feel reborn and stronger.

"Are you going to stand there and make this awkward, or are you going to come over here and eat breakfast with me?" Gabriel asks as he turns with a smirk on his face.

Instead of showing my mortification, I hit him with a raised brow. "Maybe I'm just enjoying the view."

A noise between a snort and a sputter reaches my ears as he places his coffee cup on the counter and wipes his lips.

I sheepishly walk over and set the baby monitor with a sleeping Grayson on the screen down before grabbing the cup in his outstretched hand. "Thank you."

"What are you doing today?"

A familiar alarm from my past rings through my head.

"Why?"

Here it comes. He thinks he can dictate what I do now that we've been intimate. How could I have been so stupid?

"Hey." His large, warm hand rests on top of mine. "Where did you just go?"

I blink. "What do you mean?"

"Your face changed when I asked about your plans."

"I ... why did you ask what I'm doing today?"

"I'll tell you after you tell me where you went in that pretty head of yours." When I stay silent, he continues, "This, us, after last night, things are different, and we need to communicate ... unless last night was a one-time thing?"

I stab the yellow of the egg with my fork; the yolk oozes slightly as I mull over his words.

Things *are* different, and I do want more of last night, so much more. But I don't want to be held under someone's thumb either, which sounds asinine with the current predicament and the contract not so subtly screaming in the back of my head.

"I don't want to be grilled about where I'm going or what I'm doing. I gave my ex all the power, I turned into a shell of myself, and I'll never do that again. Not even for you."

"I see." He nods, a small smile playing on his lips as he bites into a crisp piece of bacon.

Shit. What does that mean?

He clears his throat. "First off, I'd like to have open communication, so I know you and Grayson are safe. The world is a dangerous place, especially in a city as big as this. I've also made enemies along the way. I'm not saying this to scare or sway you. This is just a fact."

He's not trying to cage me in, only to keep us safe. I feel like such a melodramatic idiot.

"And I only asked because my mother mentioned wanting to take you and Grayson to the aquarium today."

"She did?"

"Yes. I told her I'd have to speak with you to see if you'd want to go or not."

"Grayson and I would love to go to the aquarium with your mom." I scrunch my brows. "Why would you tell her I might not want to go?"

"I wasn't sure if you'd want to spend time with my mother."

"Are you crazy? She's easy to talk to and incredibly sweet. You're lucky you have her."

"I know." He nods. "And she seems to love you."

"The feeling is mutual." I smile, but a frown takes its place as I think about how we're deceiving her. "I don't like that we're lying to her."

He's quiet and thoughtful for a second before a smirk tilts his lips. "After last night, I don't think we're lying as much as before, right?"

My cheeks blush as more memories of him on top of me flood my mind until they circle back around to his mom. "Right. I just don't want her to find out ... ever. I feel like it would break her heart."

"She won't," he says with such confidence I almost believe him. But that's not reality. Our agreement is for three years. Nothing more. What happens when the time is up, and we divorce? She'll still want to see who she believes is her grandson.

Then what?

The more I ponder, the more I realize that despite his

careful preparations, he fails to comprehend the possible fallout once our time is up. It's not just about us; it's about the people who will be devastated by this. Primarily Vivian, but also Grayson, once he's able to understand the situation.

Then what?

"Hey." His forefinger hooks into the worn denim of my shorts, pulling me close until our chests meet. His eyes, soft and searching, meet mine as his fingers tuck a wayward strand of hair behind my ears with a tender touch that has me swooning. "We'll figure it out, okay?"

I nod. "I just don't want to hurt her. She's the closest thing I've had to a mom in a really long time."

A look of contemplation crosses Gabriel's face as he takes a bite of his eggs. "Have you ever tried to find yours?"

His question throws me off temporarily since I had hoped we would switch to small talk. Not to jump back into murky waters.

"After I graduated from high school, I tried, but it didn't lead me anywhere useful."

I remember being so hopeful, thinking one trip back to the fire station where I'd been dropped off would lead me to a family. I was so unbelievably naïve.

"It still upsets you," he says, searching my face while it feels like a wildfire burns my throat.

"It would've been nice to find out who I was before I ended up at the fire station. Did I have a name? Was I ever wanted, or was I just a mistake to be discarded? There's an entire piece of who I am, down to my very DNA, that I have no clue about. It's like living without a memory ..." My voice catches at the end, and I shake my head to get out of that headspace as embarrassment seizes me. "I'm sorry. I didn't mean to get worked up—"

I don't know what gave me the courage to tell him one of my deepest wounds and insecurities that I like to keep buried within. Perhaps it's his raw confession of feelings and the intimacy we shared last night?

His eyes soften. "No, it's okay. I asked. I couldn't imagine—"

"It's fine."

He shakes his head as his thumbs brush against the apples of my cheeks. "No, it's not fine. Don't dismiss the way you feel. Your feelings are valid. Anyone would feel the way you do."

His words seemed to mend a piece of my soul, as if the part of me that invalidated my emotions was finally quieted, making the weight on my shoulders lessen.

I nod even as the last words I need to get out finally come. "Sometimes it's just hard to accept the idea that I'm unwanted, a burden."

His eyes hardened as if refuting my words. "You don't know that—"

"It doesn't matter," I whisper, hoping he'll drop the conversation, even though it's been nice to confide in him. None of these thoughts will help me now.

I've done this before, run through countless scenarios in my head, trying to understand my abandonment, but those imagined reasons don't change my present reality. It's best to move forward instead of looking back.

Gabriel must see my reluctance, so he decides not to push further, instead asking, "So I should tell my mother yes to the aquarium?"

"Definitely."

21

GABRIEL

"Mr. Reed, your eleven o'clock is here," Henry says, poking his head in through my office door.

"Excellent. Send her in."

With a hesitant step and a nervous glance, a woman in her late thirties walks into the room. The same black hair and porcelain skin are there, but the familiar brown cognac eyes are replaced with a deep forest green. A modest navy-blue shift dress falls just below her knees, paired with low heels of the same shade.

I don't know what I expected from this encounter, but I feel like this may go better than I originally thought.

"Gabriel Reed?" she asks, clutching her bag anxiously.

"Mrs. Thomas," I say, nodding as I gesture toward one of the two chairs on the other side of my desk. "Thank you for making the trip out to the city."

"You said it was urgent," she says, her voice tight as she takes a seat.

Instead of going into a lengthy explanation, I face the picture frame of Willow and Grayson, my mother took the other day while they were at the aquarium, toward Willow's birth mother.

A sharp gasp cuts through the silence as her perfectly manicured, light-pink nails fly to her lips, while tears well in her eyes.

"She's ... she's beautiful."

"Willow."

With trembling lips, she shapes Willow's name silently, then breathes, "What a beautiful name."

I don't respond, but decide to do what I do best: dissect her as a person.

While she appears polished and composed, can I trust her with Willow and Grayson? I'll never forgive myself if I unintentionally hurt them by bringing her birth mother into the picture.

She must feel my penetrating gaze because her eyes rise from the frame and meet mine, a flicker of unease crossing her face in the heavy silence.

Moments later, her head droops, and she retrieves a soft cloth from her bag before dabbing underneath her eyes. "Does she know you contacted me?"

"No."

"Do you plan to tell her?"

"Depends on how this meeting goes."

She visibly swallows and then nods slowly. "Understandable."

I cut straight to the chase. "Why'd you abandon Willow?" A look of surprise flashes across her face, her eyes widening before she squares her shoulders and levels a glare at me, one so much like Willow's it makes me smirk.

"If I get the opportunity to speak with Willow, that will be a conversation between her and me."

The similarity between her and Willow is showing more and more.

"If I allow this, there will be rules."

"I'm listening," she says with so much hope and desperation in her eyes that it almost makes me forget she abandoned her child.

"Prior to meeting her, you will need to sign an NDA. If she decides she doesn't want a relationship, you disappear. If you go to the press with anything, I'll crush—"

"Gabriel?" Willow's voice cuts through my words, and all I can think is ... fuck.

22

WILLOW

The letter sitting in the diaper bag feels like a lead bomb, heavy, threatening, and seconds from detonating as I rush to Gabriel's office.

From cloud-nine to the pits of hell in a matter of seconds. That seems to be how my life works. A continuous cycle of highs and lows, joys and sorrows. For me, the second choice inevitably becomes the reality.

Gabriel and I have fallen into a sort of groove since the night in his home office. Although we haven't touched each other like we had that night, it still hasn't stopped us from showing each other the promise of wanting more in each heated stare, lingering touch, and wickedly hot innuendo. These are what I'd consider highs and joys.

But everything that goes up must come down. I was enjoying the pleasant early fall weather and the view from my cute bistro table when the server brought me a white envelope. He stated that a guy in a black hat gave it to him to give to me.

Inside, a threat that chilled me to the bone. Ten million dollars wired to an account, or Grayson and I would be hurt.

The second I placed the letter down with trembling hands,

I surveyed my surroundings. Nothing greeted me besides the feeling of a million tiny ants on my flesh as I felt someone's stare analyzing my every move.

I was being watched and, worse; I was alone with Grayson. Exactly what Gabriel was worried about. Next thing I knew, I was rushing a few blocks south to Reed Equity as fast as I could push the stroller.

As I make my way onto the floor of his office, I let out a breath, place a strained smile on my face, and say hello to anyone I pass.

The last thing I need is to add fuel to the fire of the ever-growing office rumor mill. Aella told me the tea was hot in the office after the annual company party, with theories and accusations. None of them put me in the best light especially when one mentioned Gabriel and me getting it on in the storage room.

I pause at Henry's immaculate desk, outside Gabriel's imposing office, but he's nowhere to be found. I check the planner on his desk. Its pages are filled with Gabriel's meticulously planned day, yet no meetings are listed, so I walk to his door, knock softly, and peek inside.

"Gabriel?"

First, I notice his wide eyes as he sits behind his massive black desk, obviously shocked by my visit and interruption, followed by a woman sitting opposite him across the table.

"I'm so sorry ... I ..."

My eyes get lost in the reflection of an older, wiser version of myself, a stranger in a familiar face.

Gabriel rises and walks toward me with a determined stride. Paralyzed, one hand clenches the cold brass doorknob, the other on the stroller. Blood roars in my ears, drowning out all other sounds as a cold, damp film clings to my skin.

Just before Gabriel obscures my view of his office and the woman, I glimpse a lone tear rolling down her cheek.

My intuition, a voice as loud as a siren, screams at me. It's so absolute.

She's my mother.

"I don't feel so good," I say just as a ringing begins in my ears and I feel myself fall into blackness.

"Come on, beautiful ... wake up." Even with my eyes closed and a slight ringing in my ears, I clearly detect the anxiety in Gabriel's voice.

"Do you want me to call the paramedics?" the woman asks.

No, not the woman. My birth mother.

"No, she'll be okay. Just give her a minute." I hear Gabriel murmur as someone places something cool against my forehead.

"Are you sure?"

Gabriel is about to say something, but I don't give him the chance as I open my eyes and try to right the dizziness it brings.

"There she is," Gabriel says, relief in his eyes as he rubs the wet cloth against my forehead.

My birth mother's glassy gaze meets mine. "Are you okay?"

I swallow and nod. Words evade me when all I'd ever thought about was what I'd say if I ever found my parents.

"Maybe you should leave," Gabriel says to my birth mother before he gazes at me with concern.

My birth mother's face falls, but she hides it quickly and bows her head. "Of course."

A surge of alarm floods me as I watch her turn to grab her bag from the chair.

"No," I croak.

This is the day I've dreamed of since I was a small child. I can't let her leave.

The child who cried night after night from feeling unwanted, unloved. The preteen who watched all the other parents picking up their children after school so they could go to a loving home. The young adult who walked across the stage at high school and college graduation without a single parent in the audience to cheer her on. Finally, the mother who brought a child into this world alone. Every season of the girl I was deserves this moment of understanding and closure.

With Gabriel's help, I haul myself up into a sitting position on his office couch, noticing the woman's uncertain stare. "I'd like it if you stayed."

She nods just as Grayson chooses this moment to cry. A flicker of indecision crosses Gabriel's face, as if he doesn't want to leave us, before he says he'll watch Grayson, allowing us our moment.

I couldn't be more grateful to him than I am now.

"Thank you," I murmur as he nods and walks to the stroller.

I scoot to the side of the leather loveseat to make room for her.

As we look into each other's eyes, a nervous flutter erupts in my chest. A lifetime of questions has built up inside me, yet now I find myself unable to voice a single one.

Thankfully, my birth mother must realize my hesitation. "Your husband told me you didn't know about this meeting, so I first want to apologize for giving you such a scare."

I clear my throat. "It's okay."

She smiles lightly before bringing a trembling hand to smooth down her immaculate hair. "If it helps, this is just as nerve-racking for me as it probably is for you, and we can talk as much or as little as you're comfortable with."

Her words are a comfort, but I still feel the emptiness. "I ... I don't know where to begin."

I glance around the room, searching for Gabriel, and spot him feeding Grayson a small jar of baby food. He nods, a subtle yet powerful gesture of support, his eyes conveying a quiet strength that fills me with hope and warmth.

Turning back to my birth mother, I ask the first thing that comes to mind. "What's your name?"

"Abigail. Abigail Thomas."

"That's a pretty name."

"Thank you."

"What did you name me?" The question rushes past my lips before I even know if she planned on having me, and I inwardly cringe, anticipating her words, a knot tightening in my stomach.

A smile touches her lips. "I was going to name you Abby, but Willow is so much better."

"Abby, like you?"

"Abby, like me." She smiles.

"Can you tell me a little about yourself when you were younger? I'd like to know where I came from."

She nods, but a flicker of uncertainty dances in her eyes, and I almost call it off, the anticipation heavy with a sense of foreboding.

"I grew up in the conservative Bible Belt of Alabama. My father was a pastor in our small town who took his calling seriously." A melancholic smile reaches her lips. "At the time I was only fifteen, and I went to my father, thinking he and my family would help me with loving arms and acceptance, just as he always preached." She shakes her head as a tear cascades down her cheek. "Instead, he insisted on fervent prayer in my locked closet for three days before taking me to a doctor in the middle of the night to fix my problem." She stops talking as her eyes glaze over, and she clasps her hands in her lap so tightly her knuckles turn white. I wish I knew if she'd be okay with me holding her hand. With the turn the story has taken, I'm sure it's hard on her, and now I feel bad for asking. "I used the excuse of needing to use the restroom and made an escape."

My eyes water as I imagine a young girl, pregnant, scared, lost, alone, and willing to risk it all to save her unborn child from death.

Suddenly, I understand, the truth is a crushing blow, and I'm overwhelmed by a torrent of tears.

My very soul felt lighter and more at peace.

"You ... wanted me?"

Abigail hands me a tissue from her bag. "More than anything."

"Keeping me must've been so hard," I say, recalling when it was just Grayson and me; I at least had a job and a college degree.

She nods as she dabs under her eyes. "I wanted to keep you forever, but I knew the future I wanted for you wouldn't happen if you stayed with me. I had no one to help me. We were homeless."

Logically, I understand her actions were those of a responsible parent, yet the pain remains.

"What about my father?"

"Roger was charismatic and a dreamer," she says, her voice tinged with sorrow, a faint smile gracing her lips, but all I could focus on was the word *was*. He isn't here anymore. "He was in a car accident in his twenties and never recovered. I'm so sorry."

I clear my throat. "It's okay."

A beep sounds from Gabriel's phone on his desk, and I hear Henry mention something about his next meeting in five minutes. Gabriel hits the button and tells him they can wait.

Abigail's hand finds mine, her grip firm and reassuring, and I squeeze back, feeling a surge of comfort. "I should be going; I have school pickups soon, but I'd love to see you again, and your son, when and if you're comfortable with it."

"I'd love that," I say as something hits me. "I ... have siblings?"

She nods. "Lily and Lachlan. They're fourteen-year-old twins."

"That's ..." I shake my head. "Can I meet them at some point?"

"They would love that."

"They know about me?"

She nods. "Since they were little. I have baby pictures of you hung up."

The joy humming through me is so intense it feels like an explosion in my chest. I don't want this moment to ever end.

I have a family. I wasn't forgotten.

"May I give you a hug?"

"I would love that more than anything," Abigail says.

My arms wrap around her in an embrace that heals a piece of me I was worried would always stay broken forever.

"Maybe I can meet your foster parents? I would love to thank them for taking care of you and helping you turn into the woman you are today."

I pause before pulling away with a forced smile. "Of course."

There's no way I'm telling her I aged out of the system, alone and without the love and guidance of a family. She's endured enough, and this added emotional trauma will surely inflict deep wounds on her already fragile spirit.

As we part, we exchange numbers, and she tells Gabriel, "Thank you."

Once she's gone, I glance at him at his desk, where he holds Grayson. His frown is deep, his eyes worried. "I'm sorry."

"For what, exactly?"

"Today. I wanted to make sure she was safe before I brought up the topic of you two meeting up. I didn't want you to be bombarded like you were today, and I definitely didn't want you to pass out."

"How did you find her?"

A grin lifts his lips. "Do you remember the other day when you couldn't find your toothbrush?"

My head tilts in confusion. "Yeah?"

"DNA, beautiful. That's how I found her."

I'd say I'm surprised, but I'm not. This man is insane. "That had to have been expensive."

He shrugs. "You're worth it ... but again, I'm sorry. I don't want you ever passing out in my arms like that again."

The worry still etched on his face draws me to him like a magnet as I come around his desk and place my hands on either side of his face. "There's nothing to be sorry for. You helped heal a piece of me today. I'll never be able to repay you for that."

"A kiss will suffice ... for now."

My lips meet his without a second thought.

I'm falling for this man, and I never want to get back up.

23

WILLOW

With a click of the camera's shutter button, mounted steadily on its tripod, I race back to Grayson, lifting him into my arms and saying, "Say happy Halloween, Gray."

I smile just as the flash goes off and then stride to the camera to see if our first Halloween photo is a success.

A wide grin spreads across my face as I survey Grayson nestled in my arms. His eyes are wide with shock from the bright light, but he looks adorable in the crisp blue-and-white pinstriped baseball uniform and high socks Vivian handmade for him.

Being that this is Grayson's first Halloween, the costume is special, but what makes it even more so is that Vivian upcycled the worn, familiar fabric of Gabriel's old baseball uniforms, transforming them into something even more meaningful.

In shows and movies, acts of parental thoughtfulness always brought me to tears, because I never thought I'd experience the same emotions myself but Vivian ticks all the boxes and goes above and beyond for both Grayson and I, which is why she's our first and only stop to trick-or-treat tonight.

My phone chimes, and I grab it from the counter.

AELLA

Halloween at the club. Say you'll come.

WILLOW

I don't know … It's Gray's first Halloween, and Gabriel wasn't exactly thrilled when he found me there the last time.

AELLA

The party at the club will be after all, Gray's trick-or-treating. Also, don't you find it odd that he doesn't want you at the club? Like, what's the big deal? You've already been, and allegedly, his friend owns it.

Shit, she has me there. I do find it strange that he doesn't want me at Obsidian, but then again, it is a sex club.

WILLOW

Things have been good between us, and I don't want to cause any problems. Besides, he said he was there for business. Maybe he's not a member.

AELLA

Don't tell me you believe that weak-ass excuse you just gave me. Besides, there won't be problems. You're an adult. You should be able to have fun.

I bite my lip. It would be nice to go out and have fun. Maybe Gabriel would like to come too … The memory of him dancing against me at the club sparks a fire in my core. Although I highly doubt that's what he'll want to do after working all day.

WILLOW

We'll see. I'll let you know.

———

BECAUSE OF A LATE MEETING, Gabriel catches up with us later that evening at his parents' house.

As Gabriel enters, a broad smile illuminates his face. He sets his jacket down on the couch before lifting Grayson into his arms to admire the nostalgic details of his costume. "Hey, buddy."

He's been picking Grayson up more often, playing with him, and there's nothing sweeter than the sight of the man you're falling for caring for your child like he's his own.

"This is awesome," he exclaims, adjusting Grayson for his mom's embrace. "Thank you."

Gabriel stalks toward me with a gleam in his eyes as he pulls me toward him. "Hey, beautiful."

"Hi," I murmur with a shy smile, right before his lips meet mine in a kiss that makes me forget everything, especially the fact that his mom is in the room with us.

"Tha ... tha ... tha ..." Grayson babbles, making us pull apart quickly.

"He's already a little cock-blocker," Gabriel whispers with a grin as he readjusts Grayson in his arms.

I snort.

Lately, Gabriel has been happier than I've ever seen him. Though stress and exhaustion still plague him, he smiles and even laughs. He's been acting more like he did the night of our first date at the baseball cages, and it makes me think this is his true self.

Now, I understand Vivian's words about him finding peace.

As I gather Grayson's toys, the cheerful chime of the doorbell rings through the house.

"What a surprise," Vivian says, as Aella enters with a confused Gabriel behind her. "I haven't seen you in ages. How are you?"

"I'm good. How are you, Mrs. Reed?"

"I'm excellent. Make yourself at home, sweetheart."

As Aella, clad in a ringmaster costume with a structured red blazer adorned with gold tassels, a black corset, mini leather shorts, and a top hat, approaches, my eyes grow wide. "What are you doing here?"

"Making sure you go out tonight," Aella whispers as she hands me an orange Halloween basket with toys, a baby book called BOO, and a bat stuffed animal inside.

"I haven't brought it up yet."

"What are you two whispering about?" Gabriel asks, striding toward us with a wiggling Grayson in his arms.

I grab Grayson and place him on my hip. "Aella invited us out to the club."

Gabriel's poker face instantly makes an appearance. "I see."

I knew it was a bad idea to bring it up.

"I said you should have no problem letting her go because she's an adult, she should be allowed to have fun, and since it's your friend's club, it shouldn't be a big deal ... right? Unless you have something to hide?" Aella raises her brow.

I swear I'm going to strangle my best friend.

Gabriel's jaw works as if he's mulling something over before he gazes over our heads. "Mother, do you think you can watch Grayson while Willow and I go out for a few hours?"

"I'd love to," Vivian says.

"Guess we'll meet you there, Marks," Gabriel mutters.

"We don't even have costumes, so maybe we should pass," I say to ease the tension.

"I may have something that can work," Vivian says.

Gabriel descends the stairs twenty minutes later. He's a walking fantasy in a vintage baseball uniform, the crisp white jersey emblazoned with classic blue pinstripes and a blue number one with blue knicker-style pants.

He smirks as he pulls me into his arms. "There's a little drool on your lip, Mrs. Reed."

"There is not!" I say, wiping the imaginary spot.

He snorts. "It's your turn. My mother's upstairs waiting for you."

———

GABRIEL'S WARM, firm hand clasps mine, leading me through a private entrance to the club.

Gazing around as we walk, I take in the sight of the dimly lit halls, which are moody but also give off an elegant aura. Someone spared no expense in making even the rear area of the club incredibly lavish.

We continue to pass through halls, doors, and staff. Some are dressed all in black with red, black, and white masks obscuring their faces, while others wear full costumes.

"Are you sure we're allowed to go through here?" I whisper. "Aella and I had to go through the front when we came."

"It's fine," he says with a nod to someone passing us in the hall. "If we go through the front, it'll take us forever to get inside with how busy it is tonight."

I nod in agreement as he pulls me along. Both the outdoor parking lot and the indoor parking garage were overflowing with vehicles when we arrived.

Upon stopping and opening a door, the lights of the club area stream through, throwing hypnotic shades of orange in every direction.

"Let's get a drink," Gabriel says, tightening his hand around mine and pulling me through the door.

The sheer number of costume-covered bodies make it difficult to move tonight. Getting to the bar is a slow process, as we move through the crowd swaying to the beat; every available space is taken, and it seems unlikely that I will find Aella in this mass of people, as cell phones are strictly prohibited in the club, so I left mine in the car.

Within a couple of minutes of arriving at the bar, a masked figure in all black, similar to the staff we saw in the back, hands Gabriel a tall glass of amber liquid.

He says something in Gabriel's ear, which makes him nod before the masked man peers at me and presents me with two drinks, one tall and slender and the other short with a pink hue.

"Pick your poison. Either a cranberry and vodka or a mojito."

My brows scrunch together as something in his voice sounds off, like a distant memory I've tried hard to forget. My hands turn clammy while the hairs on the back of my neck stand on end.

The masked man's head tilts, his gaze intense as he waits for my answer, but my tongue feels heavy, rendering me speechless.

"I'll take the cranberry and vodka, she'll take the mojito," Aella says at my side.

I whip my head toward her as she grabs both drinks from the man's hands.

She hands me my mojito and pulls me away from the bar area.

"Are you okay? You look ghostly?"

I shake my head, trying to get rid of the unsettling feeling that has settled in my chest. "I'm good. That guy's voice just sounded weird."

"What do you mean?" she asks, taking a pull of her drink.

"I don't know ... it's nothing." I shake my head of all my irrational thoughts. "It's just him in the mask, throwing me off and bringing up bad memories."

Aella's thoughtful gaze strays to where Gabriel is still talking to the man.

"Shit. I didn't even think about that being a trigger for you. I'm sorry, Wills."

"It's okay. I didn't think it was either."

She eyes the glass in my hand. "Slam that so we can go dance the night away."

As I push the awful memories behind the door in my mind and lock it tight, I give her a smile and take a big gulp, and follow her to the dance floor.

Gabriel comes moments later with Kennedy in tow, and we all take shots and then dance for what feels like hours.

Gabriel's lips kiss and gently suck the side of my neck before he whispers, "I never got to tell you how much I love that you're in one of my old jerseys. But I have to ask ... what position are you?"

A mischievous smile touches my lips. "The one on top of you."

Shit. Did that just come out of my mouth? Damn you, alcohol.

Gabriel groans as he pulls me impossibly closer. "Fuck. I want you so fucking bad right now."

"You have me ... any way you want me," I say, pulling him down to bite and lick the shell of his ear before my mouth lands back on his.

The feeling of freedom washes over me when I realize I just spoke my mind without hesitation. Something I've wanted to do since we made our relationship more.

He pulls back, his eyes searching mine as he asks, "Do I?"

A nod and yes escape me as I lick my bottom lip, and the taste of him—dark, delicious, and dangerous to my heart—lingers, but I don't care. Everything he does to me feels too good, and I want more.

"We're leaving." Fueled by purpose, Gabriel guides me through the boisterous crowd of dancers in colorful costumes, down an unmarked door, and into the echoing parking garage at a dizzying pace.

Gabriel opens the back door of the car and gets in, much to my confusion. He grabs my arm as I peer in and sends me a hungry look. "Jump on my cock, wife."

His brazen words send a shiver of pleasure down my spine and warmth into my core. This is Gabriel unfiltered, and I love it.

With a bit of a sway and my eyes wide, I survey the deserted parking garage. No one is here, but the thought of someone witnessing us sends an odd thrill through me. Voyeurism wasn't something I'd ever considered, but now it's the only thing I crave.

"Come here, beautiful."

As I climb in and straddle his muscular legs, a smile spreads across my face, my skin tingling with anticipation.

With a swift, brutal motion, he rips my top apart; the jersey's buttons scattering with a metallic ping as they bounce off the car's backseat.

My breasts bounce freely, and my nipples pucker as the cool air from the open door hits them. Gabriel's hands, eager to touch, reach for them and give a gentle tug as his eyes roam my naked body.

"Fuck," he groans. "You've had nothing under the shirt all night?"

With a grin, I shake my head and lean in for a kiss.

"You're going to pay for being such a bad girl." His mouth captures mine, his tongue trailing against my lips before he takes my bottom lip in his mouth and bites. The sweet pain sends a jolt straight to my core, causing me to whimper.

Gabriel rips his lips from mine, hands trailing down my ribs and to my waist, where he moves me back and forth over his hard bulge. "Place your hands behind you."

My breasts push forward as my hands find the console. I lift my hips as he shifts and lowers his pants and boxers. His eyes lock with mine as he readies himself, stroking his head a few times before moving it along my entrance and up to my clit to cover himself in my arousal.

"Get on my cock but leave your hands behind your back."

I do as he instructs, completely captivated by his dominance and what it's doing to my psyche. I sink down agonizingly slow, feeling myself stretch to accommodate his thick length. "Oh, God." The curve of my back intensifies, the car's ceiling brushing against the top of my head, as I take all of him.

"Right fucking there," he groans, his fingers digging into my hips with a possessive hold. "Now roll your hips." Again, I do as he instructs. "Fuck ... just like that." His hand reaches my neck, and he gives it a firm squeeze. "Watch your pussy take my cock like the good girl she is."

Heat rushes to my face, and though his words are the dirtiest I've ever heard, I'm spellbound as I tilt my head and fix my gaze where our bodies meet. We fit together perfectly, our rhythms matching as though we are destined for each other.

His fingers graze my parted lips, and without words, I open my mouth to let them seek entrance. But he surprises me as he hooks his two fingers in my mouth, just under my tongue, as I moan, and I'm dragged into his space. His tongue licks mine while his fingers are still in my mouth. This possessive feeling of him using me as he pleases is strangely hot, and I'm left wanting more.

His eyes meet mine as his mouth opens in a deep moan. "I'm going to fuck you hard and fast, and if it's too much, let me know."

I nod as he pushes me until my back is resting on the center console where my hands just were. This new position ignites a sensation within me I've never experienced, and my legs tremble as he brutally thrusts into me with a force strong enough to rock the car.

My eyes roll into the back of my head as his palm pushes

down on my lower stomach. The pressure adds to the pleasure, and I'm soon trembling all over.

"You're strangling me, beautiful." Gabriel groans from above me. "You ready to come all over my cock?" He asks as the thumb of the hand holding my lower stomach presses on my clit in the most painfully pleasurable way.

I nod, as words are beyond me, as I continue to moan as the fire starts in my limbs and climbs into my core.

"I'm going to fuck my come so far into you it will never come out, because you're mine."

Stars explode behind my eyes at his words, and my orgasm shoots through me.

With one more hard thrust, Gabriel spills in me with a groan, but he doesn't stop as he does exactly what he says.

He possesses me, claiming ownership, satisfying me entirely, and then leaving me in a state of euphoric bliss.

24

GABRIEL

With a sigh, I silence my phone and put it back on the coffee table, all the while watching the screen flash with incoming messages.

"You can answer that if you need to," Willow says from the kitchen.

I shake my head. "It's not important right now. I can deal with whatever it is tomorrow."

I sprawl back out onto the vibrant rug beside Grayson, surrounded by a miniature town, complete with street signs and a road. Grabbing the discarded car in front of me, I make silly engine noises, and Grayson, completely engrossed, follows behind with one of his own.

We laugh at Grayson's attempts to mimic my noises, as his are mostly high-pitched and wet, since he's cutting his first bottom tooth.

I continue to push the crimson car across the carpet, pausing as expected at each make-believe stop sign or light, following Willow's request as she referenced Grayson absorbing things like a sponge. I want to tell her that this will eventually be forgotten. He's barely eight months old, but I respect the parent she is. It's pure, and remarkable, and passionate. The kind of parenting and love she gives is what every child needs and deserves.

Grayson's little fingers, sticky from the yogurt bites in his snack cup, grip the blue truck in his hand tight as he continues to follow mine, before stopping at the stop sign just as I did.

"Good job, Gray," I say, rubbing the chaotic black head of hair atop his head. He flashes a goofy grin my way, before turning to his colorful plastic blocks, and meticulously stacking them with a focused intensity.

It's extremely hard for me not to compare Grayson to Jack. Grayson is only a few months younger than Jack was when everything came tumbling down. Despite Jack's humor, intelligence, and wit, I now realize how little quality time he received. Eryn and I were both selfish. I worked too much, and she was too caught up in everything besides parenting.

Grayson's intelligence and curiosity are nurtured by Willow's hands-on teaching, and I'd be lying if I didn't feel guilt over how much more Jack could've had. Why was I so blind? Why didn't I say more? Not that it changes anything now.

A timer's shrill beep echoes from the kitchen, and my gaze immediately turns toward it. Willow stands over the stove with a messy bun on the top of her head and a taupe apron around her waist as she stirs something that smells delicious in a cream cast-iron Dutch oven. A smile plays on my lips as I observe her, captivated by her focus.

I love coming home to see what she's cooked every night.

Willow's eyes meet mine as she places the lid on the pot with a soft clink and stalks toward Grayson and me. "It should be done in thirty minutes."

"I can't wait. It smells delicious."

"Sorry, it's not ready. I got to talking with Abigail on the phone, and time just flew by."

"I don't mind waiting. I'd wait all night if I had to. How are things going with you two?"

"Better than I could've ever imagined but we're taking it slow. I don't want to rush the relationship, and I don't think she does either. We're talking about meeting after the holidays."

"You can invite her over whenever you want."

"Really?"

My eyes meet hers as she sits on the floor with us, and I link our fingers together. "This is your home too."

A mixture of contentment and shyness dances within her eyes, making them sparkle. I fucking love it.

We've fallen into a sort of routine over the past few weeks. She has dinner ready when I get home; we eat together, play on the floor with Grayson, and then talk about our day while lounging on the couch after Grayson's asleep.

The best part of my day is when I'm on my way home to them, and today was no different, as I found myself counting down the minutes. I even left early, something I never do on a hectic day, but I wanted to be home ... with them.

"How would you feel about moving to my side of the penthouse?" As I nonchalantly ask, my fingers trace the delicate curve of her cheek. The block she holds stops midair. Maybe it's too soon to share a bed? "Unless you aren't ready for that?"

She chews on her lip. "I am. I just ... I don't want to leave Grayson over there by himself."

"We're a family, beautiful. Wherever we are, he comes too."

25

WILLOW

The chilly, gentle breeze rustles through the park, its whisper mixing with the vibrant hues of fall in the trees, as I rock Grayson's stroller back and forth during his afternoon nap. With the weather calling for a high of fifty-seven, I couldn't wait to bundle myself and Grayson up and get some fresh air.

I rest my back against the wooden park bench, close my eyes, and enjoy the sweet silence surrounding me as I let my mind wander.

With Thanksgiving and Christmas on the horizon, I'm practically bursting with joy and excitement. This holiday season marks a new chapter, brimming with loved ones and the sweet anticipation of holiday traditions I've long wished for. I can envision making dinner with Vivian, the scent of herbs and garlic filling the kitchen, while Gerard and Gabriel are engrossed in a game, followed by Grayson and Aella's sugar cookie and gingerbread house decorating, and finally stealing a kiss from Gabriel under the mistletoe.

It all sounds so magical, my lifelong hopes no longer distant dreams but within my grasp.

A sense of overwhelming gratitude and happiness washes over me as my hands instinctively go to my heart, thinking of Abigail, with whom I've slowly built a connection and grown closer every day.

I'm so glad things turned out this way, even though my journey to this new family and a reconnected relationship was unconventional and at some points extremely difficult.

A rustle of shattered leaves comes from behind, and I slowly rise from my comfortable position leaning against the bench.

"Willow."

My spine stiffens, and I pivot rigidly, as a wave of cold dread washes over me, causing the blood to drain from my face. Darren stands behind the bench I'm currently occupying.

With a quick snatch, I swing my bag onto my shoulder and stand to create space between us. "Darren, what are you doing here?"

"I saw you online. You're all over the news."

Alarm rages through me as I survey his bloodshot eyes barely seen from his low-slung black hat, dirty clothes, and the acrid scent of stale beer permeating the air around him and now me. But the worst part is him finding me here. Chicago is a big city, which means he's been watching me, and he followed us here.

"I think you should leave," I say, gazing around the park to make sure there are people within screaming distance, just in case.

"I'm not going anywhere, and neither are you," he says, striding closer.

"Stay back!" The words rush from me as I jerk the stroller in the opposite direction and sprint away.

A hand wraps around my upper arm and jars me back so violently, I almost lose my balance. "Don't you dare walk away from me!" His hand squeezes my arm so tight I wince in pain. "You have the fucking nerve to call that guy you married the father of my child. My child!"

Tears burn my eyes as I try to wrench my arm free, but he just holds it even tighter. "You left me the night I had him, Darren. Grayson isn't yours. He's mine." My voice is barely audible as the old feeling of terror and pain he inflicted on me when we were together rushes back in.

"The fuck he is." His growl intensifies, a guttural sound laced with menace, his disgusting breath hot on my face, and I'm paralyzed by fear, unsure what horrific act will follow. "I want ten million dollars from your rich husband, or I go to the press and tell them the bastard child is mine, you lying slut."

A desperate plea escapes my lips as I retreat into the cold, lifeless shell of myself that I was when we were together. "Let go of my arm. You're hurting me."

A click rings out as an arm encircles Darren's neck, causing him to choke and drop my arm in a desperate attempt to free himself from the suffocating hold. My gaze drifts over Darren's head to Gabriel's face, contorted in rage, right behind him. His eyes are nearly black and blazing in a way that sends a chill down my spine.

"If you ever talk, let alone touch my wife again, I'll end you."

In the next second, Gabriel's arm vanishes from around Darren's neck, leaving him gasping for air as he collapses to the ground. Gabriel buttons his navy suit jacket, and my eyes widen as I catch a glimpse of the gun holstered against his right side, the cold steel glinting faintly.

Holy shit.

Gabriel's hands touch my cheeks as his eyes roam every inch of my face. "Are you okay?"

Overwhelmed with emotions, I nod. My vision swims as his

lips brush my forehead—a feather-light touch that sends a surge of warmth, safety, and thankfulness through me. His body vibrates with a gentle hum, a comforting sound that matches the firmness of his embrace as I cling to him just as tightly.

"Let's go home," he murmurs, placing his hand along the small of my back while guiding the stroller with the other, and escorts Grayson and me back to the penthouse.

At the park entrance, Gabriel exchanges a brief nod with a bald man whose tattoos peek out of his black suit, the crisp fabric and polished shoes a stark contrast to the casual clothes of other park visitors; the man exudes an air of warning and mystery, and his presence leaves me feeling a sense of unease as we walk past.

Gabriel clears his throat before peering down at me. "I know I promised you I wouldn't tell you what you can and can't do, but I don't want you two alone in the park ever again."

I eye him as he quickly glances behind us and follow his gaze, but only see the back of the man in the black suit and Darren a distance away.

"I just wanted some sunshine and fresh air, but I agree."

"We have the terrace."

"I'm scared of heights."

"I see," Gabriel says as we wait for cars to pass so we can cross the street. "What did he want?"

"He wanted money. He said, to give him ten mil—" I gasp. "The note." I unzip my bag and rifle through it as we walk until I find the paper at the very bottom. I hand it to Gabriel, then steer the stroller, its wheels clicking quietly against the polished marble floor, into the penthouse's lavish lobby. "Someone gave this to me at the café the other day."

Gabriel's eyes briefly flicker across my face before his jaw clenches, and a withering look settles on his features as we make our way into the private elevator. "Why didn't you tell me about this, Willow?"

"I was on my way to, but then I walked in on you talking to my birth mother, and I forgot about everything that happened. I'm sorry."

He sighs. "You need to tell me these things. Promise me you will if something like this ever happens again."

"I promise," I say, wetting my parched lips. "I don't think it will, though. Darren demanded ten million dollars, the same as on the note. I think it was him."

"We don't know that, and we don't know what he's capable of—"

"I think he's probably scared and will leave us alone after you pulled a gun on him," I say while parking the stroller in the penthouse's entry with a still sleeping Grayson. "I didn't even know you had one."

He loosens his tie as he walks to the kitchen counter. "I couldn't exactly bring a bat into the park and scare him with it."

"Yeah, I guess you're right," I say while biting my lip. "How did you know what was happening and where we were?"

Gabriel fidgets silently with his cufflinks as he looks anywhere but at me.

I quirk a brow. "Did you put, like ... a GPS or AirTag on me?"

"That's a good idea, but no."

The nod to the guy in the park cuts through my thoughts, and my eyes widen. "You had me stalked?"

A world-weary sigh escapes him as he approaches, his fingers already reaching for my well-worn pocket, before pulling me into his embrace. Once we're chest to chest, he runs his fingers through my hair, the softness a contrast to the intensity in his stare. "I hired Jaxton to watch over you and Grayson."

"Why didn't you tell me?"

"I wasn't sure how you'd feel about it."

"Probably a lot more comfortable than I am now, knowing I was being watched by someone and I had no idea."

He nods. "You're right. I'm sorry."

"Keeping things from me just because you aren't sure how I'll act is still lying."

"It won't happen again. I promise."

26

GABRIEL

With a sweet smile, Willow surveys the four-season sunroom in awe. The enormous glass walls will soon let the sun's warmth fill the space in a handful of months while offering a stunning view of a garden and its central fountain.

We've toured multiple homes this morning, this being the last and, in my opinion, the best of the day.

The property has plenty of space. I can have an office, while Willow can have a studio to pursue her photography passion, and Grayson will get a playroom situated conveniently next to the theater room.

"What do you think?" My voice breaks the silence as I come up behind her and wrap my arms around her shoulders. She grabs my forearms, her soft fingers gripping me tight as she looks out to the garden area.

"It's magical."

I kiss the top of her head. Her easygoing nature and gratitude fill me with a desire to give her the world. "Better than the others?"

Her head bobs. "It's also close to your parents' house. Your mom could come over whenever she wants without a long drive."

My mother would be on cloud nine if we bought the house just down the road.

A frown creases her forehead as she looks up at me. "It's far from the city, though. You'd have a long drive."

After her ex's sudden appearance the other day, I want them safely tucked away and far from the city.

"I'll manage just fine. My father did for decades."

She bites her lip and whispers. "I like you close."

My heart pounds in my chest when she utters such tender words. It's becoming more common for her to say things like this, and I'd be lying if I said I didn't love it.

"I like you close too," I say, giving her a quick kiss that turns more passionate as my tongue dances against hers.

As we pull apart, I give her a smile. "If we move here, I'll take an office day a week at home."

Her eyes light up. "Really?"

Footsteps sound as the realtor walks into the room. "How are we feeling about this one?"

"We'll take it," I say, watching Willow's initial surprise melt into a joyous smile.

27

WILLOW

The stroller wheels scrape against the threshold as Grayson and I enter the brightly lit clothing store, where I told Aella we'd meet her. I'm not a big shopper, since funds have always been tight, but Gabriel encouraged me to buy some new clothes before we head to the lake house in two weeks.

Between two clothing racks, Aella stands with a scrunched nose, furiously typing on her phone.

I sneak up on her. "I can't believe you haven't found anything yet."

A small smile reaches her lips as she pockets her phone. "I wanted to wait for you."

We shopped for hours, filling bag after bag with clothes, shoes, and handbags. It's like I went into a trance once I started finding things I liked. I definitely went overboard, and I'm trying hard not to feel guilty as I swipe Gabriel's card for the last time today. I should put some of the blame on Aella, who kept piling more clothes onto the racks in the dressing rooms.

As we leave the store, Aella looks behind us.

"What's up with the suit?"

"The what?"

"I thought it was just my imagination, but that bald fucker in the black suit has followed us to every store."

I turn my gaze toward her, curious, and follow her pointed finger to Jaxton, who is positioned by the door we just passed through, attempting a casual pose as he pretends not to observe us.

"Gabriel wants us safe, so I have a bodyguard," I whisper so no one hears.

She purses her lips in displeasure.

Before she can say anything, I raise my hand, anticipating the rant I know is brewing.

"Trust me, I didn't like it either," I say as I think back to the other day and how I felt like my privacy was invaded. A simple heads-up from Gabriel would have sufficed; I wouldn't have enjoyed being watched, but I'd have understood his intent to keep us safe. "But after Darren stalking me in the park," I shake my head to tamper down the feeling of panic the thought still gives me. I still have bruises from his fingers on my arm. " ... if Jaxton wasn't there, I think things could've been really bad."

"Has Darren shown his face since the park incident?"

I shake my head. "No, thankfully." I glance around to make sure no one is listening, then whisper as we walk across the street. "I think Gabriel really scared him with the gun."

Aella nods. "It's far less than the slimeball deserves."

"Agreed," I say as I stop and wait for Jaxton to catch up.

I smile at him as he stands before me. "Do you think you can take these to the car? We want to go to the restaurant across the way, and it's really weighing down the stroller."

He nods as he grabs the bags.

"How long have you been watching Willow?" Aella asks him.

Jaxton turns to her with a tight smile. "Not too long."

"Who else do you work for?" She fires back.

Puzzled by her question, I eye her.

"I sign non-disclosure agreements, so I'm afraid I can't say."

"Figures," Aella mutters as she perches her sunglasses on her nose and walks away.

Shrugging my shoulders at Jaxton, I offer him an apology and rush behind her.

I wasn't sure before, but once we're seated at the table, I can tell something is definitely off with Aella. She pokes at the pasta on her plate, not really eating, but simply moving it about.

"We looked at houses on Sunday. One was even close to his parents, like five houses down, and it was a total dream," I say, smiling, though her eyes remain fixed downward. "It even has a garden in the back. Grayson would have a ton of room to play." I tilt my head as I regard her puzzling behavior. "I'm of course going to need your decorating expertise."

Silence greets me.

"Hey," I say as I reach over and place my hand on hers. "What's going on? Is it your mom?"

Her mother, injured in a severe accident caused by her driving under the influence, has been hospitalized for months. She told me weeks ago she was doing better and moved into a rehabilitation center, but maybe that's changed ...

"What? No, she's fine," she says with a shrug. "Well, as fine as she can be. She's still begging me to smuggle her in some benzos and booze."

I frown. "She's still coming down from the drugs and alcohol?"

She blows out a deep breath as she types something into her phone. "I doubt she'll ever come down from her high."

Grayson slams his hands on the table to get our attention, followed by him forming his fingers and thumb into a circle with both hands, before tapping the fingertips of one hand against the other. "Do you want more?" I say, gesturing with my own hands. He smiles and does it again.

"I can't believe you taught him sign language," Aella says with a smile as I give him a few more of his yogurt bites.

"It's only a few words, but it makes things so much easier ... next is potty training, though," I say with a sardonic smile. "Thankfully, Gabriel said he'd help."

With a nod, she acknowledges the words but offers no response.

I blow out a breath. I'm done skating around her strange mood.

"Spill, Aella. You've been weirdly quiet since meeting me, and that's not like you."

She scans the dimly lit restaurant, eyes squinting as she absentmindedly runs her tongue along her upper teeth. I feel a prickle of anxiety course through me. She never struggles to say what's on her mind. Her bluntness is one of the many things I appreciate most about her.

Her eyes, filled with doubt and uncertainty I've never witnessed before, meet mine.

"Do you ever wish you could be blissfully ignorant? Like you're so happy ... more than you've ever thought possible. But maybe that happiness is fractured by underlying lies?"

My brow furrows as I place my chin in my hand, mulling over the many aspects of her question.

"Blissful ignorance is a double-edged sword. Sometimes, veiled lies are more comforting than the truth, but it's still not right. Happiness or not. But I guess it depends on the person and whether they can handle the truth."

As she nods, her fingers explore the rough weave of the napkin. Her silence and downcast gaze set off a cacophony of alarm bells in my mind.

"What's going on? Did something happen? Are you okay?"

Aella's sad eyes meet mine. "I'm so sorry, Wills ..."

28

GABRIEL

GABRIEL

Look at what I hung today. *Image of Willow's painting on the wall in the office.

GABRIEL

You should know that two of my prospective clients came in, and it did not scare them away.

I continue to check my phone throughout the day for a reply, but it never comes. Jaxton has briefed me on Willow and Aella's shopping adventure. I'm assuming she just wants to stay in the moment with her friend. So, I back off until later in the day.

GABRIEL

How do you feel about smash burgers? I could pick some up on my way home, so you won't have to cook.

GABRIEL

Or maybe you'd prefer Italian beef
sandwiches?

GABRIEL

We could go out if you'd rather? Somewhere
kid-friendly?

Despite every message of mine delivering, they all remain unread, and I have a terrible, sinking feeling in my gut. She always answers my text messages.

GABRIEL

Just got off work. I'll be home soon.

Once inside the penthouse, I take in how dark and cavernous it appears. Something that would have been the norm prior to Willow, but now it just feels wrong.

From the kitchen, there's no delicious scent of food, no silly sounds from Grayson, and no sight of small, colorful toys I always step on.

I can't drop my briefcase on the floor by the entry table and slink out of my suit jacket before stalking over to Willow, as she stands from her place on the floor where she's playing with Grayson, to greet me. I can't grab her by the loop of her pants and pull her toward me, watching her gorgeous, shy smile appear, or come up behind her at the stove, moving her silky hair to the side, and kissing her neck, which causes her to gasp.

As I enter the living area, a warm glow spills from my ajar office door down the hall. My footsteps thud eerily as I hurry down the long, dark hallway, yet they cease when I fling the door open fully.

On my now cluttered desk, manila file folders lie open, spilling slightly. My ears ring, a deafening roar as blood rushes in, amplified with every stride to my desk; there, on the top, is a hauntingly familiar spreadsheet.

"Tell me this is all just a misunderstanding."

I nearly jump in surprise as I turn and see Willow, her form barely visible, sitting on the couch in the corner.

"Tell me you weren't part of guns being aimed at Grayson's head while I was threatened. Tell me you didn't ruin my life and have a hand in me doing something that went against my morals to save my baby," she whispers, her voice choking with tears, her lips trembling.

"I—" the words get caught in my throat as a wave of nausea washes over me. "I didn't know that's how it was going to happen, and I didn't know you had a child at the time."

With a humorless laugh, she arches a brow before standing and walking toward the door. "Does that even matter? Really? You might not have been one of the men who held the gun to Grayson's head, but your finger was on the trigger long before it happened. Is power and money that important to you that you're willing to step on anyone, no matter how small or defenseless, to get what you want?"

"If I could take it all back, I would."

"Which part? Where you conceived a plan to scare a struggling single mother into committing a crime for your selfish gain or for letting me believe we had something special while you kept the lie in your back pocket?"

"Both—all of it."

She nods her head, but I can tell she isn't convinced.

"I'm sorry," I say, taking a step closer to her.

"Yeah, I am too." She sighs as she walks out of the office. "For being foolish enough to believe in you as a flawed but redeemable human being."

My chest burns from her words, though the heat was a small price for my actions.

"You can't leave," I say, even though I know I don't deserve her, but I'm grasping at fucking straws at this point.

She snorts. "Don't worry. I'll stick to my end of the contract out of pure hatred for myself for lying to your mom because the last thing I want to do is hurt her, but ... she will eventually get hurt when this is all over. And that hurts more than anything else. Staying tethered to you for the remainder of the contract is my punishment for my part in this." She leans down and hoists the overflowing bag onto her arm. "I'm moving in with Aella until I can figure out what to do with myself and my child. I'll collect the rest of my stuff later."

I take another step in her direction, hand out, and she shoots me daggers that pierce my heart. "Don't you dare touch or follow me, Gabriel. I mean it."

My hand clenches as I sense my defeat, and my fight slips away, leaving me with a chilling vulnerability that I guarantee she's felt multiple times since this all began.

Then she walks out, and if it weren't an elevator she's getting into, I'm sure she would have slammed the door in my face.

29

GABRIEL

4 MONTHS AGO

W ith a sly grin, Gage Gallo Moretti, the head of the Chicago Mafia, one of my closest friends and silent business partners, leans in close on the other side of his desk and asks, "What do you think?"

I meticulously examine the detailed paperwork and blueprints, visualizing his innovative state-of-the-art investment after the groundbreaking ceremony and its completion. "I'm a little disappointed you found it before I did."

His booming laughter fills the room, momentarily softening his dark aura, even as his heavily tattooed body and dark features suggest something else entirely. "Yeah, well, you can't have it all, motherfucker."

He and I met when I tried to hustle him out of a project years ago. This was before I knew who he was. Naturally, my tactics were fruitless, and instead, a partnership was created that turned into a friendship.

"I'll buy it from you with interest." I grin.

He snorts. "Not a fucking chance."

"Your loss." I shrug before taking a drink from my glass.

A knock comes from the door, and one of Gage's employees, Jace, walks in with an envelope and sets it on his desk. "The monthly debts."

"Excellent, thanks."

Gage opens the contents and lets them lie on top of the blueprints on his desk.

I raise a brow. "Debts?"

Gage nods as he flips through spreadsheets with pictures attached. "Opening the casino and fight club has been profitable, but now I have more fucking headaches. These are all the stupid mother-fuckers who owe me a significant amount of money and have been dodging my men."

I shake my head. Failing to settle a debt with the Mafia is a death sentence; the consequences are swift and brutal. I once had the unfortunate pleasure of watching Gage collect the debt himself, armed with only a hammer. The memory of the man's wails still raises my hair on end, and I'll never look at the claw of a hammer the same again.

"I told you ... that's why I didn't want in on them," I say.

"I told him it would be a mistake too," Jace says as he leans against Gage's desk.

"Says the idiot who fights in said fight club," Gage mutters, causing Jace to roll his eyes.

"I bring in the crowd with this face," Jace grins with a dimpled smile and his all-American jock look.

"Not when it's getting beaten in," Gage says, leaning back in his chair, a thoughtful look on his face as he surveys the spreadsheet he's holding. "Interesting."

"What?" Jace asks, leaning in, but Gage's blue eyes are locked on me.

He tosses the paper across the desk, and I glance down at a young woman. "You know her?"

With brows scrunching, I ask, "Why would I know her?"

I scan the paper, which includes her full name, eye and hair color, home address, car details, marital status, and employer, Reed Equity.

Surprise widens my eyes, and I search my memory, hoping to find a single, fleeting recollection of her.

An image of her in the elevator speaking with the clown, Greg Thompson, comes to mind, and then another one at one of our monthly safety meetings. She's a new hire in the accounting depart-ment. A unique W name. Winnie? Winter? No, Willow ... after my favorite tree.

"She owes you money?" I ask.

I don't really see her being the gambling type. I don't know her personally, but she gives off a quiet, reserved vibe, as though she's afraid of repercussions for rule-breaking. But I could be wrong; I have been in the past. It could be nothing more than a mask, care-fully crafted to go unnoticed and deceive the world.

"Nah," Jace says. "Her boyfriend, husband, what-the-fuck-ever owes it, but he seemed to skip town or some shit, so now she's on our radar."

"I thought you didn't hurt women?"

"We don't," Gage says, eyeing another spreadsheet. "I'm just going to have my men ask her questions. If he left her high and dry, she's probably pissed, you know, a woman scorned and all that shit. She'll probably tell us where we can find him."

"And what if she doesn't know?"

He shrugs. "We'll call it a wash for now if she can't help us locate him or pay his debt."

My attention stays locked on her photo. She has a classic, simple beauty and a soft smile. She seems so innocent, young; anyone could mold her into anything. I could mold her, envisioning every curve and angle, into anything I desire.

A thought, like a phantom, appears and becomes an idea, solidi-fying into a plan within seconds.

"What if I can guarantee you the money?"

Gage raises a brow.

"How much?" I ask.

"Little less than two hundred k."

I nod. Her ex must not care for her at all, vanishing without a word, despite knowing someone would come to collect his debt. "She'll pay it, and I'll give you an extra hundred."

"Not that I don't like the idea of getting my money back plus a little interest, but why?"

"I need a wife; you need the money."

Gage's brows shoot up. "You're going to blackmail her?"

"I think I am."

Gage is silent and pensive. "These types of things have a way of going sideways fucking quick."

I ignore his warnings.

Lack of preparation fucks plans up, but I'm always prepared.

"You think we can make this happen?" I ask.

"Of course we can."

30

GABRIEL

"Is there any way you can get them out sooner?" My leg betrays my irritation with a shake as I lie on the couch in my office at Reed Equity, carefully modulating my voice to be as courteous as I can.

"Mr. Reed, their stay just started. They rented it out until the end of next week."

I let out an aggravated breath, blowing the lock of hair that's fallen into my eyes. "I'll pay triple what they paid if you can get them out of there tonight, and my reservation after Thanksgiving can be given to someone else."

Silence follows on the other end for mere seconds before the owner relents. Money always speaks, and fortunately, I have enough of it to pay an exorbitant fee for early cabin access.

Kennedy peers in, his brow furrowed as he surveys me sprawled across the leather couch.

"I'll have a cleaning crew come in as soon as they vacate and have it ready for you by tomorrow afternoon. The key will be in the lockbox on the east side of the property. I'll send you the code."

"Excellent. Thank you, Tom," I say before hanging up.

"Tom who?" Kennedy asks as he sits on the armrest above my head.

I reach for the tumbler, feeling the cold glass against my fingertips, and polish off the scotch with a weary sigh. "Tom with the cabin on the lake I won in the auction."

Kennedy nods as he surveys me. "What's with the pink, holey pillow and blanket?"

As I shift the soft blanket, my fingers graze the missed crochet holes that were supposed to make a moss stitch but turned out more like something a moth chewed through instead. "Willow made them for me."

"Tell her she should stick with accounting," Kennedy mutters as he surveys my office with a frown. "Why does it look like you've slept here? Marital discord already?" he jokes.

"She found out I helped orchestrate her theft."

"You what?" he asks incredulously.

Fuck. Guess I forgot to tell him the whole story too.

"I pushed her into taking the money through Gage. Her ex owed him a debt, and I made it so she was backed into a corner, and the money was easy for her to steal here."

"That's ..." Kennedy's many things, but speechless isn't one of them. "That's fucking crazy. You really are out of your fucking mind."

I squint as his loud voice reverberates, amplifying the pain of my hangover. "I fucked up. I know."

"This is beyond that. I thought she ..." He shakes his head in disappointment as he peers down at me. "I take back everything I said about her. She's probably traumatized by the ordeal, and the kid? Jesus, Gabriel, what the fuck were you thinking?"

"Like I say, I fucked up—"

"That's the understatement of the fucking century."

Ignoring him, I pull up our message thread and scroll past all the apologies I've sent her over the past two days that have been delivered and read but never replied to. I've never been left on read. It's frustrating.

What's also frustrating are the questions I have. What made her want to go on a scavenger hunt in my office to find those papers? What did I do to make her doubt me? I thought we were happy. Are these questions delusional after what I've done? Yes. Do I still want the questions answered? Also, yes.

GABRIEL

> Change of plans, we have our reservation for the cabin tomorrow through Sunday. My mother already knows and is excited to spend time with Grayson.

Kennedy releases a heavy sigh as he reads over my message. "You're hoping time secluded together will fix this gigantic fuck-up of yours?"

"That's the idea."

I can get anyone to agree to anything because everyone has a weakness; Grayson, being Willow's, and she'll jump at the chance for Grayson and my mother to spend some quality time together. I feel like a complete asshole for resorting to such a low tactic, but I don't see any other option to fix this. To fix us.

The three dots blink into existence and vanish repeatedly, which makes me feel incredibly unsure, which then makes me annoyed with myself. I'm far from insecure, but Willow has brought out a deeply buried side in me over the past few days.

"She won't go for it."

I angle my head to look up at Kennedy. "You don't know that."

"She just found out you lied to her. She needs to feel safe, and she won't if it's just you and her alone in a cabin far away from everyone."

I quirk a brow. "Are you a relationship expert now?"

He snorts. "Tell her she can bring Aella."

"Why the hell would I do that?" The last thing I need is for her little pitbull of a friend to come. I'm sure she already wants to string my balls like garland on a Christmas tree.

With irritation, Kennedy shoots his hands up in the air. "Just fucking do it."

Despite rolling my eyes, I concede because I really need all the help I can get. If having Aella there makes her more comfortable, so be it.

I just need another chance.

GABRIEL

You can bring Aella with you if you want.

"It's not going to work," I mutter just as the three dots appear.

"It will."

WILLOW

Fine.

"See, I fucking told you."

"Well, now you can tell me what's going on with you. Why do you want Aella to go so badly?"

Kennedy stands and walks to the door while my question hangs unanswered. "I need to go get packed for the trip. What time are we leaving?"

"We?"

"Yeah, *we*. There's no three's company shit going on."

31

WILLOW

Since heights made flying impossible for me, Aella and I began our seven-hour road trip to the lake house, departing early in the morning and leaving Grayson with an enthusiastic Vivian. Thankfully, she doesn't know what happened between Gabriel and me, and I hope that's the way it will stay. It's a mystery how someone as sweet as Vivian could possibly be Gabriel's mother.

Throughout the entire drive, Aella has been bubbling with excitement for the week ahead. She can't wait to sleep in, guzzle hard seltzers in front of a fire as she gazes at the lake, gorge on snacks, and lastly, make Gabriel's week absolutely miserable all on his dime.

I, on the other hand, have felt a rollercoaster of emotions. Anxiety. Dread. Anger. Sadness.

It's been a few days since the fallout between Gabriel and me. Since he broke my trust and, worse, my heart. He's sent me countless messages saying he's sorry, but what kind of sorry is it? For putting me and Grayson through what he did, or the fact that he got caught?

Though he's shown me his soft and tender side, his lies and

actions remind me of his ruthless nature. Making his moments of tenderness lost, swallowed by the dark.

What he did was unforgivable, and I stand behind everything I told him.

Aella's phone beeps with a myriad of texts one after the other. "Can you grab my phone from my bag?"

"Yeah." I lean into the backseat and fish it out of her bag as it continues to beep. "Someone left you like ten messages."

"Check it for me. I've been waiting for a message from my mom's nurse."

I face her phone screen toward her and then hastily turn it toward me to swipe up. My eyes widen, and I drop her phone in my lap, but the damage is done as the image of a very large, pierced, veiny dick sits not only on the screen but in my mind. "Oh my God!"

"What?!" she exclaims in surprise as she wrenches the phone out of my lap.

A sardonic smile touches her lips as she looks at the screen. "Oops ... sorry."

Oops? That's all she has to say after my eyes were visually assaulted?

"Please tell me I didn't just see Kennedy's dick." I grimace.

She licks her lips as she stares out the windshield. "That was his brother, Kade's, actually."

"I thought you two were *just* fake dating?"

Her tongue sweeps across her top front teeth, a nervous habit that betrays her anxiety.

"Hey, if that's changed ... if you like him, you should go for it."

"No, we *were* only fake dating or are ..." She shakes her head. "I'm not sure now what we are, to be honest, but I needed a favor from him, and he wanted to collect something from me in return."

I raise a brow. "What does that even mean?"

When she stays silent, my stomach knots.

"Tell me."

"Kade's a security analyst."

"Okay ...?"

It's like she's speaking gibberish. When I fall silent, she continues, "He's a hacker and can effortlessly slip into any system, any device, no matter how secure it seems."

"That's totally illegal."

"So is setting up a single mother into taking money and then coercing her into marriage."

It all clicks.

"That's how you found out? You asked him to hack into Gabriel's devices?"

When Aella first told me about Gabriel's misconduct at the restaurant, I was in denial, too lost to accept the truth, and after the scavenger hunt in his office, I was too upset and didn't want to even talk about it, but now I crave the details. How could I be so wrapped up in myself that I didn't ask how she found the information? And worse, what price did she pay to help me?

She hums her yes.

"What did Kade collect from you?"

Silence greets me.

"Elle, please tell me."

"A date," she says with a shrug. "Sex."

"Why? Why would you do that?"

"I had to find out for you. The whole thing with you and Gabriel ... from the start, it never seemed right. Reed Equity has tight security measures, ensuring its money is well-guarded and not easily accessible. That was red flag number one. You were a new hire, no offense, but why the hell would they give you access so quickly when the head accountant would take care of the task?"

When she lays it out like that, I feel like the biggest fool in the world. When I took the money, I felt as if a higher power was watching out for me. I just didn't know the higher power was my billionaire boss with ulterior motives. I was herded like a mouse in a maze with the promise of cheese at the end.

"Kade casually mentioned that the club was owned by the boss of the Chicago Mafia. The same Mafia boss you paid Darren's debt to. Suddenly, it all came together," she snaps, making me jump. "Gabriel said he was with the owner the night we tailed him to the club, and they're friends; next, his obvious unwillingness to have you at the club; and finally, your reaction to that guy in the mask Halloween night."

Though I look forward, my vision is clouded, as a bitter cocktail of self-directed resentment and irritation courses through my veins. "I was oblivious, lost in the false high of happiness. I never saw this coming."

"Who would?" Aella says. "I wrestled with what I should do. Whether to tell you. You were so happy with Gabriel, and he with you, so I thought maybe I was just overthinking, but my intuition is never wrong, and I needed proof."

"Hence, Kade?"

She nods. "Hence, Kade."

"You can't keep sacrificing yourself for everyone else, Elle."

"It wasn't that big of a sacrifice, or maybe it was ..." She grins, lifting her brows.

"First off, gross; second, don't make a joke to lighten a very dark situation; and third, don't you dare do that again. Unless it's for you," I say, turning in my seat to face her straight on. "Swear to me ... swear you won't sacrifice a piece of yourself to help anyone, including me, ever again."

"We're sisters, Wills. I'd do anything for you. That will never change."

"As sisters, I know when to say enough is enough. I love you, and I love your fiercely protective soul, and I'd do anything for you as well, but I'm forbidding you from doing anything reckless going forward. It's time to focus on yourself, and if you do something reckless, because I know you will, do it for yourself and no one else."

"I'll try," she says, taking her right hand off the steering wheel and jutting out her pinky.

"That's called a pinky-promise. I need something a little more concrete than that."

With a twist of her wrist, she reveals her palm and arranges her fingers into a claw. I take my hand and thread my fingers through hers, feeling the warmth before we both squeeze.

"I swear it," she says with a small smile.

For the next hour, we belt out old rock songs with such sharp, shrill voices that could raise the dead. It's just what I need to keep my mind clear and quiet, and even a small thrill of excitement blooms at the thought of a vacation, my first in more years than I can count, with my favorite person in the world by my side to laze by the water in warm blankets and eat girl dinners with every night.

But my excitement wanes completely as she drives up the small, winding, tree-lined road leading to the house.

As we stop in front of the garage, I exhale a deep breath, but it does nothing to ease the tension in my chest.

"Everything's going to be fine, Wills, and if not, we'll lock the asshole out in the cold," Aella says, vacating the car. "I mean, how bad can it be? Look at the beautiful lake house and the trees. We're never in—"

"Ladies ..."

The unexpected voice makes both of us jump.

Aella, bewildered and annoyed, gives Kennedy a scathing look. "Who invited you?"

"He invited himself," Gabriel says. The porch's wood creaks under his weight as he walks beside Kennedy and grabs hold of the railing. "How was the drive?"

My skin pebbles with awareness as his eyes meet mine, and it takes everything in me not to buckle under his gaze.

I despise the way my heart races when our eyes lock, how my stomach flutters with thoughts of our cherished memories, how my body trembles with recollections of his touch.

"As fantastic as an almost eight-hour drive can be," Aella mutters as she opens the trunk. "Now, make yourselves useful and get our bags. We have a week's worth of shit in here, and it's kind of heavy."

Gabriel advances toward us without a word, while Kennedy remains rooted in place, his eyes sizing her up. "Seems like a boyfriend's job to me."

"I guess I should call him," Aella says.

"No more guests," Gabriel mutters to Aella as he passes me with a small, unsure smile on his lips.

With our bags inside the entry, we embark on a tour of the pristine lake house, admiring the surrounding views while taking in the seven bedrooms, nine bathrooms, theater room, game room, and the indoor miniature golf. The outside offers a glimmering heated pool, pergola, and a lake that reflects the endless forest. It's like a dream.

Aella and I schemed on the drive to secure bedrooms as far from Gabriel as possible, but Kennedy's unknown invite messed everything up. Gabriel grabbed the most distant room on the left, while Kennedy snagged the farthest on the right, leaving Aella and me trapped in the middle. Despite our best efforts to get the guys to take one side so we can have the other, it was a fruitless discussion. Now I'm two doors away from Gabriel, and Aella is one away from Kennedy.

The guys left us alone for the rest of the day as we sat by the dock, under the pergola, enjoying our drinks, charcuterie, and music.

As the sun dips below the horizon, the late November air has turned icy, prompting us to hurry to the house, where we see Gabriel and Kennedy setting the table.

"Mmm ... something smells amazing," Aella says, her nose twitching as she walks past and settles in front of the food.

Steak, salmon, quinoa salad, seared artichokes, and dinner rolls.

I sit down beside Aella, and the enticing aroma of a steak fills my nostrils as a plate piled high with food is set before me.

My head snaps up, and my eyes meet Gabriel, whose gaze is intense, as if he's holding back a flood of thoughts.

Taken aback by the plate he made me, I whisper, "Thank you."

He inclines his head and walks to the other side of the table before taking a seat across from me.

The meal is quiet; the only sounds are the clinking of silverware and chewing as the awkwardness between Gabriel and me thickens. We try to avoid eye contact, or at least I do, but when our eyes inevitably meet every so often, a fleeting, unsure smile dances across our faces before we look away.

The odd thing about connections is that even when they're broken, their strength still lingers.

Meanwhile, Kennedy and Aella have straight animosity and tension. Their faces twisted in silent fury, appearing ready to lunge at each other with their steak knives.

If this is only day one, I can only imagine the dumpster fire that will be the rest of the week.

32

GABRIEL

An hour passes as I drink my scotch and gaze out the window before I finally muster the courage to step onto the back patio.

The moonlight illuminates Willow as she sits at the dock's edge, a tender breeze carrying her hair as it brushes against her face and neck.

As my feet drag over the dock, the wood groans, echoing in the night's stillness with each measured step I take.

Willow glances back, surprised. "If you want to be alone, I can leave," I say, lifting my hands in surrender.

I stand motionless, waiting for her to shoot me down, so I have to make the walk of shame back inside.

"You can't sleep either?" she asks.

With a grin, I take a few steps forward. "My body isn't used to being away from work for so long. I think it's going into shock."

With a nod, she surveys my approach, her eyes sweeping over me, and I almost stop mid-stride until she turns and looks back at the moon-drenched water, the soft lapping of the waves creating a gentle sound.

"What's keeping you up?" I ask, glancing at the stars brightening the night's sky.

"I haven't been away from Gray like this before. I guess I don't know what to do with myself either."

Her tone isn't exactly upset, but perhaps a little lost? Same.

"We can go get him right now. I'll drive," I offer.

Standing beside her, I can feel her eyes on me, her lips curving into a faint smile. "You can sit. You paid for the dock for a week after all."

I don't contemplate her invitation; I sit next to her as quickly as possible and leave as little space between us as I can without her mentioning it.

"And I'd love to have him here, but I fear Aella would give me another lecture on how I need to fill my *just* Willow cup back up to be the best mom I can be for him," she says, bundling up a little tighter in the heavy cream-colored blanket as the gentle breeze picks up. Against the splintery wood of the dock, my fists clench as I fight the urge to hold her close. "And I know your mom would be sad if I got him early."

The way she says it and stares at me with narrowed eyes makes it clear she's aware of the underhanded tactic I used to get her here.

"I shouldn't have leveraged my mother's happiness and Grayson getting quality grandparent time to get you here. I'm sorry for that."

She quirks a brow. "I almost would've been disappointed if you hadn't."

"Really?"

"Yeah. You wouldn't be you if you didn't fight for the upper hand in every situation."

I turn my whole body toward her. "You understand that you have all the power, right? Or did my thirty messages saying I'm sorry, and I'll do anything to get you back, go unnoticed?"

She smirks. "They weren't unnoticed, but they were ignored."

I nod, licking my parched lips. "I deserved it, and I'm ashamed of my actions. What I did to you is by far one of the worst things I've ever done, and I'll do anything to make it right."

Willow tucks a rogue strand of hair, snatched by the wind, behind her ear. "I get that you're sorry, I do. But what you did ..." She shakes her head with a sheen in her eyes and disappointment clear from her scrunched brows. "It left a mark on me. I was terrified that those men would come back for us. Can you fathom the sheer, paralyzing terror that gripped me night after night as I desperately tried to listen for any noise beyond my window and every rap on my door? Most nights, I didn't even sleep. I couldn't ..." She blinks back tears as she continues, "And I thought nothing would be worse than that until I found out you capitalized on my fear to get me just where you wanted me and ..." A tear traces its way down her cheek, and I gently wipe it away with my thumb. Her hurt and vulnerability, stemming from my actions, make me physically nauseous; I don't deserve her. But I will move heaven, earth, and hell to have her forgive me. "Then you made me fall in love with you."

My heart hammers against my ribs, a frantic drum, as she confesses her love. This wasn't the way our love was supposed to be professed. I've fucked it all up.

"I never thought that would happen. Us. I didn't seduce you into wanting me if that's what you think. Like you, I felt the undeniable attraction that pulled me in. My feelings for you stemmed solely from your kind heart, your humor, your selflessness, and your beauty. The contract was the furthest thing from my mind."

Ignoring my words, she continues, "You never told me why."

"Why?" I ask.

"Why did you do this to me?"

The *why* is selfish, ruthless, and awful, and the last thing I want to tell her, but I do anyway because I've got nothing to lose. I've already lost the most important thing I had—them.

"My father promised me he would give me full ownership of the company if I settled down with a family."

As if processing the information, Willow gives a slight nod. "So why didn't you just settle down? Seems like that would be an easier option."

"I didn't want anyone. I ... have trouble with trusting people."

Willow snorts.

"Yeah, I fucking deserve that. I know that this is quite a contradiction considering our circumstances."

Leaning over, I pull out my wallet and locate a small photo, worn around the edges, before handing it to her.

"It's the one and only memory I allowed myself to keep of the son that was never mine."

Willow's eyes take in every detail of the old photo that was taken on the day he was born, before sorrowful eyes meet mine. "That woman at the charity event ..."

I nod. "She was my girlfriend in college. One night, she told me she was pregnant, and I blindly gave up everything—my dreams, my hopes, my life—for a family I believed to be mine, only to find out it never was. He never was."

"That's horrible. I couldn't imagine—"

"It's been a long time, but after that, I never allowed anyone to get close to me again."

I want to say *until you,* but now isn't the time. I'm not trying to manipulate her into pitying me. I've done enough of that, and I regret it deeply. I'm just hoping it will give her a clearer picture of who I am. The good, the bad, the hurt, and the plain fucked up.

Her eyes soften. "The way you acted with Grayson when we

first moved in makes so much more sense now. It must've been so hard for you."

"Sometimes shitty things just happen."

"Did you love her?"

This I won't sugarcoat or hide from.

"I've only ever loved one woman, and I happen to still be married to her."

33

WILLOW

"He's prime fucking candy and a total silver fox, Wills. It doesn't matter if he's now in his fifties," Aella says, sitting across from me on the cabin's theater room couch, as she sorts through her cards. "I'd climb that stallion and never get off."

I snort, slapping down the draw four, which causes her nose to wrinkle. She hates losing, and after acquiring half the deck, she's on the verge of faking a hand cramp, leading to her seeking a different game so she won't lose.

Gazing at the screen, I take in the A-list actor whom we coincidentally saw at the charity event. He's handsome in a Hollywood-type way, but I don't share the same enthusiasm she does.

I shrug. "Eh ... he's alright."

"Okay, so who's better?"

As I try to conjure someone, my thoughts feel like scrambled wires. Not only do I not look at men ever, but I'm also not a fan of television, possibly because it was a constant companion to keep me silent in the foster homes during my childhood.

The only time I ever watch anything beyond cartoon movies for Grayson is when Aella requests it.

"Interesting," she says.

"What's interesting?"

She ignores my question and asks a different one while changing the color of the deck to red. "Name any celebrity you find hot as hell."

My brows scrunch. "I ... you know I don't watch movies."

"Okay, what about the movie last night? The blond-haired guy or the guy with dark hair?"

That's easy. "The one with dark hair."

"Okay, and what about that guy?" She points to the screen.

"He's better than the other one."

"Have you noticed they all look like Gabriel?"

"They do not!"

"In college, we binged that motorcycle club show, and who was your favorite? The lead. Long blond hair, hot as hell, and a total red flag. The show about the family that committed armed robberies? You liked the blond. Then there's the douche Darren, with scraggly blond hair. You *had* a type, but that type changed."

I go for nonchalance even though I know where she's heading when I set down a wild card. "Blue ... and people can change what they like. I hated onions when I was younger; now I love them."

"I saw you guys on the dock the night before last," she says, as she searches for a blue card from the deck, her brow furrowing slightly in annoyance as she grabs one after the other with no luck.

She's been beating around the bush, which is so unlike her, and I feel like it's because of Kennedy's presence in the lake house. It's like it's knocked her off her axis.

"We cleared the air."

"So does that mean he gets another chance?"

Does he? A part of me wants to say hell no, yet another part longs to return to the way things were. But I shouldn't. But then there's the contract. But does the contract even count? Or could I have ended it, but didn't, because of my guilt over Vivian? God, I'm so confused.

"I don't know."

"I just need to know if I now have to play nice with him. Ah, finally." She sets down a blue card.

We hear footsteps down the hall just as Gabriel saunters in, a beaming smile on his face and his phone held out before him. "She's right here."

My brows scrunch as he sits right next to me, puts his arm around my shoulders, and pulls me into his warm chest.

"Hi, darling!" Vivian's face fills the screen. "I just gave Grayson a bath, read him a few stories, and now he's getting tired, so I thought I'd call so you can say goodnight."

"Thank you so much."

Grayson's sweet little face comes into the frame, and I melt. He looks adorable in his baseball-themed onesie, and his hair is neatly styled to the side.

"Hi, Gray!"

"Ma-ma."

I laugh. "Hi, honey. Are you having fun?"

"Da-da."

My body stiffens.

"Hey buddy," Gabriel says from my side as he gives me a tight squeeze.

"We've been practicing the flashcards you placed in his bag, and I feel like he's picking them up so fast. He's so smart," Vivian says somewhere in the background.

"Thank you for practicing with him."

My smile becomes stiff, yet I keep it in place until we hang up. I knew we'd end up here, but now I feel like an even bigger idiot, staring at the disaster I've created. Grayson sees Gabriel as his father, and I don't know what I see Gabriel as.

"Chinese is here!" Kennedy enters the room, holding up two translucent white bags, releasing fragrant wisps of garlic, soy sauce, and sesame oil.

"Oh, thank God." Aella sighs, letting out a breath of relief as she haphazardly slaps her cards onto the upturned deck.

As I try to sit up, Gabriel's arms keep me close, and his eyes, filled with a mix of emotions, meet mine before he gives me a final, gentle squeeze and lets me go.

I might not know what Gabriel is to me, but his desires and intentions for me are evident.

———

GABRIEL GRUMBLES in the back of his throat as I place another skip on the discarded pile, and it takes everything in me to keep the smile from my face.

It seems Aella isn't the only one who hates losing. All three of them seem to share the affliction. I've become accustomed to losing in life; it's par for the course, so I take it in stride.

After the last morsel of delicious chow mein, orange chicken, beef broccoli, and cream cheese wontons was devoured, the guys lingered, so we resumed our card game. With Gabriel planting himself on my right and Kennedy on my left, it gave me the opportunity to give Gabriel every shitty card in my arsenal.

I hit him with a draw four and changed the color to yellow. Prompting him to pick from the deck. Behind my drink, I grin, the seltzer bubbles tickling my nose. The card gods are definitely on my side.

Kennedy groans, and Aella looks at him in disgust. "What?"

"Can we watch something else?"

Aella glances at the screen and then gazes at Kennedy. "Does a man being chivalrous make you uncomfortable?"

Kennedy scoffs. "Not in the least ... and I'm chivalrous. Women just want too much." He throws down a blue six, changing the yellow to blue, and I check the cards in my hand.

Switching the color back to yellow, I watch Gabriel roll his eyes before selecting a card from the deck. This time, I let my smile spread across my face. His exasperation amuses me far more than it should. Possibly because I'm extremely buzzed?

With each unwanted card he picks, I snicker behind my drink; the sound draws his attention.

His eyes, dark brown like the richest chocolate, reel me in. I'm a prisoner, reveling in the exhilarating shivers that course through me at his gaze. It's a delightful torment I want to prolong indefinitely.

One thing I know with certainty, buzzed or not, is that my feelings for him haven't faded; if anything, they burn brighter now that I know more about him.

Which is completely asinine ... right?

Indeed, it is, but I can't dictate who captures my heart, the intensity of my emotions, or the extent of my forgiveness.

I take another sip of seltzer; the alcohol gives a refreshing chill as it slides down my throat, and then a cozy warmth in my stomach.

"What a massive fucking cop-out. *Men* these days feel like they don't need to put in the work. That's the problem. No fucking dinner where he calls in the reservation, no opening doors or pulling out chairs, no, here is this really beautiful trinket that I saw and thought of you. Just a 'let's fuck'. You see that right there ..." Aella points to the screen as one of the antagonists, who is the conceited, rich jock, steps on the screen. "That's all that's left in this world."

"That's bullshit, and you know it, or do you need to be reminded?"

My wide eyes meet Gabriel's, and he shrugs. We both don't know what's gotten into these two, but over the last few days, it's gone from fun and a little petty to feeling like Mom and Dad are minutes away from a divorce, and they're wanting us to pick who we want to live with.

"It's not that hard to do a grand gesture, especially after *you* fuck-up royally. You men lack the motivation. If you wanted to, you would ... period." Aella mutters, taking a drink from her can.

Okay, maybe it's not the best idea to have us all drinking together.

Gabriel finally lays down a card, followed by Aella, then Kennedy. My gaze meets Gabriel's yet again, and he mouths, *"Don't do it."*

A thrill runs through me as I dramatically drop the skip card onto the discard pile. Gabriel shakes his head and bites his bottom lip to keep from smiling. I fight the urge to lean in, wanting to feel the touch of his lips on mine.

Geez, I need to calm myself, or I'm going to end up in a pool on the floor. My eyes dart overhead to follow the movements on the screen.

On the field during soccer practice, the female character pauses as the music's opening notes begin to play. The male character's serenade fills the air as he walks along the rough cement bleachers. The female character's father makes a rule that her younger sister can't date unless she dates. Strings are pulled, and the male character gets paid to fake his affection for the female character so that the younger sister can date. Using the cash the male character was given to win the female character over, he hires the marching band to accompany his rendition of "Can't Take My Eyes Off You." He sings and dances in front of the whole school while avoiding security guards, all to apologize for not kissing her. In the end, she lets her guard down and even laughs, since this proves he's genuinely into her.

It's a bit corny, but it's incredibly special to have someone so deeply into you. At that moment, any trace of their shame, ego, or sense of superiority vanishes, and they pursue their desires fearlessly.

A burning sensation flares on my cheek, then trickles down my neck. Gabriel stares at me, his eyes moving back and forth between me and the screen.

Was bringing me here his idea of a grand gesture? Or did he just come up with an idea?

———

WITH THE LAKE house in complete darkness, save for the pale moonlight streaming through the large windows, I leave my door ajar and tiptoe down the hall. I'm determined to find a snack to absorb all the alcohol coursing through my body.

Game night seemed a lot more fun in theory.

As I head to the pantry, a glance out the kitchen window reveals the moonlit lake's shimmering surface, which casts a dreamy and magical scene amongst the glittering sky.

Though I had reservations about being here, some of which still linger, I feel a sense of calm. I've always fought to survive, fought to keep my head above water. But for the first time in a long time, I can feel the air completely fill my lungs.

A smile spreads across my face at the thought. Even with the trip being dysfunctional and slightly awkward, I found a strange peace.

Even though it doesn't justify his actions, understanding Gabriel's intentions, motives, and pain has brought me the insight I needed for closure, which I think contributes to the peace.

I tiptoe the rest of the way to the pantry, tucked behind the kitchen, which plunges me back into the enveloping blackness. Squinting, I try to discern the contents of the containers in front of me until I reach out and grab a bag of chips. This will have to do.

The loud rustling bag opens, and I place a cheesy triangle chip in my mouth with a deep moan.

"I've missed that sound."

I whirl around, the bag of chips spilling across the ground, and collide with Gabriel's naked chest.

"Holy shit, you scared the crap out of me," I whisper-yell.

"I'm sorry," he says. A barely perceptible smirk flickers across his lips.

I snort. "No, you're not."

"You're right, I'm not."

He takes a predatory step toward me, and I'd be lying if I said my insides didn't quiver and my heart didn't skip a beat.

"What are you doing in here?" I ask, trying to be strong, though near him, my body trembles with a mind of its own. It doesn't want to be strong; it wants to be taken and used by him.

"I'm hungry."

"Oh, well, you're in the right place. I'll just be going."

His arm shoots out the instant I move, and I'm instantly pulled into his rough embrace.

"I'm not hungry for food."

His mouth slams down on mine in a hard kiss, his taste a fusion of sin and whiskey, a bittersweet blend of bad decisions and the promise of heaven.

His hand tangles in my hair while the other explores the curve of my ass, prompting me to lift my leg around his thigh, seeking friction. He wastes no time picking me up and pushing me against the wall with a thud. His length is hard and ready against my core as I rock against him while deepening the kiss.

Wanting and needing more, my nails claw and scratch his back.

"I want you," I breathe, a sudden warmth spreading through my body.

His hand finds its way between us, and in an instant, my gown is over my head, and his sleep pants are on the floor as he thrusts into me.

I gasp; a choked sound lost in the sudden rush as stars explode behind my eyes. He doesn't slow but pistons into me. Hard. Fast. Brutal. Desperate. Just how I like it.

"Fuck, I've missed you so much." He groans as he picks up the pace. "You feel so good wrapped around my cock."

I groan as his deep thrusts and wicked words take over my body.

"Tell me you don't miss this ... miss us."

I opt to remain silent, biting my bottom lip to block out anything except my moans. I do miss this and us, but speaking it into existence would bring forth questions and choices I can't face yet. Not until I'm ready and I've had enough time to reflect.

"Stay with me, beautiful," Gabriel groans, his breath warm against my face as he grabs my jaw to meet his gaze. Lost in a haze, my eyes meet his, and I see a fire, half ecstasy, half raw desire. "Good girl."

His praise and tight hold on my jaw are causing a surge of desire to rush to my clit.

With a sudden click, the kitchen lights up, and both Gabriel and I swing our heads to look toward the pantry's entrance. The refrigerator door opens with a creak, and then we hear someone pouring liquid into a glass.

Gabriel's brow furrows for a second before a mischievous smile playing on his lips. Then his hand, which had been gripping my jaw, suddenly presses against my mouth, right as he pulls out and then thrusts back into me with slow, long rolling strokes.

My orgasm builds quickly, with my thighs shaking and my insides quivering. The heady combination of his deep, controlled strokes and his pubic bone pressing against my clit rhythmically is driving me to the brink of no return.

"Be a good girl and come all over my cock," he whispers, biting the shell of my ear.

A muffled cry escapes my lips as the waves of euphoric bliss wash over me. Moments later, Gabriel follows me over the edge, his forehead pressed to mine, his intense gaze locked with mine, his ragged breath mingling with mine, and his cock swelling inside me.

He holds me tight, the scent of us mingling as I descend from the peak of the most intense orgasm I've ever known.

We hear thunderous footsteps coming from somewhere in the house toward the kitchen, and we both freeze.

"So you really fucked him?" Kennedy asks.

Silence follows before Aella says, "Yeah ... I did."

"How could you do that after already fucking me?" Kennedy says, sounding ... hurt?

"Simple. You ran after that night and made it clear you wanted nothing to do with me. *Don't make such a big deal out of it; it was just a fuck*, right?"

"You know it was more than that," Kennedy seethes.

"What it was ... was a mistake."

"So that gives you the right to fuck my brother?"

My eyes widen at the thought of Aella's private business being public knowledge, and even worse, a wave of remorse washes over me, knowing she did it for me.

"Is this really what you're upset about? Me fucking him and liking it, or the fact that it wasn't you?"

Holy shit.

"We shouldn't be listening to this," I whisper.

We wait until they both stomp in different directions after passing insults back and forth, then scramble to gather our clothes before silently dressing.

Gabriel's fingers gently thread through mine. "Tell me I still have a chance to fix the mistakes I made. Tell me I have a chance to treat you the way you deserve."

"I-I don't know ..."

My mind is a battleground of opposing thoughts after everything that's happened and what we just did. Being with Gabriel feels so right, and yet so wrong.

"That's okay," he murmurs, his voice laced with defeat until a spark of determination takes over. "Can you do something for me?"

My brows scrunch.

"Give me the week to show you."

34

GABRIEL

For the past hour, Kennedy and I have been seated at a cramped table, the dim lights of the dive bar casting shadows as we talk and drink, but my focus has remained on her, on the other side of the room.

She's sin personified in a black minidress, with a few strands of hair escaping her loose updo.

Aella gestures dramatically, her hands flying as she speaks, while Willow, barely containing her mirth, finds it humorous with her head tilted back and her slender neck on full display as she laughs.

Since our talk on our first night here and then the sex we had in the pantry, she's kept her distance, leaving me unsure how to interpret her actions and where to go from here. I confessed my feelings, expressed my sorrow, and apologized, and now I'm trapped in this torturous waiting period. The uncertainty of whether she'll keep me or cast me aside is pure agony. And I know there's nothing I can do to sway her; the only thing that will help is time.

Before our moment is lost and we must return to reality, I

hope to show her how important she is and that I'll do anything to keep her and Grayson with me.

"How's it going with her?" Kennedy asks from my side, his knuckles bone-white as he holds his drink to his lips and glares at them or, more accurately, Aella.

I shrug. "It could be better, but it could also be worse," I say, eyeing my ring still sitting on her delicate finger. It's the sole piece of evidence I have that suggests things aren't over.

Just then, as if Willow knows I'm talking about her, she glances over at me. I don't turn away as if caught; I continue to hold her gaze until a small smile meets her lips, a slight blush, and then she turns back to Aella.

When he grunts but remains silent, my eyes cut a glare in his direction.

"What's with you and Aella? I thought she was too young, and you didn't want the headache."

His gaze lingers on her, the familiar look of irritation masking a hint of longing I know so well.

"She is too young and a fucking headache," he says, just as a group of young guys approaches Aella and Willow.

I watch as Aella gives them a flirtatious grin while Willow gives more of a respectful nod.

Kennedy is out of his seat in seconds as one of them puts his arm around Aella. I decide to stick back. Would I like to go over there and show them that Willow is mine? Yes. Would it win me any points with her? Probably not.

I lean back and watch the chaos unfold as he shoves his way through the crowd before getting into a heated argument with Aella. Willow sidesteps them with a sardonic smile and her hands up before walking down a hall where I assume a bathroom is.

I follow her, not wanting to lose sight of her for even a moment.

After the bathroom door closes behind her, I wait a beat

before pushing it open again. I peer around the bathroom, making sure she's alone before going inside and closing the door just as she steps out of the stall.

She doesn't notice me until she's in front of the sink, the water rushing over the porcelain, soap suds covering her hands as she looks into the mirror. "What are you doing in here?"

I engage the deadbolt and feel it click home without our eyes leaving each other.

"I missed you."

Smiling, she dries her hands on the paper towel, the crinkling sound filling the room. "I've been by you most of the night."

I shake my head. "Not good enough."

I approach her as she leans against the sink, appearing as though it were the only thing that could keep her from collapsing.

"What are you doing?" The notch between her brows forms, but I don't give her a chance to ask questions as I drop to my knees.

Her hands go to the top of my head. "We can't; someone might come in."

"You'd better be quick then," I rasp.

"I can't ..."

Her objections disappear as I lift the hem of her dress above her hips, slide my finger along the edge of her red lace panties, before pulling them to the side and burying my face into the apex of her thighs.

The first taste is divine, the sweetest bit of honey with the slightest bit of salt. By the third swipe, I'm a man possessed. She bucks against my face, her breath quickening as I focus on her clit just the way she enjoys.

As if to enter, someone bumps the door, startling Willow.

"Gabriel, stop."

I shake my head, grip her hips, and continue my ministrations while ignoring her attempts to pull away. Her eyes, heavy-lidded and filled with longing, lock with mine as she grinds my mouth against her folds. I hum my approval against her, which makes her lips part as her legs buckle beneath her.

"Gabriel ..." she moans.

"That's it, beautiful," I say, taking my fingers and adding them to her tight channel. "Come on, my fingers."

I don't ease up until I've drawn out every last drop of pleasure her body can give. Until she's barely able to move. Until she holds on to me like there's nowhere else she'd rather be.

———

IN A SLIGHTLY DELIRIOUS, still half-drunk stupor, I wake with a jolt to Willow's body intertwined with mine. I grin and snuggle back into her, but the harsh ringtone of my phone shatters the quiet of the moment. Without a glance, I silence it. Whatever it is, it can wait. My throbbing headache demands more sleep, and Willow's body against mine takes precedence.

The blaring noise echoes again, and I groan, covering my ears.

Someone better be dead.

The ringing fades and is replaced by the ping of a voice-mail, and then the relentless ringing resumes. I open one eye and squint at the bright screen before answering it with a grunt.

"Gabriel ..." My teeth clench at the sound of my mother's shrill and worried voice, the pitch only something I've heard a few times, and what followed was never good. The following words tumble out of her mouth, a confusing jumble I can't piece together.

"Slow down, I can't understand you."

The phone crackles, then my father's familiar voice comes through.

"Son, you need to get home as quickly as possible."

Willow's wide eyes meet mine as I spring to a sitting position. "What happened?"

"Your mother was taking Grayson on a walk around the neighborhood, and someone hit her on the back of the head."

My heart sinks. "Is she going to be okay?"

"She'll be fine. She needed three stitches, and she has a severe concussion."

"Okay, I'm glad she's okay. Do you know who did it?"

My mother says something from the other end, making my father let out a deep sigh before clearing his throat.

"No, and when I found her on the sidewalk, unresponsive, she was the only one there."

My eyes meet Willow's, and the look of anguish across her face is nothing short of gut-wrenching.

"Son, someone took Grayson."

35

WILLOW

Dazed and completely drained, Gabriel rushes me up the steps and into the back entrance of the police station to stay out of the watchful eye of the media.

Once the story of Grayson's kidnapping hit the news outlets, it was a whirlwind of highs and lows. The hotline rang continuously as worried citizens reported potential sightings, while others, driven by the promise of Gabriel's reward, made false claims, giving me hope.

My acrophobia was nothing but a forgotten whisper as we boarded a private jet two hours after Gabriel got off the phone with his dad.

News arrived after twelve hours: the kidnapper is in custody, and Grayson is now safe and sound.

The police chief emerges from his office and leads us through a winding series of hallways to a cramped room, where Gerard and Vivian sit on a black leather couch with Grayson nestled in Vivian's arms. Vivian hands Grayson to me, and I hold him close while peppering kisses against his head and sobbing uncontrollably.

"We're ready, Mr. Reed." I turn my head and see Gabriel

nod just as the police chief departs, and the previously opaque window suddenly becomes clear, offering a view into the adjacent room.

Blood rushes so violently into my ears; I feel like I might faint.

Darren sits at the metal table, his messy blond hair falling into his eyes, a dark bruise on his jaw, a busted lip that's still bleeding, his clothing dirty and disheveled, and his hands cuffed and clasped on top of the table.

"Do you know why you're here?" The officer who sits opposite Darren asks.

My eyes dart to Gabriel as he stands beside me, his jaw clenched, his eyes hard and fixed on Darren.

"Not a clue," Darren says smugly.

"Kidnapping—"

"If he's my kid, it's not kidnapping," Darren says with such arrogant confidence it's sickening. He hasn't spent a single moment with Grayson until he stole him. He isn't a father. He's a fraud and a thief.

Vivian inhales a shocked breath, and I freeze.

"The child you abducted is Gabriel Reed's," the officer states.

Darren smiles as he gazes up through the two-way glass as if he knows I'm here watching him. "I want a lawyer and a paternity test."

My eyes squeeze shut as I inhale Grayson's familiar scent and cling to him for dear life.

This can't be happening.

"This man is obviously ill—" Vivian says.

"Is there truth to this, son?" Gerard asks Gabriel.

I squeeze my eyes shut tighter, feeling a wave of panic, fear, and physical pain surge through me as the room falls into a tense silence.

"Son!"

With the sound of approaching steps, I open my eyes and stare into the police chief's unwavering gaze. "Mrs. Reed, do you know the man in the interrogation room?"

My throat constricts, and I desperately look to Gabriel, hoping he'll know a solution to the mess of lies about to unravel.

Gabriel gives me a tense look before gazing at the police chief. "Let's discuss this in your office."

"The hell you will. What's going on, Gabriel?" Gerard yells.

"Gerard," Vivian hisses.

"No, he's lying about something, and I want to know right now."

"Gabriel, please tell your father this is just a big misunderstanding. That man—he's just—"

"Mother ..." Gabriel's eyes meet mine before flitting over to the police chief. "Can we get ten minutes?"

"Of course," the police chief says, his voice steady as he inclines his head before walking out and gently closing the door behind him.

In the deafening silence of the room, Gabriel's eyes are fixed on the closed door, his rigid back and clenched fists reflecting the tension in the air.

"What's going on, honey?" In a voice barely above a whisper, Vivian asks, her words punctuated by sniffles.

More unnerving silence follows until Gabriel turns around and looks over my head toward his parents.

If I were stronger, I would meet their gaze while he reveals our deception, but I can't bring myself to do it.

And when Gabriel tells Vivian and Gerard the truth, I leave the small room like the coward I am, sick to my stomach from Vivian's gut-wrenching sobs and Gerard's anger and disappointment.

The following hours are brutal. While Darren will be charged for hurting Vivian, family law representatives come in to facilitate this unusual situation, prompting a discussion on abandonment laws and whether Darren might face charges for kidnapping.

In Chicago, Illinois, a parent's prolonged absence or lack of contact with a child for a year or more is considered abandonment. Although Darren hasn't seen or provided care for Grayson since he's been born, it's been less than a year, given Grayson's age, so we're more in a gray area.

Darren now wants to go to court for custody of Grayson, which is my worst nightmare. Even though I was placed in a separate room from Gabriel, the police chief stated that Gabriel had requested a restraining order against Darren for me, and that it was granted by a judge he knows, which also means Grayson will be safe with me until court.

Continuing with my cowardly ways, I text Aella and sneak Grayson and me out of the back of the police station without saying anything to Gabriel.

I jump into the car with Grayson as soon as Aella pulls up. "Hurry, but not too quickly. I don't have a carrier."

"What the hell is going on, Wills? You scared the crap out of me with your cryptic text."

I clip my seatbelt and hold on to Grayson for dear life and a silent prayer that we make it safely to her place.

"The Reeds know everything. Darren took Grayson."

"Shit."

"Yeah, shit is right," I say, tears escaping my lids.

"So it's over?"

My heart thumps rapidly as the question echoes inside my head. Is it over? With his parents now knowing the truth, I am of no use to Gabriel. The thought sends a jolt of conflicting sensations coursing through my veins and, worse, through my heart.

Yes, I despised him for what he put me through. The sleepless nights, tears, fears, and uncertainty were in his hands. But during our stay at the lake house, I felt as though I could see beyond it. Every smile, kiss, and touch reminded me of all the special moments we shared. Taking care of Grayson and me while I was sick. The dates. The hobbies he guided me into. Him finding my birth mother. All of this helped my heart soften, giving me the strength to forgive his unforgivable acts.

But none of that matters now. He will return to his life as the untouchable billionaire, while I go back to my life as the single mom and accountant.

He will look back on this moment as the instance his meticulous planning went awry.

And I will look back on this time as a test of my strength while being an interloper.

"I think so."

Aella cuts me a questioning glance. "But is that what you want? You guys seemed disgustingly happy just last night."

A wistful smile touches my lips as resolve takes the place of any sorrow I have left. "This was always supposed to end. The time just ran out quicker than we expected. Besides, I don't think I can ever look Vivian in the eyes again. The pain and heartbreak I heard coming from her will forever haunt me. She didn't deserve any of this."

"And you did?"

"I ..." Leave it to Aella to ask all the hard questions while I'm still trying to process them. "In some ways, I think I do."

"That's absolutely asinine, Willow."

I don't comment because to me it isn't. My decisions led me here.

"Can we make a quick stop at Gabriel's penthouse so I can grab the rest of my stuff and drop off the keycard?"

"You think he's just going to let you leave?"

I shrug. "He doesn't want or need me now that his plan is ruined."

"So this is a good thing?"

"I think so."

I need not dwell on what could've been but on what lies ahead. Like finding a job, a place to live, and creating a new normal for Grayson and me. Thankfully, he's too young to remember any of this.

"I have a huge favor to ask ... maybe the biggest yet."

My bank account has the money Gabriel gives me monthly. I didn't use it because he provided everything we needed, but I can't touch that money now, even though I need it; it feels wrong. Or maybe it's just my pride? I don't know. But what I know is that I won't touch a cent.

"Yes, you guys can move in with me."

"It will only be until I can get back on my feet."

"You can stay indefinitely for all I care. I love you guys."

"Thank you, Elle. We love you too," I say, passing her Grayson, and rushing to the elevator from the penthouse garage.

36

GABRIEL

I slam on the horn, nearly colliding with another car as I switch lanes, while Henry's voice fills the car through the Bluetooth system. "Do you want me to prepare a statement?"

Blowing out a breath of frustration, I survey the streets, but see nothing but a hue of red. "No one deserves a statement. My personal life is no one's fucking business."

"Understandable. If you change your mind, let me know, Sir."

After I end the call, I drive home as if in a trance and completely disconnected from my body as I maneuver into my usual spot under the penthouse.

Things are fucked in the worst possible way. Far worse than I imagined them to be. My mother's devastated, my father's pissed, and Willow has completely ignored my calls and texts since she snuck out of the police station without even a goodbye when I thought we were really making headway.

Once I'm in the penthouse, I can feel the stillness, the silence, the abandonment. It's as if the bright, warm light of Willow and Grayson was never here.

"Willow?" I yell, walking toward Grayson's bedroom, which

is open, and as I peer in, my fear is validated. A pristine, uncreased bedspread covers his small crib; the bathroom and walk-in closet are clinically clean and completely bare, and not a single personal item remains; everything is gone.

Just as I feared.

With a shaking hand, I walk into our bedroom and dial her number for the tenth time, only for it to go straight to voicemail again.

"Fuck!"

My hands find their way into my hair, and I tug until a sharp pain shoots through my scalp. This can't be happening.

A slight knocking echoes from the kitchen, and I instantly lift my head and hurry over.

Willow places her keycard, bank card, and diamond wedding ring on the counter as she hefts a bag over her shoulder.

"Where do you think you're going?"

Willow startles; her teary eyes meet mine. "This was always supposed to end, Gabriel."

Shaking my head, I close the distance, gently gripping her arm, and turn her to face me.

"I don't want us to end."

"It has to. After everything that's happened, after everything we've put everyone through."

"Fuck everyone. I've never cared what anyone thought, and I won't start now."

"What about your mom?"

My chest tightens at the mention of the pain I inflicted on my mother, whom I love more than anything. "She'll come around."

She shakes her head, a silent protest on her trembling lips, a silent plea for me to let her go, but I don't want to.

I can't.

"No. We aren't doing this," I say with a certainty that's

waning as I continue to stare into her eyes and the resolve that shines through. "You aren't going to push me away at the slightest problem. We are stronger than this. I told you that you were mine, and you are. Not for three years, but forever. You belong by my side. Grayson belongs by my side. And that will never change. Not because of your stupid fucking ex, or anything else."

"But—"

"No fucking buts, Willow. While you were trying to make a family, hoping to find what you've always yearned for, I was trying to stay away from one. I was scared. You changed that. I love you so much, and I can't live without you."

"Gabriel ..." Her voice breaks at the end.

"Bring Grayson back upstairs, Mrs. Reed."

She shakes her head in defiance. "It's over, Gabriel."

"Please ... don't go—"

She shakes her head, her bottom lip quivering, as tears well in her eyes. "We're done."

Reality cuts through me with the stinging force of a whip. Nothing I say or do can alter the damage that's been done. Her mind is made up. Begging, pleading, or trying to manipulate her would be a repeat of the past, and I won't go down that road again.

What's the saying about how things that are destined to be will always find their way back?

God, I hope so.

She turns to walk away, and my grip loosens, sliding down her arm until my grip on her hand is barely there, and then I release that, too.

37

WILLOW

A single tear escapes and traces a path down my skin as I scan my reflection in the elevator, my lips trembling in the silent, mirrored space. A strangled sob escapes, but I quickly smother it with my hand as I replay the hurt etched on Gabriel's features.

Unbearable devastation.

His plea for me to stay was a desperate whisper, laced with raw pain and heartbreak.

He may have sparked the demise of our relationship with his deceit, but I ignited the fiery end when I left him.

Wrapping my arms around myself, I rock back and forth. Once the elevator pings its arrival, I take a few deep breaths and walk to Aella's car.

She furrows her brow, yet doesn't comment on my appearance as I put my bag in the footwell and grab Grayson from her.

I clutch him tightly, as if my recent losses threaten to steal him away too.

Incoming calls flood my phone, beeping insistently, but I silence them all.

Leaving him was hard, and I'm scared I'll lose my resolve if I hear his voice.

"Are you okay?" Aella asks, pulling into her apartment's garage.

"No, I'm not."

38

GABRIEL

The sharp ding of the elevator is jarring, the fluorescent lights are blinding, and the day feels endless even though it just started.

As I pass Henry's desk, he slams the phone down. "Mr. Reed, wait ..."

"Not right now, Henry," I grumble as I step past him and open my office door.

I head right for my mini-bar off to the side, grab the neck of an almost empty whiskey bottle, and polish off all of its contents in one gulp.

The alcohol seeps into my system like a warm hug, and I can't stop the sigh of pleasure that leaves my lips.

"This is quite disappointing."

I pivot at the voice.

There in my seat, behind my desk, sits my father.

I exhale a deep, shaky breath. "To what do I owe the pleasure?" I slink out of my coat and place it on the rack near the door.

When my father remains silent, I glance at him. His hands

rest on my desk, the steeple of his fingers a symbol of his deep thought.

Great, exactly what I need to add to this awful hangover.

"Since you haven't answered any of my calls since the police station two weeks ago, I thought I'd come here to let you know I'll be overseeing the company for a little while."

"For what reason?"

"Your motives and business tactics."

I snort and nod my head. "My motives and business tactics? You mean the way I've made this company successful?"

"At what cost, son?" he asks with tired eyes and disappointment in his tone. "You're ruthless, relentless, and after what happened with that poor girl." He shakes his head. "You blackmailed her into marrying you, son. And your mother ... she got hurt because of your lies, and I've never seen her so upset. When does it end? When do you decide you've gone too far?"

He's right. Every single word he speaks holds validity, but I choose to ignore every word, even though I hear them. My focus shifts away from that because my work is all I have left, and now he's trying to take that away from me, too.

"So what is this? You're taking the company back? After all the countless hours I've poured into it?"

"I'm only overseeing the company until you get your shit together." His eyes survey me from head to toe. He's not impressed. "You've been drinking heavily. I can smell it from here."

"What I do on my personal time is my fucking business."

"It is my business when I see your life falling apart before my eyes. You are better than this. Stronger than this. You need to get away and get your shit together, son."

"Fuck you!" My father's face pales as I yell, but I'm too consumed by rage to worry about the fact that I have never disrespected him like this before.

"Excuse me?"

"You heard me," I say, gazing around the office with a sneer. This was never mine and will never be mine. "Take the fucking company and shove it up your ass. I'm done."

My father rises from his seat. "Son, stop."

I don't stop; I walk out without a second glance.

Fuck him.

Fuck the company.

Fuck everyone.

I retrieve my phone and send Kennedy a quick text.

GABRIEL

Are you ready to start our own company?

KENNEDY

Say less ... when?

GABRIEL

Now. I just quit.

The three dots appear and disappear, but I close the message thread and decide there's one more thing that needs to be rectified.

As I slide into the cool leather of my seat, I hear Gage's voice as he picks up the phone on the second ring.

"What's up?"

"Are you still watching her ex?" I ask. He was released two days ago after a week and a half in prison for hurting my mother and abducting Grayson. What a fucking joke the justice system can be. I ensured jailhouse justice was served, but the punishment felt hollow and unsatisfying.

"Yeah, I have a guy on him. He's been staying close to Willow's friend's building. I think he's taunting her. I told my guy if he gets too close, to take him out."

My knuckles are bone-white as I grip the steering wheel. "I want him gone."

Though silent on the other end, I could hear the telltale clicks of his laptop, confirming he's still there.

"I thought we were going to do it my way," Gage says.

His way is fucking him up to within an inch of his life before letting him heal, only to repeat the process over and over again. I went with the plan, but I no longer want delayed gratification. I want him dead.

"Not anymore."

"Once you step into this side of life, it sticks with you. It will be on your conscience forever."

Leave it to the head of the Mafia to get philosophical about taking someone's life.

I clear my throat. "I can live with that."

The series of clicks on the other end of the line comes to a halt. "This isn't like you."

"He fucked everything up," I say as Willow's face fills my mind.

"Vengeance," Gage says.

Is that all it is? Right now, yes, but also no.

"Safety. She'll always be looking over her shoulder, worried if he'll come back, and so will I."

"Okay."

"That's all?" I ask.

"We keep the ones we love safe. There's nothing more noble than that."

The war within me, fueled by anger and spite, erases any trace of nobility I've ever had.

39

GABRIEL

ONE MONTH LATER

The club's bar is shrouded in shadows, save for the red lights that make the towering bottles of liquor gleam.

Music is booming through the speakers, but the shrill screams of that dumb fuck Darren, from the basement, still cut through the noise.

My left hand clutches the neck of the single malt scotch, the liquor inside mirroring the ominous red light, but my thoughts are consumed by the ring on my finger.

Taking it off is not an option, as it would signify my defeat.

My phone glows for the third time in the last twenty minutes, and I contemplate throwing it against the fucking wall. I want to see only one name illuminate the screen: Willows. Not my father's for the fiftieth time over the past month.

"It's done," Gage says while settling onto the seat next to me, his hands stained red.

I take a long pull from the bottle, waiting for the familiar burn, but it never arrives. I just feel nothing.

"Is it strange that I don't feel any better?" I ask.

"The joy of exacting revenge ... taking someone's life, is fleeting. The more you do it, the less you feel, until you feel nothing but emptiness."

I take another drink as I contemplate his words.

Gage eyes the bottle as I place it back on the bar. "The appeal of alcohol will wane as well."

I snort. "It hasn't yet."

"In time it will," Gage says, rubbing the deep scar across his bloody palm. "There are few things in this life worth living for, but I think you already know what they are." He eyes the ring on my finger. "Get the fuck home and sleep off the alcohol. No one likes a fucking drunk. Then figure out a way to get her back."

With a roll of my eyes, I push myself up and stumble away from the chair. "Fine. Will you make sure his body gets found, so she knows he's no longer a threat?"

"Done. I'll have Jace take you home. No way I'll let you drive home and kill someone innocent."

Disheveled, I enter the penthouse an hour later, ripping off my jacket, and seek solace at the bar, desperate for another drink. I grab the closest bottle and eye it like it's my prized possession.

I yearn for the incessant chatter in my mind to cease. It's like a never-ending roar.

My phone rings again, making my anger flare, and this time I hurl it against the fucking wall. It offers a nice crack as it dents the drywall and clatters to the floor.

As I open the bottle, the scent of the liquid wafts out, and I toss the cap into the sink. No use in keeping it when I plan to polish the bottle off in the next few minutes. The liquor meets my lips, and my phone rings again.

With a low growl, I stalk toward it. The screen is cracked, but the fucker still works, unbelievable. I pick it up, and I see my mother's picture smiling serenely across the front. Although I don't know what compels me to answer, I do it anyway.

"Mother, I'm not in the mood. We can talk tomorrow."

"Gabriel ..." My mother's voice sounds breathless and broken.

I stand a little straighter as I ask, "What's the matter?"

"Your father ..."

"I don't want to talk to him—" I shake my head. Why can't they see I don't want to have anything to do with him right now?

"He-he's gone."

My brows scrunch. "What do you mean?"

"He's dead ..."

The world seems to fall from beneath me.

"What?" I gasp.

"He went to the emergency room with a horrible headache, and it turned out to be an aneurysm."

My throat closes as my eyes swim with tears. "I don't understand."

"He went in for emergency surgery, and he ... and he didn't make it. He's gone. What am I going to do?" My mother's crying is drowned out by my own sobs as the liquor bottle falls from my grasp and shatters onto the floor.

With a single step, the world swims, and I grab at the wall, but I can't stop myself from falling.

40

GABRIEL

AGE 7

"**R**ight here, son," *my father yells as he bends into a squatting position from the other side of the yard while hitting the inside of his catcher's glove.*

I nod, digging my cleats in the dirt as I take my stance just as he taught me.

His instructions repeated in my head: Balance, pivot, lift my left leg, lower my back hip, bend my back leg, lead with my front hip, twist my upper half, pull down my front arm, and then follow through with my right arm as I let go of the ball.

The ball sails through the air and lands with a smack into my father's glove. He pulls his hand out of the glove and shakes it out, which makes me laugh.

"That was excellent, son!" he says, rising with a smile on his face.

AGE 14

The bleachers are cold and hard beneath me as I sit, replaying the disaster of a game in my mind. A sharp clank echoes as my metal cleats scrape against the cold aluminum bench.

The seat groans, and I don't have to look to know it's my father. I avert my gaze, wanting to conceal my bloodshot eyes and the lingering coolness of tears on my cheeks.

"Hey, son."

"I messed everything up," *I blurt out like word vomit. If I say it first, he can't, and I won't feel crappier than I already do.*

"Hey." *My father's hand grabs the back of my neck, and he places his forehead against mine.* "Not every game is going to be effortless or without flaws. Your performance in the game showcased your persistence and refusal to quit. Those are both phenomenal qualities to have. And even though your team lost, without you, it would've been way worse."

"You think?" *I say, blinking back tears.*

"I know," *my father says as he pulls away and cracks a smile.* "Let's go celebrate."

I eye him, confused. "I lost my game, though."

"Even a loss is worth celebrating if you learn from it, and I remember a home run in the second inning."

AGE 21

You are not the father. You are not the father. You are not the father.

The paper trembles in my unsteady hands as I struggle to maintain control, but I feel myself unraveling as my eyes swim over the stark words in black and white.

This can't be happening.

"Son, are you okay?"

"She lied to me. I——" *As the words got caught in my throat, I shook my head, feeling the sting of unshed tears.* "I can't believe he isn't mine. I love him so much."

As his arms gently wind around my shoulders, I fall apart in his embrace, succumbing to the feeling of utter devastation and true heartbreak.

"I know, and I'm so sorry."

Tugging away from him, I'm met with sorrowful eyes. "How do I move on from something like this? I gave up everything for a family, and now I have nothing." Tears stream down my cheeks in rivulets. "I have nothing," I whisper.

The air around me feels like shards of ice, stealing each breath as my heart continues to break with a sharp sting to my soul.

My father shakes his head. "You have your mother and me. Family is what you have. We will get through this together."

41

GABRIEL

ONE WEEK LATER

T he pastor's words fill the crisp morning air, describing my father's life, legacy, and spirit, while I stand rooted to the sprawling green grass at the cemetery claimed by countless marble and granite headstones, my body vibrating, my legs stiff, and my stomach contents rolling.

The cruelest twist of fate is that the same pastor who helped orchestrate my sham marriage, a union that indirectly led to my father's death, is now delivering his eulogy. Or maybe it's the fact that after giving the order to take a life, one was taken from me. It's twisted, it's fucked, it's my nightmarish reality, and just where someone like me belongs. Talk about a full-circle moment.

My mother's hand, clammy with tears, clenches mine while she sobs into my father's silk pocket square. I wish I could offer her more, but I'm numb. Words, feelings, thoughts, and the world seem to fade away, leaving me delightfully detached. If we weren't preoccupied with the burial, would she notice my slight swaying from the effects of the alcohol? Would she even care after I've ruined every special thing in her life?

Surrounded by the hushed sniffles and heavy scent of flowers, I survey the crowd gathered to mourn my father. Everyone shrouded in black, here to pay respects before going back to their pristine lives. Even Eryn came, and although I didn't want her here, I kept my cool to avoid a scene and hurt my mother more.

I blink away my stupor as the crowd approaches my mother and me. Empty words and salty tears, a painful duet that lasted a long hour. Leaving me with a parched throat and a craving for another drink.

In the chaos, my mother is pulled away, and as one of my father's mourners leaves me, I see Willow hugging my mother across the lawn. As they exchange words, I'm struck by her. In a black shift dress, with her curled hair perfectly styled, she looks beautiful. They exchange smiles and another hug before my mother is intercepted by someone else.

Willow's gaze meets mine as she turns, and a sensation of being utterly seen washes over me; my body becomes a symphony of sensations, a rollercoaster of blood coursing through my veins, and a dizzying, free fall into raw feelings. I know with a certainty that defies explanation that I want her, need her, would do anything to have her back in my life.

I start toward her, drawn by the warm glance of her milk-chocolate eyes and the sweet curve of her cherry lips, but something holds me back.

"Not here," Kennedy says near my ear.

"What?" I ask, surveying Kennedy's hand on my arm.

"You smell like a bar floor, and you can't string together coherent words. Don't let her see you like this."

I wrench my arm from his grasp, irritated that he ruined the moment with Willow, only to stare at the space where she stood.

It's empty, and she's gone.

———

WITH MY HEAD BOWED, my forehead rests against the cool tumbler in my hands while my elbows rest on the dark and deserted bar. I don't know how long I've been here or where I am.

The last thing I remember is feeling as if I was being strangled from the inside out. The knot in my tie was like a noose, the stiff suit felt like a prison, and a thousand tiny bugs seemed to crawl across my skin.

The reception after the funeral was set for the ballroom at Reed Equity. I couldn't even make it out of my car. The second I saw the building with its imposing tall glass and concrete, I peeled out. All I could envision was my father's face, contorted with hurt and disappointment, when we had our fight in the office.

That was the last time I laid eyes on him, the last time our voices mingled. The last time they ever will.

Though the music plays and a dizzying sensation overwhelms me, I can faintly hear someone speaking close to my ear. Their scent is nauseatingly sweet, like cotton candy. Not the flower field I crave.

My eyes flutter open as I feel a touch on my upper thigh, and I squint to see a flash of bright pink nails against my dark pants. Not the deep red I yearn for.

Willow. Where is my Willow? Why did she have to leave me when I needed her more than air to breathe, more than the blood in my veins?

The thought of having her back consumes me; desperation claws at my insides. Without her and Grayson, I am nothing.

Nails scrape against my neck, but they feel wrong, leaving a churning in my gut.

"Let's go, baby."

An urgent warning screams through my mind as I'm pulled up by my upper arm as if to stand. I shake my head groggily, the world a blurry mess before my eyes, but no words come out. The glass in my hand falls from my fingertips.

A sudden shout rings out, my arm falls uselessly to my side, and a growing disturbance begins just behind me.

I slump against the bar, the scent of stale beer and desperation filling my senses.

I'm so fucking tired.

Arms suddenly wrap around me, and I'm lifted from my stool. "It's time to go, man."

My head swings toward the voice, and I peek at Kennedy. Why's he always saving me?

"Fuck. You're heavy. A little help would be nice," he mutters, straining as he hefts me up, the screech of tires echoing as we make it to the parking garage.

I'm tossed into the passenger seat, the door slams shut, and I close my eyes.

"I understand that this is a hard fucking day for you, but you need to pull it together."

"I can't."

"Can't or won't?"

I stay quiet. Can't. Won't. What's the fucking difference?

42

WILLOW

I quickly finish my shower and dry off as my phone's shrill, repetitive ringing, the tenth time in a minute, pierces the silence.

"Where's the fire?" I ask Aella as I answer instead of saying hello.

"Turn on the news."

"Why?"

"Just do it."

"Okay, going ..." marching into the living room, I turn Grayson's movie off since he's asleep in his playpen and run through a few channels until I stop on one. The blood leaves my face, and I fall onto the couch as I turn the volume up.

"—*believed first to be a homeless man from where his body was dumped—he was identified through dental records as twenty-five-year-old Darren James. The authorities believe it's a gang or drug-related incident given his prior record, but if you have any information, please call the authorities.*"

A mugshot of Darren with sunken cheeks and bloodshot eyes is broadcast on the television.

"Are you there?"

"Yeah," I choke out.

"You think he ran up another debt, and the Mafia got him?"

"Maybe."

"Good old-fashioned justice if you ask me."

"Yeah." A tear cascades down my cheek.

"Are you okay?"

"I ... I think I'm in shock."

"I just parked. I'll be up in a minute."

I remain silent, my head nodding, the plastic of the phone screen protector still stuck to my ear after she ends the call.

Aella's hands wind around me seconds later, and I release the breath I'm holding, finding comfort in her familiar scent as I hold on. We remain in this position for what feels like hours before Aella whispers, "Talk to me, Wills. What are you thinking? How are you feeling?"

Darren was a year older and initially treated me like someone he needed to look after when we met in foster care, but our bond blossomed as time passed. Darren insisted it was *us against the world*, and we were self-sufficient, requiring no one else.

He promised me a great life once I fostered out, where we'd both help each other follow our dreams. I followed mine, but he never followed his. With time, I realized our relationship was toxic, fueled by his need to keep me isolated from my relationship with Aella and the world while he drank to excess and gambled our money away. Then he left me with a debt owed to the Mafia. They could've killed Grayson and me for all he knew, and he left anyway.

The image of Darren hurting Vivian and kidnapping Grayson for money is still fresh in my mind. And for weeks, since the police released Darren, he has been persistently bothering me, always visible from afar, never close enough to violate

Gabriel's restraining order, yet still able to instill a sense of dread. His presence was a reminder that he could still hurt me, still take Grayson away, and now that's gone.

"I feel ... relief," I rasp.

43

GABRIEL

Footsteps echo, but I remain still, unmoving, under my blankets, until the loud rip of curtains being pulled from the wall catches my attention.

"Why don't these fucking things open?" Kennedy grumbles as he continues pulling at the curtains.

With my eyes still closed, I fumble for the remote on the floor and press the button, and the curtains silently slide open, flooding the room with an unpleasant glare of light.

"What the fuck are you doing here?" I groan.

"You've had months to drown in alcohol and self-loathing. Your time is up. You fucking stink. This house is an empty, depressing shithole, and I'm tired of doing all the fucking work at the company."

I sit up and instantly regret it as my head swims in a haze of pain and dizziness.

"My father died," I state the obvious like an idiot, as if that makes my behavior acceptable.

"Yeah?" Kennedy hits me with a questioning look. "And so did mine. Shit happens. Get your ass in the fucking shower, Gabriel."

"For what?"

Kennedy, scrunching his nose in disgust, grumbles as he gathers up the empty Jack bottles and takeout food boxes littering the floors.

"We're going on a trip. Pack for a week or two."

With my head buried in my hands, I shake my head in defiance. "I don't want to go anywhere."

I want to stay here, in the house I bought for Willow, with no furniture but endless booze, in the dark where the nothingness of the void holds me tightly.

"Tough fucking shit. I can't watch you self-destruct any longer. Your mom needs you; I need you; our company needs you."

Embarrassment flares within me at how far I've fallen, but the wave of self-loathing quickly crashes, engulfing me. It's warm, and in my warped, over-alcoholized brain, it feels like my only friend. The only thing that won't leave me.

"If you care about anyone besides yourself, you'll get up and get your shit together."

When I remain in bed, because I don't give a fuck about anything right now, Kennedy continues, "Willow would be disappointed."

I glare at him. "Don't bring her up."

"She showed up for you at the funeral. That has to mean something, right?"

"Don't bring her up," I repeat.

The thought of her creates a dull pain in my stomach that only intensifies as it travels to my chest and then into my throat. Despite believing I've cried all my tears, I still feel the urge.

I need a fucking drink.

The moment I eye the half-drank bottle on my air mattress, Kennedy snatches it up. "The last thing you need is another drink; do you want me to remind you again about how I saved you from Eryn that night in the bar? How you were too shit-faced to realize she was trying to weave her way back into your life?"

My glare is my only answer.

"Get your ass up. We need to head out."

———

THE LATE AFTERNOON gives way to the dark night as we drive until early morning. As we finally pull onto a dirt road, the sun's rays are just warming the air and casting beams of light along the rolling hills. A wooden sign, just like one you'd see at a camp, hangs overhead: "Tranquility Ranch."

I whip my head toward Kennedy. "Where the fuck are we?"

"Iowa."

With a groan, I drag my hands down my face, the rough stubble scratching against my sweaty palms, as my frustration builds. After he woke me up yesterday, I've been enduring a brutal hangover throughout the entire drive, feeling my skin crawl from the absence of alcohol, my body feverish, all thanks to Kennedy and his tiresome sobriety talk. I'm at my fucking limit.

"No fucking shit. I've known that for hours. Why are we here?"

We drive past horse stables, a garden, and half-built buildings, their wooden frames catching the morning light, before pulling up to a ranch-style house where an elderly man stands, a warm smile on his face.

"It's a retreat."

I gaze around. "The fuck it is. It looks like a rehab facility."

"You catch on quick," he deadpans.

"I'm not a fucking druggie."

"No, but you've been drinking alcohol like it's water for months, maybe longer, since you're so good at hiding, and while it's been an absolute pleasure to sit through the drive with you while you slowly come down from all the alcohol. It ends now."

I can't believe this shit.

"You're not leaving me here," I hiss as I watch the smiling man in the doorway speak to another man dressed in black medical scrubs.

This can't be happening.

"No fucking shit," Kennedy grumbles, grabbing a bag and slinging it over his shoulder as he gets out of the car.

"You're staying too?"

He nods.

I raise a brow. "Why?"

If he came here to babysit me, my temper will flare with the heat of a thousand suns.

"We all need some guidance every once in a while. Just because I don't have a drinking problem doesn't mean I don't have *a* problem."

The only problem he has is not leaving me in drunken solitude.

With a groan, I force myself out of the car and grab my two heavy leather bags from the back seat with more strain than I'd like to admit. I feel weak as fuck.

"Gabriel, welcome." The older man holds out his hand, and I reluctantly take it. His handshake, firm but warm, and his steady gaze somehow puts me at ease, which is unsettling but also reassuring. Or maybe I'm still a little drunk.

"Kennedy," he says with a smile while embracing Kennedy in a hug.

"John, thank you for taking us on such short notice."

"You're both welcome whenever you need to find peace."

Peace? Yeah fucking right.

44

GABRIEL

TWO MONTHS LATER

With our hands, we build houses; we hike and hunt in the woods; we plant fruits and vegetables; we talk about life; we ride horses along the stream; we read; we rest.

For the next two months, this was my routine, and I savored every moment.

Coming clean from alcohol was a battle, especially at the beginning, as my body fought to adjust, with fever dreams, clammy skin, tremors, and mood swings, but as lucidity won, things transformed, and the actual work began.

You don't know what's been suppressed, buried deep inside, the hidden things that live within, until you allow yourself to face them. I let everything come to the surface, things I've been numbing for decades.

The hurts. The faults. The inadequacies.

The good, the bad, and the fucking ugly.

When you look at yourself with complete clarity and focus, without pride and superiority, you experience a metamorphosis, and an odd tranquility washes over you, similar to the feeling of coming home after a long absence.

My pride blinded me to the fact that I had a problem when it first began. I went from occasionally drinking to unwind after a tough day at work to needing a drink every day, and then to being an alcoholic, entirely dependent.

I've gently yet definitively repaired the bond with my mother, the innocent party in my destructive behavior. She deserved better from her only son, the last of her family, and I utterly failed her, a failure I vow to mend for the rest of my days.

The gut-wrenching regret of the way I left things with my father will never fade. It has sat with me like a cancer since coming out of my drunken stupor. The remorse for never telling my father that I loved him and that I was beyond fortunate in having him as a father in his final days will haunt me forever. I'd relinquish my wealth, pride, and contentment to rewind time and spend those final precious moments with him. I can only hope that repairing my relationship with my mother will bring peace to his spirit.

It turns out both Kennedy's father and my father frequented this location for decades, finding solace when they were feeling like the walls were caving in, like the world was a little too loud.

During the fifth week, John showed me photos of them over the years—fishing, cooking, laughing around a bonfire. He and my father had been friends since grade school, and I never knew. He told me stories of their friendship, of good times, and of how he saw my father, which is all I have to hold on to now. His words made me consider how much I resemble my father, not only in looks but in personality and struggles. Maybe he and I weren't that different after all. It gave me hope for the future I crave.

A week ago, I finally mustered the courage to listen to my

father's last voicemail, recorded just before his emergency surgery that ended in his death. His voicemail sounded like a regretful goodbye, like he knew he wouldn't make it out the other side. His voice cracked as he confessed his love and pride for being my father; even now, I don't feel I deserve it. But I will honor his legacy by being the man he wanted me to be.

Willow is still a hard subject to articulate. She reminds me of my greed, failure, and loathsome behavior. She was the beacon of light I needed, but her radiant presence, like a dying star, was unexpectedly consumed by the darkness of my atrocious behavior.

Insomnia held me captive for many nights, during which I replayed our memories. She made me feel life, not just observe it passing me by.

And her love? Her love was something truly extraordinary.

Willow is at the peak of my comprehensive list of failures that I hope to set right. If she ever forgives me.

Despite vowing to let her live her life, I still reach out to Aella to check on her and Grayson. And I may have made Willow's transition easier behind the scenes so she gets everything she wants out of life. Everything she deserves. She has always fought her battles alone, and I want to support her, even if my help is a secret. It's the least I can do, considering how badly I messed up with her.

And finally Eryn. She was the origin of all my trust issues, and I never took any steps to heal or move forward. I was trapped in a cycle of unending sorrow. How can I mend myself and repair the bonds I share with my loved ones if I don't first deal with what started it all? Forgiveness, I've discovered, is a gift you give yourself, not the other person. And ever since then, I've felt more like my old self.

I give John a tight hug and thank him before hefting my bags over my shoulder and heading to the entry.

Kennedy stands by his car out front. He left a month earlier to hold the fort at our new company, which we merged with Reed Equity, while I stayed behind.

"Ready?" he asks, the jingle of his keys filling the otherwise silent air.

I gaze behind me, at John in the entry, who inclines his head, and then back at Kennedy.

I'd be lying if I said I wasn't a little heartbroken to go. This new way of living has offered a sense of immense peace to my mind, body, and soul. I was reminded of a time when life wasn't so complicated, before the daily pressures and the coldness of ambition took hold.

"I think so," I say, putting my bags in the car and waving goodbye to John.

45

WILLOW

FOUR MONTHS LATER

"Thank you." I smile quickly, hoisting my black camera bag over my shoulder and grabbing my to-go chai latte.

On a whim, I ran the three blocks to get a coffee to give myself a little energy before work, but found the usually quiet shop unexpectedly full for a Monday morning. I glance at my watch and see I have around twenty minutes before I'm expected back, so I have to hurry.

My right shoulder shoves the door open, and I sprint forward and straight into a tall figure's frame. Luckily, the coffee has a lid, or we'd both be drenched in the sweet, hot liquid.

Strong hands steady my shoulders as I slowly let out a breath I didn't know I was holding. "Oh my, I'm so sorry," I rush out, my eyes traveling up his muscular chest with a tight black shirt, which shows multiple tattoos running down his arms, and finally to a devastatingly handsome face. My eyes widen. "Gabriel?"

He gives me a dazzling smirk, his eyes crinkling at the

corners, as we move from the entrance to let another customer enter. "Willow ... how are you?"

I manage a smile, but the familiar nerves, absent since I left Gabriel, surge back, as intense as a tidal wave. Especially with the way he looks. He's bulked up, inked more of his skin, grown a beard, and radiates a tranquil aura—a stark contrast to what I saw seven months ago.

"Good. Really good, actually."

"And Grayson?"

"Good as well. He's so independent and is in the discovery phase, so he's into everything and likes to run everywhere," I say, shaking my head as I think about my sweet but busy baby boy. "He definitely keeps me on my toes."

Gabriel nods his head before surveying me with an odd look. "That's great. You look ... good."

There's a lot of *good* going around, apparently. Can this get any more awkward?

I raise a brow. "Thanks ... I think."

He bites his bottom lip as he attempts to hide a smirk. "You look breathtakingly beautiful, but I didn't know if saying that was appropriate."

Butterflies. So many damn butterflies take flight in my stomach.

Get a grip, Willow.

"We were married, so it's only slightly appropriate."

"*Are.*"

I scrunch my brows. "Excuse me?"

"We *are* married." He gives me another dazzling smile.

Shooting him an incredulous look, I say, "I signed the divorce papers months ago."

"I think I may have misplaced them." He shrugs.

Misplace them? That's not part of his Type A personality.

I snort as I check my watch to escape his intense gaze. My eyes widen. How have six minutes already passed?

"Convenient, Mr. Reed," I mutter, walking away.

"Indeed, Mrs. Reed," Gabriel says, catching up to me.

I raise a brow but continue to walk. "Are you following me?"

"Yes, and no." He points to a large building just up ahead with the name Heartwright & Reed in bold but sophisticated black lettering on the side.

"So it seems Kennedy won the '*whose name would go first*.'"

I shrug. "I gave it to him. The best always finish last."

A smile creeps onto my face as I observe his casual clothes, completely out of sync with a typical weekday. "Casual Mondays were his idea too, I'm assuming?" I ask while pointing to his light-wash denim jeans.

"We can't win them all, right?" He gives me a tight smile.

Before I can utter a word, he carries on with a clearing of his throat, his face etched with a serious frown as he stares at his feet. "I wanted to thank you for attending my father's service. It meant a lot to me."

His words cause my heart to clench painfully in my chest. Aella told me he descended into a dark spiral after his father's passing, and the guilt gnawed at me, understanding my lies and our sham of a relationship deepened their divide. He wasn't able to mend their relationship before his father's passing, and I can't fathom anything more devastating than that. I wanted to reach out to him, but I just couldn't. Every time I picked up the phone, I talked myself out of it.

I went to the funeral to silently show my support for him and Vivian; initially, I wasn't sure if it was appropriate, but Vivian lit up when she saw me.

Blinking away the tears burning my eyes, I reach out for his strong, warm hand and stop in front of him. "Your father was a good man, and he raised an even better son."

From the ground, his eyes lift to my hand holding his. I give it a reassuring squeeze, ready to pull away, but his other hand envelopes mine, his dark gaze pinning me with its intensity.

The devastatingly sincere look hits me like a physical force. "Thank you."

As I nod, I attempt to draw in a calming breath of air, focusing on the sensation of it filling my lungs before I glance at my watch. "I'd better get going."

"Of course," Gabriel nods wistfully as he gives me a tight smile.

God, I have to get out of here.

Even though time has passed, my heart still yearns for him, and my mind has struggled to forget him.

Even after everything he's put me through, I still want him.

"It was good to see you," I say as I turn and head toward South Holden Elementary School to photograph the entire student body and faculty.

His hand grabs hold of mine, and my heart beats so erratically I think it might leave my chest. "Was it ... good to see me?"

A genuine smile spreads across my face. "Of course."

The problem is that it was more than *good* to see him. It was like reuniting with a beloved friend after years, but with an irresistible allure and yearning that causes me to shiver. A desire for his arms to wrap around me, for his lips to find mine.

"You can see me again."

I raise a brow.

He licks his lips and smiles. "Go out with me."

His words take me by surprise, and part of me wants to say yes. Hell, I want to scream it.

The thought of not being lonely after a long day. To have someone to come home to every night, someone to eat dinner with, someone to talk to. The thought of taking a chance, a second chance to get everything right ... with him ... it has the potential to be amazing.

However, the other part reminds me of how well I'm doing. I manage my own photography studio and hold annual photography contracts with six schools and two corporations. Grayson is flourishing and happy.

What if everything falls apart again?

But what if it doesn't? What if it's what you've always dreamed of? A small voice in my head says.

Even though it pains me to say it, I do it anyway. "I don't think that's a good idea."

Another smile touches his lips. "Please."

"I ..." I don't know what the hell to say.

"Give me a chance."

When I offer no response, he drops to his knees at my feet.

What the hell is he doing?

My eyes widen as he clasps my hand in his.

"What are you doing?" I hiss, the sound cutting through the air as people pass by, their expressions a jumble of surprise, shock, and nosiness. "Gabriel, get up."

Gabriel's fiery eyes lock onto mine, and I feel them burning through me. "You see, the thing is ... I can't let you go. I've tried the noble act of walking away, leaving you alone, and I can't any longer. I love you, Willow. I love Grayson. Please let me make this last year up to you. Let me love you the way you deserve."

I shake my head as tears well in my eyes. "Gabriel ..."

"Willow, *still* Reed, please go out on a date with me."

EPILOGUE
GABRIEL

ONE YEAR LATER

The opulent tan marble floor echoes with the clicks of our feet as I mutter resort fixes to Henry, who scribbles them on a tablet as we go.

Despite the resort's excellent framework, a multitude of updates are necessary to bring it up to par. As a luxury five-star resort, I want to provide a unique all-inclusive blend of opulence, hospitality, and history, creating an unforgettable destination fit for royalty.

This resort is the first in a series we'll be assessing in the coming weeks.

I glance at my watch. "I think now's a good time to stop for the day."

Henry stares at me, a look of bewilderment etched across his features. "Sir, it's only eleven."

"Enjoy the rest of your day, Henry. Use the company card for anything you need." After patting his back, I turn to leave, catching the flicker of a strange expression. He's been doing that a lot lately. He still seems puzzled by how to approach my relaxed and easygoing personality.

As the sun warms my skin and the ocean breeze swirls around, I kick off my sandals, letting my feet sink into the warm sand, and unbutton my shirt.

Gazing at the beach dotted with just blue and white striped umbrellas and chairs, I can imagine the soft comfort a private cabana would bring, with a stocked mini-refrigerator and a server on standby. The waterfront would be elevated, offering a touch of elegance enhanced by the shimmering, crystal-clear sea and ...

Like clockwork, I shake my head, seeking to silence my work thoughts and welcome the calm and happiness of life.

At John's ranch, while detoxing, I promised myself to cherish the here and now and develop a healthy work/life balance, ensuring I never drink again, and although some days may be harder than others, I haven't touched one drop of liquor.

I scan the waterline, hunting for the treasure I crave the most. Dancing in the breeze, a head of long black hair under an oversized, wide-brim sun hat immediately catches my eye.

As I creep toward her, a smile spreads across my face, the anticipation of holding her growing with each sandy, silent step. My arms embrace her, my chest flush against her back, her heart beating a steady drum under my arms.

Home.

Her head tilts up toward mine, and I have to angle my neck to see past the brim of her hat. "You just left a few hours ago. There's no way you're done with work yet."

"I couldn't stay away," I whisper, unable to resist as I bite and suck on the soft skin of her neck.

A soft moan leaves her lips. "I'm glad. I was thinking about last night ..."

"Were you? Which part? The part where I fucked your tight—"

"Dad! Mama!" Grayson yells from behind us.

I reluctantly pull away from Willow and flash a big smile to the cutest cock-blocker I know as he sprints toward us, my mother's flustered expression visible behind him.

"Hey buddy," I say, hoisting Grayson's sand-covered body into my arms. "Are you enjoying the beach?"

"Yeah. Look, a sandcastle!" he says, pointing up to where the chairs and umbrellas are.

"Very cool. Can I help later?"

He nods enthusiastically before wiggling out of my arms and showing Willow a few seashells along the shoreline.

"I swear he's getting faster and faster every day," my mother says, grinning as she hugs me.

"How are you liking the resort?"

"It's beautiful. I couldn't imagine one nicer than this."

"I suppose we'll see when we visit the next location later this week."

With a big smile and eyes sparkling with anticipation, she says, "I can't wait."

It fills me with joy to see her happy, which is a welcome change after the hardship she's endured since my father died. She was struggling with depression, and my actions only made it harder for her to cope and mourn. Thankfully, she has found the strength to keep forging ahead despite my father's absence.

"Did you bring it?" I whisper to my mother, hoping my words won't carry to Willow's ears.

My mother gives a slight nod, reaches into her bag, and discreetly hands me the small red velvet box where a custom wedding band sits.

Despite any missteps, I'm fully committed to making sure Willow's life is a fairytale, starting with tonight's proposal, surrounded by loved ones who are currently en route to the island, followed by the hope of growing our family soon.

I give the box a tight squeeze before placing it in my pocket and mouth a thank you. She winks before walking over to where Willow and Grayson are digging in the sand.

Moments like these always feel bittersweet.

Though losing my father has left a gaping hole that will never heal, it brings me peace to know he's watching with joy and pride. He would've loved it here—the air filled with the sounds of laughter, surrounded by family, and warmed by love.

The way life is meant to be lived.

THE END

———

THANK you so much for reading COERCED VOWS! If you liked it, please leave a review. Your support means the world to me.

MORE FROM THE AUTHOR

———

ALL OR NOTHIING SERIES
All Your Firsts
All Your Lies

Deceitful Vows- Kennedy & Aella's story coming December 2026